Praise for Growing Up on Route 66

(The first novel in this series)

"I finished your novel . . . and was struck by how perfectly it seemed to encircle (of course) the world of childhood and its heady veering toward adulthood. It's a loving and funny book . . . and made me recall with mingled pleasure and embarrassment all the twinges and itches and passions of adolescence. Well done, and thank you or putting it into my hands."

--Carrie Brown, author of Lamb in Love and The Hatbox Baby

"A wonderfully well-wrought novel, set in a place that's still the stuff of myth, about coming of age in a simpler time when sex was giddily mysterious and life was filled with endless possibilities."

--Bernard Edelman, editor of Dear America: Letters Home from Vietnam and Centenarians: The Story of the 20th Century by the Americans Who Lived It

"*Growing Up* does what every good novel does: creates a time, place and characters that the reader can see and feel. And like every good serial, you want the next installment. Mr. Lund has learned the lessons of Dickens, Anthony Trollope and the other great serialists. Having grown up in a small town on Route 66 myself, I felt Mr. Lund had been reading the childhood diary I never kept."

--Harry Fuller, TV Executive, currently with CNBC Europe

"In *Growing Up on Route 66* Michael Lund gives us a loving look through the telescope of memory, resurrecting forgotten feelings in the idiom of adolescence sharpened by the lens of age--and wisdom. He takes us back to a time when the road ahead was a winding one, just right for joyrides, meant to be wandered, with curious roadside attractions and shady stops along the way. Reading this book is like returning to a summer night when you were young, when life was full of promise, mystery, and terror, that time at twilight, before your mother called you in to wash up and go to bed, when you were playing a leisurely game of kick-the-can and wished that the game could just go on and on. Fortunately, Lund promises that it will go on, in the second book in his series, *Route 66 Kids*, and, I hope, many more to come."

--Eric Kraft, author of The Personal History, Adventures, Experiences & Observations of Peter Leroy

"A book that takes us back to a quieter time - when learning about life and love was a pleasant journey, and the nights were full of childhood adventures."

--Bob Moore, managing editor, Route 66 Magazine

"The novel is in the rich tradition of the American novel of stories of initiation, or coming-of-age. The opening chapters recall Mark Twain's *Huck Finn*, although instead of Huck and Tom Sawyer planning a pirates' raid on a Sunday school outing, Mark Landon, his semi-steady girl friend Marcia Terrell and five other 'Circle Children' start out on a 'Great Expedition' into the woods west of town . . . . But make no mistake: *Route 66* is clearly an original!"

"Mike Lund has assembled a wonderful cast of main and supporting characters in this first novel . . . "

"Lund's novel is a process of discovery--discovery of self, of others admired or feared, of relationships among peers and family members, or between older and younger boys and girls. It is also about acceptance of responsibility, recognition of limitations, and a discovery that many people whom we most admire when we are young and innocent actually possess the same character flaws we discover in ourselves."

"As Ishmael says in *Moby Dick*, 'me thinks' we will see more of Mark in the not-too-distant future, as Mike Lund moves beyond the boyhood of *Growing Up on Route 66*."

--From Bill Frank in the Farmville (VA) Herald:

GROWING UP ON ROUTE 66

A critical review by Larry Parks

More pertinent than Salinger's *A CATCHER IN THE RYE*. More optimistic than Wolfe's *LOOK HOMEWARD, ANGEL*. More realistically humorous than Bradford's *RED SKY AT MORNING*. Michael Lund has taken a frank look at the coming of age sexual anxiety of baby boomers as we tripped through the late 1950's and early 1960's in smalltown mid-America. This semi-autobiographical first novel by Lund is crafted with sympathy and candor. When you finish *GROWING UP* you will look forward to a next installment of the lives of youthful Michael Landon, Marcia Terrell, and Cathy Williams. They have so much life in them, so much promise, and some hope of incorporating a healthy sexual identity into the culture of the first post-WWII generation.

Salinger's *A CATCHER IN THE RYE* is so focused on the experience of one lonely and confused youth that it fails to get in touch with my experience and view of reality. Really, why would anyone choose to read it? One wonders who keeps placing this on required reading lists anyway. Lund draws on his own (rather normal) experience in a compact neighborhood of children of the men and women who returned from WWII and settled down to lives of relative peace and prosperity.

Information about sex was not easily obtained and that which was available was not very clear. Teenagers in 1960 did not have many resources--certainly not the new millennium bombardment of sexually explicit television, movies and magazines of today. In 1960 neither the churches nor the schools provided the frank and informative sex education of today and parents were not so adept as parents of today. Rather than reading Salinger and asking "Why?" just read Lund and say, "Okay, I get the idea."

Wolfe's Eugene is surrounded by parents, siblings, and women (young and not so young) who are so burdened with unhealthy views of life that Eugene is going to be screwed up--we just don't know when his crazy world is going to finally crash. Eugene is not real. He is not believable enough to make me care about what will happen to him next.

His life is more bizarre than encouraging or optimistic. Lund's main character, Landon, on the other hand, is more straight forward, easier to identify with, and much more hopeful. Perhaps I am reading more into Landon than the story justifies because I knew Michael Lund as a youth and know him now to be a thoughtful and accomplished college teacher.

Having made that disclaimer, I offer you Mark Landon as a more representative character of America's youth in the 50's than Eugene was of the second decade of last century. Eugene is just too screwed up to care about but one wants to pat Landon on the back and help him along.

Bradford did a masterful job in RED SKY AT MORNING at presenting likable characters through episodes of humor--both situational humor and artful use of dialog.

How can one not fall in love with the sharp and sassy Marsha? Lund's characters are composites of real kids in a real neighborhood. Because many of the events described in GROWING UP happened much as Lund tells in his story, you will acknowledge that truth and believe the tale that he is telling. The discomfort of youth with the opposite sex is worth watching up close with Lund because he handles it gently and fairly. It is not all rosy but it is more frank and quite real.

Finally, there is a chapter that stands out to me as the finest example of Lund as a craftsman. Chapter II of Part Five: On the Town is the story of the delivery of a small town daily newspaper by adolescent and early teen newspaper boys. They pick up the newspaper weekdays after school as it comes off the press and deliver it to businesses and residences all over this small town. Lund's description of the holding room of the delivery boys, the bag and book, and the method of folding the sixteen-page edition like a rectangular frisbee is truly wonderful.

His description is so careful and precise that you can see in your mind the delivery boy doing exactly what they have been doing for decades.

Read it and cheer.

Here is the bottom line. If you want to impress your literature teacher, read Salinger and Wolfe. If you want to read something fresh and fun, read *RED SKY AT MORNING* and *GROWING UP ON ROUTE 66.* You will be pleased with your choice.

Larry Parks--Schoolmate and friend of Dr. Lund during their youth, now a trial lawyer in Texas.

Route 66 Kids

by Michael Lund

BeachHouse Books

Chesterfield, Missouri

Copyright

Graphics Credits:

Graphics Credits:
Cover by Dr. Bud Banis. The front cover is composited from a satellite photo
courtesy of the US Geological Survey and photo Objects from Hemera
Technologies (www.hemera.com) with text and enhancements by Dr. Bud Banis.
Picture of the Banner Hotel is extracted from an old postcard, ca. 1950 from the
National Printing Company in Hannibal Missouri. The Photo of the St. Louis
Arch is from the Library of Congress American Memory Collection.
Publication date February, 2002
ISBN 1-888725-70-2 Regular print BeachHouse Books Edition
ISBN 1-888725-71-0 large print (16pt) MacroPrintBooks Edition
First Printing, February 2002

    Library of Congress Cataloging-in-Publication Data
Lund, Michael, 1945-
  Route 66 kids / by Michael Lund.
     p. cm.
Sequel to: Growing up on Route 66.
  ISBN 1-888725-70-2 (alk. paper) --
  ISBN 1-888725-71-0 (large print MacroPrintBooks ed. : alk. paper)
  1. United States Highway 66--Fiction. 2. Teenage boys--Fiction. 3.
Missouri--Fiction. I. Title.
  PS3562.U486 R68 2002
  813'.54--dc21
                              2002002261

an Imprint of

BeachHouse
Books

𝕾cience & 𝕳umanities 𝕻ress
PO Box 7151
Chesterfield, MO 63006-7151
(636) 394-4950
www.beachhousebooks.com

Route 66 Kids

by Michael Lund

ACKNOWLEDGMENTS

I wish to express my sincere gratitude to Dr. Bud Banis, a publisher of the old school (an educated friend of the author) and of the new (a skilled man of business and technology). We have worked happily together on the basis of an electronic handshake, surely a modern-day miracle.

Robin Sedgwick has graciously offered editorial advice in the course of this book's production, and for that I am also grateful.

Any inconsistencies or errors remaining in the pages that follow are, of course, attributable solely to the author.

FOR ANNE

Toward whom this book is moving.

Route 66 Kids

Michael Lund

Prologue: Stolen By Gypsies

Happiness is something one can't explain. You must take my word for it. Troubles enough came afterward, but there was that summer, high and blue, a life in itself.   Willa Cather, The Professor's House

Nothing was more exciting in my Midwestern childhood than the announcement that something had been spotted coming over the horizon, an object or objects seen above the distant line of rolling Ozark hills when we were out in the open or above the more immediate treeline within our neighborhood.

It might have been a low flying plane, dropping leaflets across town, a flock of birds on their annual migration, or the low rolling bank of storm clouds bringing snow. But no matter what the cause, whenever one kid called out and pointed to the sky, the rest of us felt our pulses quicken and anticipation mount.

Nothing exceeded the sense of childhood promise-- tinged,I must admit, with a touch of embarrassment-- caused by the aerial sighting Billy Rhodes and I experienced one lazy Sunday afternoon late in August. The two of us were lying on our backs on the unshingled roof of a new house under construction on Ridgeview Road, an extension to the south of the Circle proper.

"The Circle" was what we called our neighborhood, a name derived from the configuration of three streets-- Limestone, Oak, and Hill--that connected in a kind of elongated loop on the western edge of this small town in south-central Missouri.

Billy and I were in the midst of one of those typical teenage boy talks about sex.

"Think about Marcia Terrell's lips," commands Billy.

"OK, I'm thinking about them," I respond. Marcia catches her lower lip in her teeth when she's worried, and I generate considerable pleasure in my contemplation of kissing them.

We were not supposed to be on this rooftop, of course. This is a three-quarters finished house, with framing, plumbing, and wiring complete and a tar papered roof above. But none of the carpenters was there on Sunday, so we were ignoring any unspoken prohibition that would have been expected from our parents.

From our present vantage point, three town landmarks are visible: the regional hospital, a two-story beige brick building about three quarters of a mile due north; the massive red brick and sandstone Phipps County courthouse only half a mile to the east; and the impressive four-story Banner Hotel, famous Route 66 establishment perched on a ridge clear on the other side of town. (You'll learn the history of the Banner Hotel later.)

"Think about Sheila Knight's hair," says Billy. And I do that too. Hair is a turn-on for Billy, so I know he's getting excited about this project in fantasy.

"Umm!" I offer, willing to see where this is leading. I decide not to let on to Billy that I'm thinking about more of Sheila than her hair. Though still a teenager, she has a woman's full body.

I called parental instruction "unspoken" a minute ago because this is a feature of our current, mid-adolescent stage. Fathers and mothers around the Circle, it has occurred to us, have at last given up repeating the rules they expect us to go by: "be home for dinner; stay away from the railroad tracks; don't play rough with girls."

Of course, this change could be as much in us as in our parents. That is, we might no longer be hearing my father assigning regular and odd chores or my mother announcing limits and prohibitions. Growing boys with hormones surging and rebellion in our bones, we could have been consciously or unconsciously turning deaf ears to whatever our parents dictated.

"Think of Cathy Williams' legs, and, oh, that sweet rear end!"

This isn't hard because our legendary neighborhood beauty has legs, as we used to say, without knowing exactly what we meant, 'that go all the way up!'

"Think of Patricia Stewart's knockers."

This too is no challenge, as her chest, just arrived from Texas, is, as you'll learn later, remarkable.

I understand at this age, by the way, about how lips, legs, and knockers are all linked in the process of human reproduction, that eternal event that continues the human race. I think I even know, as I'll explain, the specific event that led to my own appearance on this planet. Of course, Billy's instructions right now fit within a different context--idle pleasure.

Certainly, I understand, though, that kids derive biologically from parents: my friends and I are the sons and daughters of the generation that survived the Depression and World War II, the "Big One," as we've heard from our earliest days.

We don't, however, fully understand how we are the kids of other things too, forces and events that shape our destiny and will give us the name "Baby boomers." It might be a little like the "stolen by gypsies" tale.

In that ancient formulation, a young man or woman, having known no other family since infancy, grows up as a member of the adopting group. However, the young gypsy realizes that he or she doesn't quite fit in. The boy doesn't want to steal chickens from the farmer's barn; the girl wants to read books instead of wash clothes along the riverbank. Their true identities cannot be hidden forever, and at the end the hero/heroine discovers an origin, true parents.

I didn't feel like this often as a young child, nor, I think, did many of my generation. So satisfied were most of us with our lot in Middle America in the 1950s that to desire anything different was almost impossible.

Oh, of course, there were exceptions. Raymond Guthrie was convinced he was the unacknowledged son of St. Louis Cardinal great, Stan Musial, And Patricia Montgomery just knew that she was Princess Grace of Monaco's forgotten little sister, abandoned somehow when the movie star left Hollywood.

Several decades later I would even come to understand that there were whole groups of the disenfranchised in our midst all those years. White Anglo-Saxon Protestants like me were just pretty good at not seeing them.

Still, by and large, most of the kids I knew figured we were who we were, ordinary folks destined eventually to take our small parts in the large scheme of things. And I was no different from the rest: Mark Landon, second son of Richard and Susan Landon of Limestone Drive, moving steadily and unspectacularly through grade school, junior high, and high school on the road to a productive if conventional adulthood.

There were some stray moments along the way of a dozen years or so in which the constructs that held me securely seemed suddenly to shake loose and reveal completely unpredicted alternatives, selves I had never until those moments imagined I could be. I might have been stolen by gypsies.

And now I realize it could be said I was born of social systems and intellectual structures that also contained my father and mother, my older brother and younger sister. I might have been, one might say, a child of Route 66, that famous highway representing westward expansion and the idea of a better America.

Route 66 ran just north of our neighborhood on the other side of the Missouri Pacific railroad tracks, which lay at the bottom of the Cut. The highway had passed through town for many years, but one of the recent phases leading to Eisenhower's national system of interstate highways meant the building of a bypass around town for through traffic.

In the chapters that follow you'll hear more about the local reasons for such a bypass and how that change reflects altered hopes and dreams for people like me. And you may conclude that all of us growing up in the Circle are "Route 66 Kids" as much as we are the children of individual parents.

Now, did I mention that at least one of the two boys on that Ridgeview rooftop is feeling a bit crowded in his pants at this moment? No, I guess I didn't.

Well, we're lying on our backs on a slanted roof, remember. And there is gravity. So our bodies are probably sliding earthward, and some things we're wearing are riding up.

Then Billy asks all of a sudden, "Why is it so dark?"

"I don't know!" It is dark; we're suddenly in shadow.

Both of us crane our heads backwards, to the south where the sun sits high. And we both see the same thing: a huge hot air balloon, flame orange, sweeping majestically over the treeline no higher than one hundred feet above us. The giant bag rising from the tiny basket is another hundred feet tall, and the whole thing has cast us in momentary shadow.

It's not really the balloon that has mesmerized us, of course, but the couple in the basket below.

In my adult memory's picture of her, the woman in the basket combines Marcia Terrell's lips, Sheila Knight's hair, Cathy Williams' legs, and Patricia Stewart's bosom. She is stunning.

"Look!" I gasp. Billy responds, "Ah!"

The man in the basket, whose arm rests comfortably across the woman's shoulder, has the lips, hair, legs, and chest I expect to have in the future. He too is gorgeous.

This couple represent, I realize at once, my future--daring adventure, thrilling romance, the achievement of great things. I will travel, I will fall in love (and be fallen in love with), I will become famous.

Billy instantly grasps this concept as appropriate to his own destiny as well, and we lie enraptured of this sight and our own prospects. The grand pair glides over the Circle, crosses Route 66, and drifts lazily north-northwest.

Before that, the two riders had looked down at us, this pair from heaven. Turning in the basket, they saw, I understand decades later, two goofy teenage boys lying spread-eagled on a rooftop and up to . . . well, let's just say, up to no good.

Before they are out of sight, Billy and I will convince ourselves that they couldn't really have seen us very clearly, that they wouldn't have had time to decipher what they observed. They were probably just viewing the neighborhood in general, more interested, we're sure, in each other than in the ordinary world below them.

And who, you ask, was this flying couple crossing America, perhaps following Route 66 to California? Gentle reader, I wish I could tell you. In fact, one of the reasons I'm writing this continuation of my life story is to see if anyone out there can answer this question. While a number of other people later remarked on the event, I at least never found an explanation of who the balloonists were or why they would have been journeying on that particular day. They remain a mystery.

Other pieces of my universe, however, did come together in meaningful patterns in those years of my growing up, years when the world was an open book for me and my friends to read and come to understand. It didn't happen all at once, of course. But many a day brought a flash of insight into the workings of adulthood, for gypsies and for children in their own families.

So I close this prologue with the image of something coming over the horizon because it stands even now for that great happiness of childhood, summer high and blue. Such a serendipitous event catches us by surprise, forecasting pleasure, companionship, genuine fulfillment-- all things I hope for you in the pages that follow.

Mark Landon

St. Louis, Missouri

Volume One: Ancestry

Part One: Sons of the Father

Chapter I

"They're going to build a new A & P," my mother observed one September evening after dinner as we glided north up Route 00 toward the distant Osage River. Jefferson City, the state's capital, lay some 25 miles beyond that.

"Mmm?" my father commented. We were cruising at a modest pace down this two-lane highway, which crossed the more famous Route 66 at the heart of Fairfield, my home town.

These "drives" occurred frequently at a time, the 1950s, when gasoline was cheap and small towns featured few recreational activities. Our regular outings marked an increasing satisfaction with America at peace and prosperous, with a stable and growing community, with a region of the country that we did not yet call but felt nonetheless to be "the Heartland."

"Yes, a new A & P, but not downtown."

"Where then?"

Between these parental questions and answers, by the way, you might want to look out the window at rolling, oak-covered hills and patchy fields of yellow corn. It's what we children in the back seat are doing.

9

"Betty McGregor says it'll be by the Holsom Bakery, off Kingshighway." Kingshighway was what Fairfield called Route 66 as it passed through town.

"A lot of traffic at that corner. Doesn't sound like a good idea to me."

"She says the mayor's family owns land there."

"So?"

We had reached one of my father's standard turn-around places on this highway, a pulloff with a pair of picnic tables. After several cars passed, he pulled back onto the highway, beginning the return to town.

During this return, where we'll have a bit of a family scare, let me suggest what I was thinking about as my parents discussed local politics, the growth of the town, the making of money.

Not yet in high school, I was enjoying the last summer of my youth without the responsibilities of school or job. That is, the wonderful time of childhood innocence was still not quite over for me.

And yet I had already begun to confront a central issue of my future: competence. Was I going to be able to function in the adult world? Or would I be doomed forever to struggle with their mysterious forms of behavior and their unaccountable standards of conduct?

The question had already been framed in at least two key contexts: the world of work (along with best friend Billy Rhodes, I had tried to start a neighborhood kids' store); and the area of personal relationships (I had had moments of sexual experimentation with our neighborhood's most attractive sisters, Tricia and Susan Bell).

The primary arena in this search for competence continued to be "the Circle," a neighborhood established by the connecting streets of Limestone, Oak, and Hill along Piney Ridge at the western edge of Fairfield, Missouri. But I was also having to face the strain of performance beyond the Circle, where boys my age began to be rivals more than pals, where competition had a new fierceness that puzzled me, where early growth and development turned some males into terrors for the small and the young.

Often this battle with peers was for the attention of girls like Marcia Terrell and the Bell sisters, sexually charged encounters emerging from seemingly innocent games of Kick the Can and less childish encounters in neighborhood bomb shelters.

Every few weeks brought for me a new understanding of what could go on between male and female, between male and male. And in the next few days I was to take several more steps in that lifelong education.

My father, driving the brand new family car, represented a primary model in all the challenges males faced in life. I've since learned that most fathers, from the perspective of their children, represent competence, even when they don't possess it. They have such authority over the lives of children and speak with such certainty about all matters, that we assume they understand themselves and all things.

Richard L. Landon, a slim, neat man noted for his good looks and quiet manner, was the Assistant Director of the State Geological Survey, second in command of a virtual army of mappers and rock hounds who filled a three-story, downtown Fairfield office building. These geologists and their assistants regularly fanned out to the state's many counties, studying and recording features of the land on which we lived.

In the central office statistics and samples, measurements and chronicles, projections and surveys were funneled across one desk before presentation to the State Geologist. At the heart of this vast network, that is, was my father, a man who shaped, honed, and sharpened information into manageable, useful packages. From his hands came the basic units of knowledge that determined policy and achieved results, as far as geological studies of the region were concerned.

And in our modest house on Limestone Drive, this same person was the manager of our family. It was, remember, the 1950s, where men were men and everyone else was not. So Richard Landon's vision of the world determined the places of mother and children in the home as well as within the family car on such leisurely rides as the present one.

"If they build a bypass," my mother resumed as we rode back toward Fairfield, "that'll make Kingshighway a good location for a new grocery store. Trucks and long-distance travelers would be going around town, reducing traffic at that corner." The state would, in fact, begin building the Route 66 bypass that fall.

"Ahh. Now that I think about, Paterson's boy owns several lots there. It all fits, doesn't it!" My father tapped the steering wheel with the palm of his hand, absentmindedly underscoring his point. At the same moment, a sporty red convertible, a foreign make I couldn't identify, came up from behind and passed us

"Son of a bitch!" whispered my father through clenched teeth.

This expletive, by the way, startled me in my seat behind the driver's. I had seldom, if ever, heard my father swear. And my attention shifted suddenly from what was flying past the window to my parents in the front seat.

To be precise here, I should say that I had never noticed my father swearing before this moment. As I try to reconstruct the events of my childhood in memory, I sometimes get confused. Some things may have been happening all along in these years, and I just suddenly became aware of them at certain points. Or I might have been alert to new events when they occurred, sudden changes from previous activity.

My father may have always sworn in this manner, somewhat under his breath and rarely. Or this little explosion may have marked the beginning to a new phase in his behavior.

Perhaps hearing such expressions on the schoolyard and from older kids in the neighborhood had recently sensitized me to the issue. I do know that such restrained uses of almost polite profanity ("Damn!" "He's a real bastard!" "The hell with it.") did characterize my father's speech from this time forward. But I don't know if that beginning was in him or in my own perception of him.

In either case, my mother went on: "Well, the A & P does need a bigger building." She had not heard or was ignoring her husband's exclamation. "The one on Main Street's too crowded, narrow aisles. And the parking."

"Mmm." Father was watching the red convertible ahead of us, perhaps no more than a football field away. It had passed us on a level, straight stretch, and it was now approaching a set of fairly sharp curves along a hilly section of the county.

My father disliked drivers who accelerated on the straightaway, then slowed for curves, especially those in cars not made in America. To his mind, good drivers selected an appropriate speed for a given highway and locked in on it. Today he was cruising at 62 miles per hour, exactly.

I could see the convertible slowing already. We were catching up, and I knew what would happen shortly--my father would pass him back on the curves.

Perhaps all American men felt themselves at this time to be great drivers, owning, as they did, such expensive and powerful cars. And, though we had not yet begun that national project of connecting all major cities with four-lane interstate highways, our roads (especially Route 66) were impressive engineering achievements. So to own the highway in your American-made automobile was a heady, almost patriotic feeling. And to impose your standards of driving on others was simply a further assertion of your authority.

Although I am struck now by how this sometimes maniacal mood affected the rest of the family, I am convinced that at the time we didn't notice. Whenever my father leaned forward in his seat, tightened his grip on the wheel, and set his jaw, our bodies instinctively prepared to be thrown left in one turn, right in the next, back during the acceleration of passing.

Because he held onto the wheel in front of him, and knew when he would begin and end these sweeps around bends in the road, my father's body departed from the vertical in a pattern exactly reversed from ours. When he leaned into a left turn, my mother and the three children in back were tilted to the right. And at other curves, we went left as he angled right. Seen from behind as silhouettes in the car's rear window, we must have made an entertaining puppet show.

Because we children had been thrown this way and that since we were infants, we accepted it as a regular part of travel. My mother, too--having recognized my father's need to challenge other drivers--did not suggest to us or to him that there were alternative methods of handling these situations. She was resigned to the knowledge that she would sometimes find herself passing with the narrowest of margins on a climbing curve.

She could not always, however, conquer a deep, inner reflex at such moments. When the space to pass ahead was shorter than she thought it should he, when the difference in speed between the two vehicles suggested we would have difficulty getting around in time, a single sound might escape her--one, sharp intake of breath between clamped teeth, "Ssssss!"

It was an exclamation not of terror, really, or of warning, but, I think, of some elemental, intimate knowledge of human mortality. "Ssssss!"

She made that sound now.

II

We did not run head-on into a bus on Route 00 that September evening thirty years ago.

True, a northbound Greyhound, the 4:30 out of Little Rock carrying perhaps a dozen travelers, did rise up above the hill in front of us at the very moment my father, having pulled into the opposite lane, committed himself to pass. But the driver of the irritating little sports car in front of us, seeing the danger, slowed abruptly and let us slip back into the right lane ahead of him.

An exchange between my parents followed this close call, the essence of which was repeated many times in my childhood.

"Richard!" my mother hissed.

"What?"

"That bus?"

"Plenty of room."

Despite the growing traffic on this north-south road and the more famous Route 66 which crossed it, my family would, in fact, never even come close to a wreck in the area of Fairfield. Statistics then and now suggest that you are in most danger within a circle twenty-five miles from the spot where you live. But our closest calls--and our one serious accident--came on long-distance travel, far from home. With that one exception automobile fatalities were for me as remote as the casualties in Korea had been when I was somewhat younger, items included in newspaper reports and radio newscasts, but never involving people I knew or places I had been.

Did I connect the apparent safety within which I, my brother and sister, and the children I knew at school moved with the absolute authority and power of my own and other fathers? Perhaps I did.

Not that I thought it out in any rational way, but I do believe I had an unspoken sense that the men of Fairfield met regularly somewhere, discussed the things that needed to be done to preserve peace and prosperity, charged their representatives (the police and military, also men and fathers themselves) to implement the necessary programs. Cars arrived intact at their destinations, factories safely produced durable goods, furnaces warmed the houses of neighborhoods and cities because knowledgeable men, who experienced no doubts or weaknesses about their roles as family breadwinners and pillars of society, stood watch in their rightful places.

Of course, the stature of these fathers and the extent of their power were dependent in part on where we were when we viewed them. There were few situations in the Landon family history where any of the rest of us--Mom, Charles, Beth, or myself--dominated events, re-defining our father from that different vantage point. For many years, the structural lines of the family unit were shifted only when we moved outside our house on Limestone Drive, when we traveled to other towns and states or when we attended events together in Fairfield.

On the weekend after this almost routine close call on highway 00, I did, in fact, see my dad in an unfamiliar situation, at least unfamiliar to me. At the Geological Survey's annual fall picnic, I saw my father play the fool. It happened when I nearly got my head knocked off during what started out as a friendly game of baseball. In chronicling my personal progress in these years, I will explain both his antics and my risky play.

A novel feature of the Survey's regular picnic was the unusual mix of people who attended. Most of the people I knew at this time in my life were defined by two sets: members of my class in school and residents in the neighborhood of the Circle.

I was usually in one set or the other. And their individual interests were shaped by a fairly stable group identity. On only rare occasions, like this picnic, did I find myself with members of both groups mixed together. Here kids from the Circle mingled with my classmates. And their different visions of the world, and of individuals like my father, were sometimes juxtaposed in ways that surprised and enlightened me.

Marcia Terrell's father, for instance, was in charge of the Survey's personnel office. So Marcia was one familiar Circle kid I would see on the Survey's spacious grounds, a single square block along business Route 66 not far from South Central Missouri State College.

From my class at school (modestly named Fairfield Junior High) came Jimmy Donaldson and Sam Blount, boys who were beginning to show an interest in the younger Marcia. Their interest had recently inspired me to take a closer look at my childhood playmate, my Circle neighbor.

Jimmy, whose father worked in the map department, was a pretty good guy, easy going and consistently happy. He and I often ended up on the same teams when sides were chosen for basketball or touch football, and I had learned to appreciate his cooperative style.

Sam was a year older than everyone in our class, half a head taller, though thin. He explained that he was older than others in his class because he had transferred when his family moved from Memphis to Fairfield a year and a half ago. I know now, of course, that he had failed a grade. His size and reputation made him stand out in school and at the Survey's picnic.

Mr. Blount worked in building maintenance, and I'd noticed that father and son shared a singular crooked smile. I disliked the younger Blount on principle, but also because of the male "sport" he brought with him from Tennessee.

Although this was an era when sexual expression was pretty much forbidden, young boys, especially at the exciting stage of puberty and just beyond, naturally had a great need for physical contact, with the opposite sex when possible but with anyone when not.

It would have been nice if there had been for me and my friends an innocent, accepted way to touch and hold girls of approximately our age. But with the rare and unsatisfying exceptions of school dances (usually square dances!) no such opportunities existed.

The energy and desire of Fairfield's junior high school males generally were channeled into contact, some of it no doubt homo-erotic, with each other. Wrestling, hitting each other on the arms or shoulders, getting someone in a headlock were all standard ways of releasing the tension generated by restrictive social codes.

When Sam Blount entered our school, however, he started a more overt and intimidating version of such expression. Or, at least, I believed he initiated it. It might be that it broke out of its own accord, like an incubating virus, at the same time he moved to town.

Sam Blount's "sport" was generally referred to as "squirreling," and it involved one boy's suddenly grabbing another boy by the crotch and holding on. Done from the front, with a sudden lunging reach, this was a wrestler's move, the off hand of the aggressor protecting against a counterattack. Equally unnerving, squirreling could come from behind, a rapid reach between the legs, sometimes causing the victim to jump in the air or at least up onto his toes.

Although the intention of "squirreling" was not really to harm, and often involved friends as much as boys who didn't get along, it was one more way in which the bigger and stronger established their dominion. This form of assault and the fear of it governed life on the playgrounds and around school for nearly half of the twelve- to fourteen-year-old citizens of Fairfield.

Among the more vivid of my mental pictures from junior high school is a view of the playground and adjacent playing field directly behind the building. On the far side of that playing field a chain link fence separated us from the grounds of the high school. A line of tall trees on one side and a hedge on the other completed the enclosure of our space. In this memory, I seem to be standing on the higher edge of the playground area, near those trees, observing dozens of seventh and eighth graders randomly scattered.

On closer observation in my memory, however, I see that the arrangement of many of the boys is not entirely random but determined in part by the possibilities of squirreling. Some individuals are checking nervously over their shoulders; others are contemplating a sudden lunge; several are already squared off against each other.

Somehow this all goes on in sight of but is not recognized by the girls in our classes and the few teachers who are officially on playground duty. How this can be I don't really understand. Squirreling is obviously an unacceptable social act.

But girls in pony tails and plaid skirts, men in sport jackets, women with purses on their arms stroll about the landscape as if the individual boys before them are reading history books as they walk, discussing plane geometry and set theory in small groups. Yet significant numbers of them are crouched in grinning attack or sidling away in quiet fear, wondering if the next stage of growing up will contain even more gruesome assaults on their persons.

A fear of squirreling was, however, significantly reduced at an event like the annual Survey picnic. Here the odd mix of boys from different neighborhoods and classes at school undermined our ability to pursue the usual courses of action.

I fell in with Jimmy soon after my family arrived, both of us hoping this year to be thought old enough and big enough to join in the ball game, which preceded the supper. We were presently trying to stay out of the sight of fathers, who, having delivered their families to the picnic in the gas-guzzling automobiles of the day, were moving conference tables out on the lawn to hold the picnic food and would have commanded help. We had already been told to report at some point and help mothers carry containers from the cars and set them up on the tables.

Jimmy and I stepped into a little garden of hedges on the south side of the Survey building and found Sam Blount at the center of a ring of four or five boys. I knew most of them, also junior high-schoolers, by sight, but none of them well. Jimmy turned to leave, and I would have also, but Sam called to us.

"Come here, guys," he insisted. "Wanna see something?" He pointed with a stick to a patch of dirt by his feet. I could see some sort of drawing scratched in the dust.

"These four guys went duck hunting," he said to Jimmy and me, at the same time grinning and nodding to the others. He was giving the two of us a brief summary, catching us up with a story already begun. And in the dirt he was providing a map or diagram to go with the tale.

I knew what kind of story this was and why there had to be a picture. Sam was telling a special kind of dirty joke. I

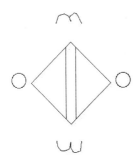

had run into this once before, when Archie Baker wanted to shock a group of younger kids in the Circle. I knew also that I was going to stay and listen.

III

"Two hunters set up in a blind along each side of a pond," said Sam. I could see the pond drawn diamond-shaped in the dirt, with two circles at the sides. Above one corner of the pond he drew a curved line, sort of a somewhat flattened "m," to represent a large bird flying toward the pond. Then he drew a second huge bird approaching the opposite corner, a shallow "w" from my perspective.

"Now, across this pond," continued Sam, pointing with his stick to the dirt. "Across this pond was a bridge." He scraped two parallel lines from the top corner of the pond, where one bird hovered, to the bottom, where the second appeared. Half of his audience had crouched down to hear this story and to see what he was drawing. The rest of us were bent at the waist, looking over shoulders. I studied the whole configuration of pond, birds, blinds, and bridge; but I didn't get it yet.

Sam looked around the circle of boys' faces that surrounded him, showed one of his twisted smiles. And then just as be leaned forward to add the final figures and finish the story, Sam's sister Barbara and Marcia Terrell stepped through the hedge behind us. His looking up alerted us, and we turned to face them. We were all embarrassed, though we weren't sure exactly why.

Sam frowned and stepped forward onto his drawing, trying to keep the girls from noticing it. "What do you want?" he asked his sister angrily. Then, remembering that Marcia was here too, he tried to look more friendly.

Barbara, a large girl though two years Sam's junior, was holding two sky-blue oven mitts in one hand. "Mom wants you to bring things from the car," she said, holding the padded gloves out to Sam.

"Aw . . . Tell her I'll be there in a minute." He dropped his stick and took the gloves. In a minute the little group hiding in the bushes had dispersed, Sam's drawing and story left, for the time, unfinished. (You'll hear the rest shortly.)

I wasn't terribly disappointed at being unable to hear the rest of this joke right now, however, in part because Marcia had flashed me a restrained little smile as I slipped past her. She had grown rapidly in the last year; and that often worried girl look she used to have had been replaced by a wistful but womanly appearance.

She still chewed her lower lip. But now that I knew so much more about lips and had even kissed some, this gesture was alluring to me. I saw it not so much as evidence of trouble, but as a sign of interest in matters that interested me. It was not that she was *chewing* lips, but that she was chewing lips!

Hmm, I thought, and this young beauty is right there in my own neighborhood!

When Jimmy and I came around by the portable conference tables being set up on the front lawn for the dinner, my spirits picked up even more. I saw men, dressed in old clothes they could afford to get dirty, making their way toward the main lawn behind the building, where the ball game would begin shortly.

Our fathers and older brothers, ordinarily stiff and restrained figures of authority, were dropping their usual poses of restraint to become boys of play once again. I saw my own dad rounding the corner of the building with Charles, who had played with the men for several years now. Others following them carried bats over their shoulders, gloves dangling from their fists. There were gestures of camaraderie and good cheer as they walked, the slapping of backs, issuing of challenges, and the flexing of muscles before friendly competition began. As soon as Jimmy and I had made a show of helping the women carry dishes and drinks, we would be free to take places alongside these seasoned veterans.

Our two family cars were at the opposite ends of the long parking lot parallel to Kingshighway, so we agreed to meet back at the conference tables and then hurry on to the field. As I sprinted off, I was excited not only by the prospect of playing ball but also by the memory of what we had brought to eat: two of my mother's famous apple pies. They would still be warm from the oven, sitting in a basket on the front seat.

It was not just these pies that offered themselves to me on this occasion. Other mothers had made other special dishes, and we sons would eat only the things we loved. I was at this time, I should admit, interested in desserts of all kinds, especially cakes, specifically chocolate cakes with thick chocolate icing. And this was one of those few places I could indulge myself without restraint.

I had been indulging myself just a bit too much in recent months, having grown a little pudgy around the middle, in the upper legs, and across my rear end. Since I was at the beginning of a growth spurt, I would lose this extra padding during the year. I would shoot up long and lean so quickly that few people have known since that I endured this short period of chubbiness. But right now I was conscious of some binding in my blue jeans and of shirts that clung where they might have hung.

Even as I took the pie basket and closed the car door behind me, I pictured myself already savoring a thick piece of someone else's chocolate cake. From memory of earlier picnics and in my imagination of what I hoped to find today, I saw in my mind's eye the round circle of cake covered with rich brown icing. My hand emerged from the bottom of a movie-screen frame of this future event. One pudgy forefinger--no wait! make that a slim forefinger--arched for a sample. I saw myself scoop out a fingerful of icing from a layer so deep you couldn't find, among the swirls and peaks of the artist-baker-mother's masterpiece, the place from which I'd subtracted a mouthful!

Back in the real world, I added my mother's basket to the table, now filling rapidly with other cake boxes, covered plates full of cookies, dishes of fruit cobbler, deep bowls of pudding. Later, main courses and side dishes would be added to the other tables: mounds of fried chicken; giant bowls of potato salad; slices of ripe watermelon; crocks of peas, corn, and beans.

This row of tables with dishes of all kinds would, in fact, shortly represent the multiplicity and variety of the Fairfield community. Arranged in basic groups of meats, vegetables, breads, desserts, and drinks would be the products of homes scattered throughout town and county. Each kitchen brought a sample of its essence or genius to find a place among others. As families found parking places along Kingshighway, as car doors opened and slammed shut, and as individuals walked from lot to lawn, the order of community was affirmed.

While all this was continuing, my eye was running hungrily up and down the one display of plenty in which I had the most interest. And I saw the very cake of my dreams descend onto the far end of the table held by a pair of small hands. A metal dome, carried by a second set of hands, immediately covered the cake. But I had captured in memory the beautiful cylinder of chocolate, the ideal object of juvenile appetite and a ball player's just reward.

Following hands up arms to faces, I saw Marcia Terrell, the cake carrier, and her mother, the dessert coverer. Mrs. Terrell, who, remember, had always disliked leaving her house in the Circle, frowned at me.

She frowned for no specific reason that I could imagine, for she certainly must have recognized me as a neighbor (her house was directly behind ours on Oak Street). I was also her daughter's friend and schoolmate, though she was a grade behind me. I couldn't think she knew, say, what Tricia Bell and I had once done in the family bomb shelter, or that I contemplated anything like that occurring with Marcia.

Perhaps Mrs. Terrell's frown took a precise shape because she was suspicious of anyone when she was out in public. Her frown certainly included Jimmy, who had just arrived beside me with his mother's angel food cake.

As Marcia had begun to blossom in recent months, her mother's uneasiness about the outside world had accelerated, though I didn't know it at the time. Like most kids at this age, I never noticed changes in adults, never acknowledged that, if we matured, they too had to grow older. As we grew taller, broader, stronger, they shrunk, thinned, grew less able to carry the burdens of life. It was almost as if, in order to fulfill their purpose in this world, they had to let us rob them of strength and vision.

Shifting my gaze away from Mrs. Terrell's frown, I watched her daughter turn and head toward the field behind the building. Ah, she will be watching the ball game, I thought. This will be a chance for me to impress her. Not only would Jimmy and I join the older boys and the men in this annual ritual, but we would also perform in the national pastime before a girl approximately our own age, a girl who might just appreciate new, more mature schoolmates.

As Marcia walked across the grass, I realized that she was nearly as tall as her mother. I saw also that her body and legs no longer had the thin, bony look I had always associated with the girl who lived over the back fence. The scruffy, scrappy core of the child had been fleshed out (and that's the right word) by age, rounding her jeans and swelling the deep maroon Fairfield High sweatshirt. She looked, in fact, rather fine to me.

She looked fine to Sam Blount also, I discovered in the very next moment. He had slipped in between Jimmy and me, though I had not become aware of him until he grabbed us each by an elbow.

"Hallo, boys," he said. And then he nodded at the departing Marcia: "Now, wouldn't you jus' like that honey to give your thang a squeeze!"

IV

Sam's appearance between Jimmy and me at the table of deserts broke the train of my reverie and inspired a temporary disorientation.

'Hallo boys' What was he trying to do here, I thought to myself. If we were 'boys,' so too was Sam Blount. So what's the point? And the other word he'd used, 'hallo'-- was he thinking he was British, putting on airs?

The different elements of Sam's short question at the Geological Survey's fall picnic, then, made me aware of the different contexts surrounding me and my contemporaries. He had even made me think suddenly of my grandfather.

'Thang'! I said to myself first, however, suppressing for the moment the fact that I had been reminded of my father's father. There were plenty of terms available for what Sam meant, especially given the man-to-man, side-by-side situation in which the three of us young people stood. There was no need for indirection, novelty, new terms.

True, Sam had a reputation for slang, especially off-color observation. It seemed connected to or derived from his practice of squirreling, that improper sport. But I certainly knew most if not all of the customary names for individual manhood, words used regularly in my neighborhood as well as at school. And one of those terms would have served easily here. Sam, however, threw me off with the unexpected 'thang', which required, in fact, several moments of reflection and then interpretation before I understood fully what had been said.

Sometimes, it is true, the item pointed to in expressions like the one Sam had delivered was hidden in metaphoric constructions, which disguised the exact nature of the literal. Furthermore, most of the figurative phrases I was familiar with at the time (many rested simply on the neuter term "it") involved the action of the man or male

27

animal in isolation, rather than with another person, someone of the opposite sex.

I was surprised not only by Sam Blount's distinctive vocabulary (thang) but also by a new element this word had introduced into my reverie. Squeezing someone's thang! What he was suggesting went beyond customary imaginings.

Fantasies of my future love life tended to start with kisses and lips but then grow vague and indistinct. True, other body parts were occasionally involved, as objects of curiosity, things I might touch. But these desired shapes generally remained inert. I did not routinely see them in their roles as functioning organs. Sam's announcement suddenly put the physical elements of male and female sexuality into a more dynamic relationship.

My grandfather, who came to mind at the same time I was decoding Sam's innovative reference, was a typically taciturn Scandinavian, a Swede who came to this country around the turn of the century and whose English vocabulary was lean and functional. The most my brother and I generally heard him utter in the course of routine Sunday visits to his home was "Hallo, boys."

In Sam Blount's joking pronunciation of "hello" I heard an echo of my grandfather, which started a train of associations and memories in my mind that moved steadily beneath a surface reaction to Sam's interest in Marcia.

Now that my father's father has appeared in this narrative, I realize that his ghost or his spirit has all along been behind some of the events I want to remember and understand. I'll have to take you back another generation in this account, then, moving from the present (myself), to the life of my father, and finally to the turn of the century and the time of my grandfather.

I visited my grandfather in Jefferson City regularly throughout my growing up on the Circle, although for the first four or five years of my life I saw him only rarely. At that time he and my grandmother were still living in

Wichita, Kansas, where, before the Depression, he had owned and operated a saw mill. When that business closed down in lean times, he went into construction, building houses in a number of small cities and towns of the western counties. After a series of moves, he returned to Wichita, where my father, the only child, went to high school and then on to Wichita State.

Just about the time I was born, my grandfather retired from full-time employment, though he kept up a small, part-time trade making furniture. And when my father took a permanent position with the Missouri Geological Survey, his father moved to Jefferson City, sixty-some miles northeast of Fairfield.

Sam's comment about Marcia and thangs, apparently, was an almost idle observation, a statement of the obvious. For he turned immediately and headed back toward the hedges where his story lay in the dust ready to be resurrected. And he waved us on with him, the hand that had been gripping my elbow sweeping along his side to include Jimmy and me. Beyond him I saw several of the other boys gathering.

At the age of 68 my grandfather began building a new house in Missouri, singlehandedly. Now, this was a small house, basically two rooms for an elderly couple. The living room with its sofa turned down would become their bedroom at night. And the large kitchen provided space for seven of us to eat sumptuous Sunday dinners without crowding. But Grandpa drew up the plans, laid the foundation, installed plumbing and wiring, cut and nailed every board from support beam to rafter.

And then a wing was added off the kitchen for a cabinet shop. Although this large area was not finished living space, the building of workbenches, the making of storage places, and the installing of power tools required considerable effort for one already in his retirement.

As Sam moved off toward the bushes, I remembered the game. "Go on ahead," I said, pointing to Jimmy. "We're going to play ball."

"Uh-huh," replied Sam, his head turned over his shoulder to look at the two of us. I saw again his off-center smile. I did want to hear the rest of his joke, but I also didn't want to be late to the field. If we were left out at the beginning, it would be hard to find a way into the game later.

That L-shaped house on the outskirts of Jefferson City was where we Landons would often be headed on a Sunday trip longer than the traditional "drive." We would go up Route 00 past the turnaround near the Little Piney River (where the red convertible had passed us) and then the Osage River. Not every week but more than once a month the five of us paid a family visit. When we arrived, Grandpa, rising from his favorite recliner, would shake Charles and me by the hand, intoning flatly, "Hallo, boys." And that was all we heard from him through the day, unless, perhaps at dinner, he asked Grandma for sugar to add to his dark Swedish coffee.

Ahead of us, Jimmy and I saw mothers and sisters carrying folding lawn chairs and blankets to sit beside the field and watch the game. I scanned the crowd for Marcia, but could not find her.

Although Grandpa never spoke about his youth, our father had filled in through favorite anecdotes much of the family history. Like the building of a new home at the age of seventy, these events in my father's eye always reflected great strength, determination, purpose.

Grandpa, for instance, had gone to work at the age of thirteen in the old country, hard times pushing him out of school and into the grim labor of coal mines near his native Helsingborg. Then he had served his mandatory time in the national army, becoming, according to my father, a crack shot with rifle or pistol even as he learned basic woodworking skills.

His sharpshooting was demonstrated several times with our boys' BB guns down in the basement on Limestone Drive. "You see, you see!" my father would exclaim, holding up a paper target whose bullseye had been riddled with holes. Even more telling was my father's repeated story of how, on a bet, his father had once sent an empty shotgun shell on a dirt road--so far away it could barely be seen--sailing with a single pistol shot.

Glancing behind me for a sign of Marcia, I could make out the heads and shoulders of four or five boys above the hedges. They were looking down, intent, I guessed, on the drawing Sam had made in the dirt.

Another demonstration of my Grandpa's character was also regularly set in motion by my father on our visits to Jefferson City. As someone who had worked with his hands all his life, my grandfather had a grip that was legendary. He still built furniture on consignment, even in his seventies turning out beautiful walnut sideboards, cherry dressers, custom designed desks. And, though he had power tools, he more often used the finely made saws, hammers, chisels, and screwdrivers he had brought with him from Sweden more than half a century ago. So his large, rough hands were steady and powerful.

To prove his father's strength, and perhaps to inspire us boys, my Dad would often want us to match grips with our grandfather. "Go ahead," he would say to Charles or me, squaring us off with Grandpa. "Squeeze as hard as you can."

Reluctantly, we would grab a hand, appear to put on the pressure, and then break away with an exaggerated cry of pain.

"Wow!" I would say, shaking my hand as if the fingers had been crushed. "That's enough for me!"

Of course, my father had put all of us in an awkward situation: Grandpa didn't want to mash these young boys' fists, so he must have held back to some extent. And we didn't really try all out, fearful of what might happen to our hands should he overpower us.

As we began to mature, we had other worries. After all, grandfathers do inevitably grow weaker. And young boys do increase in stature. There would come a point where

Charles first and then I would be something like an even match for Grandpa. So we broke off the contest early. And later, whenever the situation required, we confirmed for Beth and our mother the undiminished grip of the quiet man who had come across the Atlantic to help build a new country.

From behind the hedges, where Sam and the other boys had disappeared, I heard a burst of raucous laughter.

V

Right after the explosion of giggles from Sam Blount's little gathering behind the hedges, I was confronted by my brother Charles and one of his neighborhood pals, Heavy Joe Martin. I knew we were now in for one of the ancient rituals of older boys bullying younger ones.

Jimmy and I were just short of the small embankment that ran along the edge of the field behind the Survey building. Here some spectators would spread blankets to sit and watch the game. Others would open their folding chairs along the top of the little ridge.

"What are you two doing here?" asked Charles. "You don't think you're playing ball with us, do you?"

He and Heavy Joe had positioned themselves between us and the field. Where Charles was tall, already close to six feet, Heavy Joe was wide. His size was not at this time all fat, but his huge frame and an enjoyment of fine things would eventually make him weigh nearly 300 pounds. Now he was probably about 5' 8" and close to 220.

"They're just here to cheer," laughed Heavy Joe, suddenly stepping forward and grabbing me in a head lock with one of his giant arms. He began to rub his knuckles into my scalp, giving me "the noogies."

"Hey! Lemme go!" I cried, jerking back and trying to keep my voice from sliding up the scale. Jimmy, trying to help, pushed Heavy Joe in the chest, but the big guy didn't even notice. Charles put his fists up in a boxer's style, punching Jimmy a couple of times quickly on one shoulder.

"Now, now," warned Charles. "You little guys should just be watching us. You can get some tips."

"We're playing this year," countered Jimmy. He had his fists up too, but this was a flimsy defense against Charles. My brother was bobbing and weaving all around him,

33

slapping him with open palms on the arms and on the top of his head.

"Charles, leave him alone!" I yelled, again trying to make my voice rough and forceful. Of course, my head was poking out from under Heavy Joe's arm like the target in a water balloon toss at the carnival, and I didn't sound too tough. I was not, however, afraid of Heavy Joe or what he would do here.

It's true that he was mammoth, more than twice my size. But the idea of him never really frightened me. I had formed an understanding of him derived from a view of his entire family.

Heavy Joe's father ran a tire shop downtown, a successful sales and service operation that was one of the enduring businesses in Fairfield. And he too was large, though his son would be almost half a foot taller and considerably heavier. The father, a happy, outgoing man, was known as Big Joe. When his son began working at the shop the next summer, the younger would be called "Little Joe." Even years later when he was far larger, our generation's representative remained "Little" Joe to all the older customers.

The Martins lived on the back side of the Circle, in an Oak Street house that had been added on to in almost every place where an extension or addition to the basic two-bedroom frame structure could be imagined: extra bedrooms in the attic (Joe's bedroom and one guest room); a large den and TV room out the back; a playroom for table tennis and pool in the basement; the garage, which was connected to the house at the kitchen, finished as sewing- and sun room where Mrs. Martin entertained her friends or, more often, sat alone on warm sunny days painting miniature watercolors. (A tiny woman, she kept the books for the family business.)

Big Joe's bulk was concentrated in a pot belly, and his pear-shaped profile was a familiar sight on Fairfield's Main Street for nearly fifty years. Little Joe was big all over, like a refrigerator. When he took a place beside his father on the sidewalk greeting customers, he looked big enough to fill one of the great garage doors through which cars came and went in a steady weekday stream.

But for all their size, neither Joe was an intimidating individual. Big Joe's success came from his cheerful attitude, hard work, and long hours, not business shrewdness or political power. He made little profit on the individual customer but over the years had built up the store's volume.

Little Joe's mass was expansive, but somehow soft. He would play football his last two years in high school, in response to relentless pressure from the coach, who thought he had in one man his entire defensive line. But Heavy Joe/Little Joe never dominated play from his nose guard position. Although opponents could not block him backwards, he was unable to advance or run well laterally. Other teams learned to go around his position or to occupy him with a decoy back who ran right into his soft embrace.

This instinctive knowledge that the boy who held me by the neck was not really a dangerous enemy did not, however, bring with it any strategy for gaining my release. I squirmed and wiggled, pulling on Heavy Joe's elbow with one hand while my other pushed against his gigantic back. Charles then closed with Jimmy and put him in a head lock. I figured we'd have to endure this hazing, but hoped it wouldn't be severe.

My father always bought his tires at the Martin's business, convinced that an independent dealer like Big Joe would give better service than car dealerships and general repair shops. And all his dealings with his neighbor had confirmed this opinion.

The decision to patronize one tire shop was not an idle one, because my father cared about his automobiles. A regular subscriber to *Road and Track* and *Car and Driver*, he knew more details about models, engines, horsepower, 0-to-60 acceleration, and gas mileage than I would think anyone ever needed to know. When he bought tires, it was with a specific knowledge of his car's needs and a thorough understanding of construction, tread design, and performance. The same orderly, scientific approach that made my father a successful Assistant State Geologist governed his approach to buying and maintaining his automobile.

It was an incongruous pairing in some ways, my father the careful, restrained administrator and Big Joe the voluble businessman. I have in my memory a vision of the two of them--a slim, quiet customer and the large, chatty store owner--standing on the sidewalk discussing a sale.

Did I actually once see them there, when I was old enough to be traveling on my own, by bicycle or by car? Or am I extrapolating from several different memories, combining images from separate occasions? I'm not sure. Nevertheless, I have great confidence that this picture is an accurate one.

My father would have parked in the lot beside the building, not yet allowing his car to enter the front doors, where the lifts, wheel balancing equipment, and noisy air wrenches did their work. Big Joe, smiling and talking steadily, would be gesturing, holding up brochures, pointing toward racks full of tires in all sizes and styles. My father's hands would be in his pockets, his mouth set beneath a traditional men's dress hat pulled down firmly on his forehead. But the two Circle residents would be moving toward common ground, working out an agreement, a shared assessment of car and tire, buyer and seller, need and fulfillment. Eventually, they would shake hands on a deal.

"Come on!" Charles said to Heavy Joe. "They're choosing up sides." Jimmy and I felt a final rub of knuckles on scalp, a wrench of forearm on neck. And then we were free. Pushing our hair back into place with the palms of our hands, we hurried after the two older boys. We had endured the required initiation, and now were going to play ball.

At one end on the other side of the field a group of men and boys were gathered in a circle. At the center of the group stood Chester Johnson, the State Geologist, and my father. They were performing that ancient ritual of making teams: tossing a bat to see who will choose first.

I believe this custom is pretty universal in America, though there are, no doubt, regional variations. In the Midwestern version of this practice, one man throws a bat (handle up) toward another, who catches it one-handed somewhere near the middle. Then the one who threw places his fist around the bat just above and touching the other's hand. The man who first caught the bat then puts his other hand just above the second man's hand. And then they alternate grips until there is no more room for a hand at the top. The one who last fits at least some fingers at the handle end must demonstrate that his hold is a solid one by flipping the bat over his shoulder behind him at least six feet away. That man, the winner, gets first choice of teammates in the subsequent division into opposing players.

On this occasion (and perhaps, I realize now, not by accident) Mr. Johnson won and began the picking. Jimmy and I were excited that we too were chosen, even though we were among the last to join a team. He was on my Dad's side, and I ended up with Mr. Johnson. Without anyone's objecting that we were too young to play, we were in the game!

There was no established playing field on the Survey grounds, just a long expanse of lawn running parallel to the building from a small parking lot at the north end to a high wire fence at the south end. That fence served as a good backstop behind home plate, but the men had to find things to use as bases, measure off distances from plate to pitcher's mound and along the baselines, and then set up out-of-bounds lines in relation to trees and hedges, sidewalks and street, building and parking lot. This was the work of the more experienced players and long-time employees of the Survey, so Jimmy and I milled around with the younger players waiting for the game to begin.

I was getting pretty nervous now that it was clear I would get to play. I hoped I would not appear to be completely incompetent at the nation's pastime, that all my playground and neighborhood experience would prove adequate training for this new arena.

Glancing over to the ridge, where I hoped Marcia might be watching, I grew even more apprehensive: there were a lot of people coming. I was standing next to a large oak tree, and now I rested one hand on it and took several deep breaths to calm myself. I even had to lean forward and put my other hand on my knee to get control.

In this bent over position I saw an odd thing, a hand, palm up, appearing between my knees. This was not my hand, of course, so what . . . ?

The hand shot up and grabbed me by the crotch. I leapt up on my toes in a sudden unhappy dance and, turning my head, saw behind me the crooked grin of Sam Blount. I had been squirreled!

Part Two: Fathers of Sons

VI

Let me tell you why I looked forward to this game with such an intense mixture of enthusiasm and apprehension. My father could really play baseball.

Oh, he was not a professional player with a record in the major or minor leagues. But at a local level, and among men past the time of early athletic prowess, my Dad was easily the best pitcher and--more impressive to me--the best hitter I had ever seen. I knew that he would drive at least one ball from the fence deep into the outfield.

Although he had been a high school standout, Richard Landon had not played varsity sports in his university days or sought tryouts at a higher level. Growing up in a harsh climate of hot summers and cold winters, in an area where the building industry regularly went bust through the 1930s, he did not have time in his youth for the long daily practices or extended periods of summer training characteristic of more recent times.

In addition to regular chores of stoking coal furnaces, tending a small vegetable garden, and even, for a time, keeping a small herd of goats, he worked with his father after school and all summer. Through four years of college he held a regular job as a shoe salesman in a downtown department store. Then he spent more than three years overseas with U.S. Army Intelligence, mapping plans of advance and retreat in Africa and for the Allied march up the Italian peninsula.

After the war he wanted nothing but the chance to follow his profession as a geologist. Recreation for him did not mean sports or travel, but a rest from the relentless, focused effort to chart the rivers, mountains, and plains of the American Middle West.

Two specific images told me what was likely to happen before the staff of the State Geological Survey proceeded from game to picnic on the fall day Jimmy Donaldson and I first joined the men at play. One image came actually from a time before I was born, from a snapshot in the family album. The other came from the previous year's ballgame.

The black-and-white photograph had been taken in a New Jersey buttercup meadow on my mother's family farm north and west of New York City. There uncles and cousins, boyfriends and brothers had gathered to play a friendly game of ball only months before Pearl Harbor. My mother kept the picture, I think, as a memento of those distant, happy, pre-war days. But I always saw in it the prowess and skill of my father.

Although the picture was taken from behind first base and focused on batter and catcher, my father was also visible on the mound, already through his windup and halfway into the delivery of, I have always thought, a slider.

The right arm cocked behind his head, the left arm stretched toward the plate, he looks to the catcher's mitt. In the style of the time, he is wearing wide khaki pants and, over his shirt, a vest that must be open in the front because it stretches loosely across his shoulders in back. He is a man absolutely in control of what he is doing. And I can see even in the two-dimensional profile that he is happy.

I know my father can pitch not only from the photograph but also because catching for him was a chore that later fell to both Charles and me. In fact, the first baseball glove our father bought when we were old enough to play was a catcher's mitt, rather than the traditional fielder's or first baseman's glove. The mitt was not for him, of course. We two boys alternated as catcher, kneeling down in the dirt as he popped fast balls into the soft pocket, stinging our palms, or snapped off curve balls that slid across an imaginary plate.

Though his fast ball hummed and hopped, my father's breaking pitches were to me more remarkable. He had what he called his "slow" curve, a nifty change of pace. It did not leave his hand going very fast, it seemed. But about ten feet in front of the mitt it seemed to duck and shoot sideways with sudden new speed.

When we were older, in years after this Survey picnic, he also threw us the harder stuff, fast balls that threatened to knock us off our knees if we didn't cushion the force by pulling back on the mitt at the moment of impact. But it was always the curve that seemed magical, hanging out there in the air toward third base, stitches spinning in a blur, dipping toward the dust.

Although I gradually learned to throw fairly hard and with some accuracy, I never mastered a curve ball like my father's. I still don't know whether the problem was physical or mental, whether I just didn't have the ability to perform the necessary actions, or if I lacked some basic understanding of the process.

"Just turn the wrist as you throw," my father would say, rolling the ball casually in one hand. The white leather sphere with its ribbons of darker stitches seemed at home in these long, lean fingers. It fit in his soft palm, drew the curved fingers around itself. Then my father held the ball out straight before him, the first two fingers on his throwing hand arching over the top of the ball. He raised the hand, bending his arm at the elbow, and brought it down, twisting the fingers to the side. "See?"

This reminded me of how he'd taught me to rig and fly a kite years ago. For him it was simple, even obvious. But in my mind there always seemed room for questions, for doubt.

"Now, do you twist at the top of your delivery?" I would ask, puzzling. "Or on the way down?"

"Right here, right here," my father would answer, and the arm would move again, the wrist turn and the fingers roll. But as I looked up at him, a sort of haze or film

41

would come between us. The sound of his voice grew fuzzy and distant.

It was dreamlike, my father become a phantom instructor or a magician surprising his audience. I expected doves to fly up out of his sleeves, rabbits to be lurking inside the glove, a ball to come out of my ear.

And then when I tried myself, I could not be sure if the fingers were to come down and to the side at the top of the arm motion, or forward and to the front as the arm descended toward the horizontal.

How much twist should I give the wrist? Was it just a turn or more of a snap? Was the motion completely overhand or should it be somewhat side armed? Do I try for some kind of whip action, or is it a steady, straight follow through? I never did get it.

At the time of the Survey picnic, however, I was not yet trying for the fast ball or the slider. I could loft a high arching lob across the infield or bounce one in from the outfield. And I knew that would be all I had to attempt. But at bat things would be different. There the measuring of my maturity would be more conspicuous, and possibly devastating.

In this case, images of my father's ability came directly from memory rather than through photographs. I had been seeing him play at this annual picnic for some years, and I recalled in particular last year's performance.

Carrying my first full-sized fielder's mitt (purchased at the beginning of the summer with an advance on my lawn-mowing earnings), I had thought I might be allowed to join the men, but my father told me I wasn't big enough yet. So I stayed with the mothers and younger children watching along the embankment.

I probably maintained a disappointed expression while everyone else played, failing to cheer at the sound of a hit or clap at good plays in the infield. Nor would I have laughed at the expected accidents or mishaps that occurred on the field: Jimmy's dad booting a grounder,

Charles' losing (or claiming to lose) a fly ball in the sun, the husband of my father's secretary colliding with the third baseman. I kept thinking it was unfair that I couldn't play, and between pitches I pounded my fist into my glove.

In the last inning of the game, my father was due to bat. And I entertained a secret belief that, when his final turn came, he would let me take his place. I might not have been able to play the whole game, but I could have one chance to show that I would be ready next year.

There had been no evidence for this conviction. My Dad had said nothing once the game began and didn't even seem to remember that I was sitting up here along the side of the field. Since food would be served after this last inning, my mother had just taken Beth to help set up. So I watched alone, hoping that somehow I would get this one opportunity.

And, sure enough, when he was on deck, down on one knee, his cap tilted back in a relaxed position, my father looked over his shoulder at me and winked. I smiled at his wink, and he pointed to the bat. I'm sure my eyes went wide.

Then he looked over at the man by the plate, got up from his kneeling position, trotted over close to me. Leaning down to my face, he whispered. "Go long," he said.

"Long?" I responded. I didn't know what he meant.

Standing up straight again, he looked to the outfield. "Go down to the parking lot. I'll hit you one."

"Huh?"

"Hurry up." He walked away. The batter ahead of him, Heavy Joe Martin, had walked, and it was his turn.

Go down to the parking lot? That didn't make any sense. No one hit the ball that far, the full length of the field, beyond the deepest fielder. And what I wanted was not to watch my father play but to swing the bat myself.

Still, what else could I do? I was, remember, the kind of son who followed directions, even if I didn't understand them. If he said go long, long I went.

He must have had to take a couple of pitches while I sprinted down the little ridge behind the others who were watching. Whether they were balls or strikes, I didn't know. I just turned my back to the game and ran, pounding my fist into the glove.

A dozen yards beyond the left fielder, I reached the low cement curb of the parking lot, a row of cars facing me. I turned and looked back in time to see my father taking several deliberate practice swings. Each swing brought the bat straight out in front of the plate, and it pointed directly at me.

VII

I don't think that at this time in my life I was aware of the famous Babe Ruth story. After several strikes in some important game, the Sultan of Swat reached a hand out toward center field and then hit the next pitch over the fence exactly where he had pointed. So I doubt if I could have understood my father's signal, several practice swings ending with the bat directed at me, as an echo or imitation of that event. Still I felt instinctively that this moment was dramatic, impressive.

On the next pitch my father swung, and there was a crack as bat hit ball.

Was I far enough away to experience a delay between impact and sound, time for the *whack!* to travel the length of the field to me? Or is this pause an element I have added to the event in my memory as a result of later experience? I'm not sure, but I tend to believe that there was a gap between action and my apprehension of it, that the ball was already on its way out to me when I heard the sound of contact.

In that pause after the swing and before I heard *whack!* the ball was rising over the infielders, and the heads along the bank were turning, following its arch. My brain switched on an alert signal and my body tensed, as I began to understand my father's instructions of a few moments earlier: "Go long." I should try to catch this ball hit all the way out to me, hit for me! I was to pound my glove no longer in frustration but now in hopes of the ball's landing right in the pocket.

The assignment contained two primary requirements: my body needed to be where my father was sending the ball; and my glove should rise to meet what he had hit. This was a hands-and-feet operation, although my mind had to complete some calculations about the path of a projectile and to send some appropriate signals to leg and arm muscles. I started moving in, toward the center fielder, who was running out. But then I stopped, paused, and began to backpedal, for the ball was, miraculously, still rising.

My father had hit the ball very well, better than anyone in memory at this annual event. But he still had not hit it hard enough to reach the curb on the edge of the parking lot, where I, after coming in too far and then backing up too much, finally stood. Having in the end misjudged the ball twice, I could not reach it on the fly. But, as much through luck as skill and experience, I was able to one-hop the ball a dozen yards behind the center fielder, juggling it for just a second before it settled into the pocket of my glove.

And I understood my role enough to quickly flip it to that player, who fired it in turn back toward the infield, holding my father to a stand-up triple. Not a bad defensive play, actually, though it had made use of an extra outfielder.

A year later almost to the day, as I prepared to play legitimately on this same field, I was intimidated by this memorable event. (In the family we had come to call it "the Deep Ball.") The son of that father would be expected to perform, not as well surely, but at some level of respectability. And I was already showing myself such a little leaguer as to be squirreled by Sam Blount beside a huge oak tree and held in an embarrassing headlock by an older kid!

I did, by the way, spin free of my fellow junior high schooler pretty quickly. Of course, Sam would not have held on for long in sight of this crowd gathering beside the field, although the large tree trunk had given his attack some cover. And his goals of surprise and embarrassment had already been achieved. He just laughed and shrugged his shoulders. I did what most boys caught in such situations would do: tried to recover my dignity through some brilliantly cutting remark.

"You jerk!" I said, shaking a fist.

"Time to play-ay," he sang, pointing beyond me to the field, where Jimmy Donaldson's team was already taking their positions. My group, the Director's team, would bat first. So I scowled at Sam and trotted over to join that circle of players. A batting order was being established.

I should add one final note to my account of the Deep Ball, last year's game, before going on with the present contest.

It would be a number of years before I fully realized what had been accomplished by this hitting and fielding operation, since for a long time I focused only on my failure to catch the ball in the air. Having a father who can do something like hit a baseball is a remarkably fine thing. Yes, it pressures you to be a chip off the old block, to follow some footsteps. But at least there is substance there in the first place, a path to follow. And in meeting the challenges one faces day-to-day in growing up, it is no small comfort to understand that it has all been done before, that someone very close to you has survived the same ordeals and gained in strength.

In middle age now, I derive great pleasure still from calling up the image of my father at baseball. I see the arms and shoulders come around, hear in my mind's re-creation of the past a satisfying *whack!* Or I suck in my breath at a slow breaking curve magically suspended over the earth.

I guess my picture of him combines a number of specific events--pitching on my mother's family farm, hitting at the Survey picnic, throwing in our own backyard. But in this composite and all its individual components my father is a person who can do things. And I have tended to conclude in recent years that my own, perhaps delayed discovery that I too am able to do things can be traced to this source. There are other kinds of fathers, you know.

I had assumed, once he had gone off behind the hedges a second time, that Sam Blount would not be playing baseball. But he now followed me away from the oak tree to join my team.

"I'm gonna show the girls who's a star," he said, nudging my elbow. I glanced back to the ridge, looking for Marcia Terrell and her mother. There they were, behind third base. I winced to think that Marcia might have seen me up on my toes.

"Did you hear this one?" Sam whispered, trying to pull me off from the other players. "These three boys were having a contest, to see who had the longest?"

"Hm-mm." I wasn't really listening, wondering if I'd have to play outfield, wondering if Marcia would be watching. I did recall, in a flicker of memory, Sam's other story, with its drawing in the dirt of hunters in blinds, a pond crossed by a wooden bridge.

"So Billy pulled his out . . . really long. 'I think you boys owe me a dime just to see this,' he bragged."

When my neighborhood friends and I played ball on the Circle, by the way, it was usually in the street, since the yards weren't big enough, and most were full of trees, doghouses, small gardens. Our baseball diamond, thus, was a thin one, bounded by curved cement curbs. And the size of our outfield was determined by where in front of their houses various neighbors had parked their cars that day. Coming to the Survey would give us enough space for once to experience all parts of the game in their correct proportions.

"And then Freddy showed his . . . whoa! Much bigger than Billy's. 'I'm afraid this here is gonna cost you each about a quarter.'"

Of course, at school we had a playground. The outfield was not regulation size, but the infield was standard. The bases were kept in place by metal spikes driven into the ground, and a high fence around the home plate area kept balls from being fouled off into the street.

However, the games most often played here were organized by overweight and out of shape physical education teachers. They inevitably involved more drills and practice than actual competition. I seem to remember standing forever in one place, say, at second base, while a wheezing, bloated basketball coach tried to explain the conditions, steps, and possible outcomes of the squeeze play.

"But when Johnny unzipped . . . humongous!"

On the elongated street field of the Circle our games also involved fewer than the usual number of players--six against six, perhaps, or five against five. Often we had enough only to play what we called "Work-Up."

In this variation there were only three batters, and everyone else was in the field. When one hitter made an out, he took the right fielder's place. The right fielder moved to center, center went to left, left to shortstop, and so on until everyone had changed position. The pitcher became the third batter. Generally, everyone got a chance to hit and the game was exciting. But the very good players could sometimes stay at the plate all afternoon.

"So Johnny went home and told his father that he'd won a contest of who had the biggest."

"'Johnny!' his father said. 'You didn't take that awful thang out in public, didja?'"

Of course, when you were down to only four or five players, you went to "Flies and Grounders," also called "500." Here one person threw the ball up in the air himself and hit it out to all the others, each of whom had rights to a certain area--deep back, middle left, front center--behind where a pitcher might have stood. Whoever had the section of the field where the ball came first got the chance to catch it. You had to make the play cleanly (no bobbling one-hoppers here), but grounders earned you 50 points, flies 100. Whoever first reached 500 won, trading places with the batter.

"Shucks no, Pa. I jus' took out enough to earn me a dollar."

I gave Sam the obligatory chuckle, even though this was yet another version of a thang joke I'd heard many a time. And now it was finally time to begin the game.

Mr. Johnson had finished explaining who would bat when, and my place in the order was a not surprising last, right after Sam. At least I would have time to prepare myself.

Looking out at Jimmy (right field), my dad (shortstop), and others in the field, I concluded that it must indeed be right for me to join the big time. The diamond seemed smaller than I remembered. The pitcher, Heavy Joe, was right there in front of the plate. And the outfielders had not receded to the size of toy figures at a distance but stood within the range I thought I might actually reach. In fact, it all looked a bit too easy, though I didn't understand then why that was so.

I scooped up some dust to rub on my hands like a big leaguer. "Batter up!" I said to myself optimistically, little guessing what was in store for me.

VIII

Did my grandfather, like my father, play sports? I have only recently realized that I do not know. In fact, I find that I can say very little about his childhood in Sweden and that there are tremendous gaps even in the fullest chronology I might construct of his life.

There were a number of brothers and sisters in his family, my father has told me, many of them immigrating to the United States in the 1890s and early 1900s, settling in Kansas. Others remained in the old country, and their descendants are apparently well off in that socialist society, although we (the American cousins) have never been in direct contact with them. The first American-born generation in any immigrant family, of course, often has such a desire to be accepted by the dominant culture that foreign customs, accents, and habits are quietly expunged. And their children (my generation) know almost nothing of ancestral history.

I do recognize several primary landmarks in the family past, as represented by my father: one of my forefathers reportedly played the clarinet before the king (which king, I cannot tell you); and one early Lindstrom held vast estates near the city of Malmo and maintained a small army of servants. (The name Lindstrom, by the way, was simplified to Landon by a lazy immigration clerk when the first family member arrived. And others changed to maintain consistency.) The family fortunes had declined in my grandfather's time. As he and his siblings approached maturity, they knew they would have to set out on their own to establish a new prosperity.

My grandfather was the oldest and did do well, as I've said, in the construction business, although he lost one fortune in the Depression. His younger brother ran a grain elevator in a mid-sized Kansas town for over fifty years, becoming moderately famous and very nearly wealthy by his diligence and sound business practice. And the brother who stayed in Sweden reportedly went into metallurgy, eventually managing several large coal mines owned by the company my grandfather had worked for as a young man.

But all this is, in a sense, hearsay, perhaps even once removed. What I present here are things mentioned in passing by my father, who would receive general summaries of past and present family events when he visited relatives and friends in Wichita. I would hear or overhear him talking with my mother, but I cannot be sure if I heard correctly in the first place or if I am remembering accurately now.

My father claims to have gathered up much of this information in files he started more than ten years ago. But he has still not found time to organize it or communicate its particulars to me. I tell him in our long distance phone conversations that I want to get all this down for myself. But with work and other interests I too never seem to get around to it.

These large holes in my sense of the past remind me of something I realized about my father's relationship to his father. (I realize I have a ball game in progress here, but give me just a moment, OK? It may be that I'm reluctant to arrive at the climax of that tale.)

My father and his father must have talked a lot in the years of his growing up. And the older man must have advised the younger when I and my siblings were young. Oddly, however, I can remember no such discussions.

In my grandparents' house, which was, as you recall, quite small, perhaps the noise of children and the mechanics of preparing and consuming dinner (our primary event on those regular Sunday visits) made talk between the adult men difficult. But they did get away together. And, I now believe, in regular sessions the older passed on his wisdom to the younger. Why was I never present? Why did I not overhear?

You'll need the logistics of the situation to fully understand the answer. Our Sundays with the grandparents generally proceeded through three phases, bracketed by the hour-and-a-half drives up and down Route 00 from Fairfield. In the first phase (the second half of Sunday morning after we arrived in Jefferson City), my mother, sister, and grandmother went into the kitchen to finish preparations for a lavish mid-day meal. My father stood in one corner of the living room, on top of the main furnace vent, and told my grandfather of recent events. We brothers sat respectfully quiet on the sofa (which became a bed at night), or one of us might have been in my grandmother's easy chair by the radio (a Motorola). Grandpa rested in his favorite recliner, tilted back to a two-thirds position, and took in the news from Fairfield. If he said anything more than "Hmmm?" or "Yeee whiz!" I do not recall it.

This was, as you might guess, a difficult assignment for young boys. We tried to stay still, to confirm when necessary our father's account of recent happenings. If our comments were not called for, we could perhaps thumb through the Sunday paper (comics and sports) or recent issues of *Mechanics Illustrated*, Grandpa's one magazine subscription.

Then there was Sunday dinner, always an elaborate affair in terms of food, but a generally restrained one for conversation. My Mom held the floor here, sprinkling neighborhood anecdotes around the Ozark country cooking of my grandmother (who had grown up on a farm near tiny Tuscumbia, Missouri).

After chicken and biscuits, mashed potatoes and fried apples, creamed corn and stewed tomatoes, Charles and I escaped for the only possible chance at adventure that day, a walk down the hill to a creek where frogs jumped and sometimes snakes could be seen. When we were older, we would take a half-mile hike to a small park on a high bluff overlooking the Missouri River.

Now, there are some things that could be said about what the two of us saw and did on those afternoon excursions (we sometimes walked all the way into town, following the railroad tracks along the flat riverbed, passing the walled and fenced--ominous looking--Missouri State

Penitentiary). But more important in the present context is the fact that, during the time Charles and I were out of the house, communication must have occurred between my Swedish grandfather and my Kansas-born, Missouri-residing father.

In fact, I have within the last few years brought back out of the files of my memory a picture I had always passed over as unimportant in order to see this central event, knowledge being passed on from one generation to another. It occurs in the cabinet shop my grandfather had built as a wing to the cozy, two-room house of his retirement.

When Charles and I step out the front door of the house, we walk down a short sidewalk to the street. That walk goes across the front yard of Grandpa's L-shaped house. To our right is the shop, its small door close to the bend of the L and a window beside it. I look through the open door or the window, I can't be sure now which, and see the Landon men in the shop.

Grandpa is not running any of his loud power tools, though he might be holding one piece of the fine cherry, walnut, or mahogany molding he keeps stored above the rafters. My Dad leans back against one of the work benches, his hands in his pockets, looking perhaps at the floor. And they talk.

As I observe this scene now, I remember something else about my grandfather, something I have not mentioned because it doesn't seem to fit in the picture I have of his life.

At some point in his construction career, Grandpa lost the end of the thumb on his left hand. Using a big table saw, he had a single moment's break in concentration, and it cost him that thumb at the first knuckle. This happened years before I came along in the world (he didn't marry until he was 35; my dad was born when he was over 40). And he could use the hand with a partial digit almost as well as his other hand. I generally noticed the defect when we were inside the house, when Grandpa would be resting in his recliner. In an unconscious gesture, he would rub the fingers of his injured hand over and over that thumb, perhaps a habit begun during the healing just after the injury and continued ever since.

As I peer into the shop window to see Grandpa run his hand along a smooth piece of cherry to check for flaws, then, I notice that hand. It is so incongruous with my sense of the whole man, whose success in life came against such odds, whose ability was so evident that people sought him out into his eighties to custom design and build furniture, that I cannot imagine even a second's carelessness in his past, one failure of attention to detail. Nor, I know now, can my father.

This snapshot of memory, the two men talking quietly after a fine meal in the middle of a Sunday afternoon, freezes the past for me and enables me to reconsider what was happening then. Because Charles and I went right down the walk and crossed a little wooden footbridge to the road, we did not hear a word these two were saying. But now, years later, I stop on the sidewalk opposite the shop and listen.

I imagine that Grandpa talks of his youth in Sweden, of hardship and crisis. It was a bitterly cold winter, he is explaining, and because of some larger economic factors, a national recession or company reorganization, the coal mine where he began work was letting people go. He has lost his job.

Training in the military qualified him as a carpenter, but there was no work in this town. Nor were there jobs elsewhere. He would go to America.

There is more to my grandfather's account, but this I do not hear distinctly, something about another element in my grandfather's past. A girl, a woman? He must leave her behind? He promises to come back to get her? She becomes ill? She does not live? Or is it that he does not come back, after all? The business keeps him too long in this country? He finds someone else?

My father nods his head slowly, admits he does not know what he would do in such a situation. Grandpa strokes the wood, its beautiful grain . . .

Now I can get back to the game. Heavy Joe Martin goes into his windup. A new employee, someone I don't know, is batting first. And I see that the bat he holds is smaller than I expect, long but thin.

I look out at the diamond, amazed again at how small it is, how close the bases seem. I must be growing up, so large myself that everything once huge has been reduced to a reasonable size, or even smaller.

The ball flies from the mound to the plate, and it too is tiny, like an egg. But what a curve Heavy Joe has put on it! It dips and dives at the batter, striking him on the foot and bouncing all the way to where I stand.

I bend over to pick it up and am astounded at how light it is, like plastic. It is plastic--it's a wiffleball!

IX

The substitution of plastic for wood and metal, for leather and string, for canvas and rubber, was, of course, going on all around us in those post-war years. Household items, tools and machinery, building material, clothes and toys were all being transformed or redesigned using new substances that had been invented and produced for American industry, spurred by the engines of war.

If I had known how and where to look at the State Geological Survey's annual picnic, I could have traced the presence of plastic from the interior trim of automobiles, through bowls, plates, and storage boxes holding food on the conference tables, to new map-reading and drawing equipment inside the building before arriving at wiffle-ball equipment on the field of play.

The reduction in size and change of material in the national pastime was only one instance of a much larger phenomenon, a reorganization and restructuring of America. I suppose, in fact, we were lucky in this particular case that the changes were no more monumental than the evolution of equipment. The bat being used, for instance, was still wooden, though scaled down from the traditional shape, much skinnier from handle to tip. In another few years there would be large plastic bats, some fatter if not as long as Babe Ruth's.

The ball thrown by Heavy Joe was about three-quarters as large as a baseball and had holes in one hemisphere that made throwing a curve easy, if not inevitable. And, though it would leave the bat quickly when hit, this ball went perhaps a tenth as far as a regular ball, almost floating to the ground rather than dropping.

I had, by the way, seen wiffleball being played earlier that fall on the campus of South Central Missouri State. Then I had only watched the college men clowning around with their dates on the quad, hearing my father explain why the ball went *pock* rather than *whack*, why some players were barefoot and everyone seemed to laugh rather than bear down in concentration.

A genuine baseball enthusiast himself, my father thought softball a comedown for his generation of hard-ballers. Wiffleball had to be a joke for him.

The game of baseball was altered at just about the moment in history when I arrived to take part at an adult level. Not only had the game changed, through the advance of science and technology, but the nature of the players was being redefined now as well, for younger, littler people could be involved without fear of injury.

At this picnic where I joined my father we would play on a field much smaller than normal; we didn't need gloves to catch flies or field grounders; and the ball and bat weighed a fraction of the standard amount, creating a sense that we were playing on the moon or some smaller planet.

I felt a sudden, deep sorrow for my father, who had lost this one annual place to excel outside the ordinary routines of his life. In fact, I could see, in my imagination, disappointment register in his look when he realized that the game this year--and probably for all future years--would be wiffleball rather than softball. He could not have disguised the shock, his face falling, the mouth hung open.

I should say, however, that I did not literally see this unhappiness. For, remember, when my father was on the field learning that we would play wiffleball, I was probably struggling in Heavy Joe Martin's headlock. So I guess this is one of those "memories" that are not actual registers of past events. We extrapolate over time from a number of experiences, combining knowledge gained in different situations often separated by months or even years. And then the mind creates a composite picture that so fits the larger patterns that we are convinced by the structure of history and we gradually endorse it as an actual happening.

I have a vivid, detailed image of my father's face when he first sees a wiffleball or wiffleball bat, looks up at the others gathering to play, and realizes what the game will be today. Some of his colleagues are pitching aside gloves that will not be needed. Others use exaggerated motions to emphasize how light and small this equipment is.

Perhaps my father tries a question. "We're not going to use this, are we?" He grins, hoping it's a joke.

"Come on, Richard," says one. "It's fun."

"You long ball hitters just want your own game," says someone else.

"It's the same thing," adds another. "You pitch, you swing, you run."

He tries to put a good face on it, I suspect, but I already knew how he felt about softball as opposed to hardball. He never did accept that larger ball, the lessened distance from mound to plate. And he always talked about playing "real baseball" on the sandlots of his Kansas youth. There was even the chance there of injury, which you accepted as important to the sport. It wasn't the same, he said, pitching underhand, even though fast-pitch softballers could get more stuff on their curves and were notoriously hard to hit.

I too was crushed the moment I realized that now even softball was lost and we would be paying wiffleball. I knew my father would take this loss of opportunity hard, but I also wondered how I could prove myself in this lesser arena. How would muscles be tested, tendons and ligaments strained to their limits, the heart pound out its desire with a ball that could be squeezed flat in one hand, a bat that even a twelve-year-old could whip around like girl's baton, the distance from home to first so short that breathing would never be labored? No, my entry into manhood could not occur in these circumstances, not at this time in this place.

And, of course, for a long while I was not even in this new game, as, with Sam Blount refusing to leave my side,

I rested on one knee near the fence behind the plate and watched everyone else come up to bat.

"So, lissen," said Sam, picking up a small stick and scratching in the dirt in front of me. "These hunters were waiting for the ducks to land on their pond." He drew again the diamond, the bridge from top to bottom.

In the game, things quickly went our way. We watched the outfield misjudge our teammates' pop-ups, saw infielders bobble shots that dipped and dived erratically, applauded runners who beat throws to first base because balls died in the grass before they could be scooped up.

There was also, I noticed, a lot more goofing around and laughter than usual. Part of it was just reaction to the new dynamics of plastic, people running out too far for balls that lost their momentum and sank just past the infield, others swinging the slim bat so hard they nearly sprained their wrists or spun themselves to the ground. But there was also a general wacky freedom involved here, as if not just the shape of the game but the rules and the purposes of the event had been altered.

"These are the blinds?" I asked, pointing to two small circles on the sides of Sam's diamond pond.

"Right. Now this hunter here fires at this bird." Sam pointed at the "m"-shaped bird above the top point of the pond and drew one long line from the blind on the right to one wingtip. "And he hits it. Ker-splat!" He made a wet, sucking sound with his mouth.

"Good shot," I conceded.

"And the hunter over here shoots the same bird." This line went from the blind on the left to the other wingtip of the top bird. "Ker-splat!"

"Um-hmm."

Our team was scoring run after run on fielding errors and through an apparent refusal on both sides to take the game too seriously. Heavy Joe was breaking everyone up with a routine as zany pitcher, grimacing ferociously, taking elaborate windups, grunting with effort as he threw the ball in to the plate.

But he had figured out that if he backed up far enough, his pitches would die in midair just as they reached the batter. The ball was almost suspended right over the plate, and anyone could hit it. And though no one was used to the thin, lightweight bat, they all seemed to be

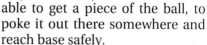

able to get a piece of the ball, to poke it out there somewhere and reach base safely.

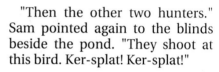

"Then the other two hunters." Sam pointed again to the blinds beside the pond. "They shoot at this bird. Ker-splat! Ker-splat!"

He makes that ugly sound with his mouth again and scratches two more lines, one from each hunter to a wingtip on the bottom bird. Now I see that the four lines representing the gunshots are parallel to the four sides of the diamond-shaped pond.

I didn't know that Heavy Joe was such a card, but he's not the only one out there. My father is even funnier!

I can't believe it, but there he is, crouched in the traditional ready position of a shortstop, keeping up a steady stream of hilarious chatter: "Atta boy, pitcher--he can't hit--throw him the good stuff--rock and fire, baby, rock 'n' roll--he ain't got nothin'--easy stick, easy stick--le'em hit, le'em hit."

Who is this guy, I ask myself? He can't be my always serious, always controlled, always quiet father?

I wonder if Sam's joke involves a variation of one of those clichés, shooting ducks in a barrel, getting your ducks all in a row, so many ducks on a pond. I look again at the drawing.

Then there's a hit by one of the Survey's older employees to the shortstop. My Dad charges the ball, scoops it up one-handed, starts to whip it underhand across the field. He'll get him easy.

But all of a sudden he pretends to lose control of the ball. It dances around on his fingertips, bounces onto his shoulder, rolls down his back. He screams in mock anguish, pounces at it, but kicks it with one foot. By the time he is up again and throwing, the ancient runner has made the turn toward second. My dad fires an overhand pitch that rises just before it reaches first base, sailing three feet over the infielder's (my brother Charles') head!

"And that's called 'gettin' a good duck'!" hisses Sam in my ear. He says it so fiercely that I turn and see his crooked grin. I look down at the drawing in the dirt one more time and finally see it: the parallel lines of bullets and the pond's edges make two sets of legs; the two birds are rumps, one poised above the other; the bridge is . . . well, you know . . . a thang.

"Come on, Mark," Mr. Johnson calls. "You're up!"

X

I was not really hurt.

Of course, at first everyone raced over to where I'd fallen in the dirt, convinced I'd been knocked unconscious or worse. But, as I've said, a wiffleball is remarkably light and can even be easily squashed flat. So when the line drive hit me right between the eyes, I really fell down more from surprise than from the force of the blow. And, of course, I was tremendously embarrassed that, having volunteered to play the "hot spot"--third base--I had demonstrated my inexperience so dramatically, so quickly. It had been our first defensive play.

At least the person who hit the ball right at me was my brother Charles, someone I had well established rights, as a sibling, to blame for what happened. And I did bounce right back up out of the dirt, pretending that there was still time to make the play.

Perhaps I even hoped for a crazy moment that I could make my antics look intentional, as if I had taken the ball on the forehead deliberately, in the only way to handle this particular situation. Yeah, when the ball's hit that well, you try to kick the ball up into the air with your head, see. Then you let it bounce on the ground once before firing to first.

But they were all around me before I could figure out exactly which way the ball had ricocheted (it had rolled out to short center field). And my eyes, from the force of the blow, a real thwack, started to water ferociously, so I probably couldn't have seen the ball to field it anyway. In the excitement, too, my legs didn't seem to get going quite right, thrashing against each other and refusing to put their feet ends down at the bottom of my stance.

So eventually I just left my body in the sitting position it had arrived at on its own, leaning back against my father's shoulder, as he kept asking me, "Are you all right? Are you all right?"

I had, of course, been playing too close in at third. Perhaps I was positioning myself as I would have at home on the street where we played so often. Or I could have been operating with the model of our school's playground field in mind, where sports in physical education classes were more often discussed than played. And I had also been a bit too excited, crouching down in an exaggerated ready position, arms dangling and hands tickling the grass in anticipation.

So when Charles' bat caught that plastic sphere just right, and it shot off the stick like a rocket, and nothing slowed the ball's momentum between the plate and the base, my forehead was positioned just right to receive the full impact. There wasn't any time at all between the crack of the bat and the pop of my skin.

A wonderful red circle appeared on my forehead, but that was the only real sign of injury I carried away from the incident. It was remarkable, however, how long that bright spot lasted. My mother, turning around in the front seat of our car on our ride back home, smiled and reached out a hand to touch it in its final receding phase and ask one more time if it still hurt (it had never really hurt, only stung a bit). And I felt, sitting in the seat behind my father, that I was still glowing, a clear, round beacon in the diminishing light at the end of the day.

When I had been playing ball, I didn't mind the red circle on my forehead. It almost served as an emblem of my arrival in the game. When we were all getting food and eating later, however, I became a little self-conscious, worrying that it might be swelling up, not just a different color but a growing lump. I hoped it wouldn't be black and blue tomorrow.

If there were any lasting physical effects from the picnic, however, it would have been the slightly queasy feeling I had in my stomach. And that was caused, not by fear or blows, but from eating too large a piece of chocolate cake at the dessert table.

I did have one good memory to offset the mark on my forehead and a slightly rocky feeling. I had not hit the ball well, though I did reach base once. I grounded to the pitcher in a late inning (after striking out once and popping up to the shortstop). Heavy Joe Martin pretended he couldn't handle the squibbler and rolled it around in the grass long enough for me to race up the line. And it was as a base runner that I achieved a moment's modest distinction in this memorable game.

As we rode down Kingshighway on the way home, I assumed that the conversation going on in the front seat was about me, about how well I had done, but it wasn't. I was ignoring the fact that my father had been a hero again, driving even that silly little plastic ball farther and more often than anyone else. His team had also come from behind to win.

There were some preliminary comments concerning town matters, but then, I erroneously believed, my parents' attention naturally focused on the achievements that day of their middle child.

"That's where the store's going to be," observed my mother, gesturing out her window.

"The A & P?" my dad asked.

My mother twisted her head back, still looking at the corner. "Mm-hm. They'll have a huge lot in front of the store."

The downtown stores depended on street parking, though most had small areas in back for perhaps twenty cars. One of the big attractions that would draw all the old grocery stores to new shopping centers or highway locations in the future would be guaranteed parking spaces.

After I reached first base, the better players at the top of the order came up: that new employee (who flied out to right field), Marcia Terrell's father (who singled, advancing me to second), and then Mr. Johnson.

We were, at the time, ahead by one run, though our opponents would have a final time at bat. So we were trying for any insurance runs we could score in our final opportunity. It occurred to me that, if I could steal third, I might make it home even on a sacrifice hit to the outfield.

From my spot behind the driver on the way home, I watched the dark shapes of buildings roll past in the window. We were moving down Kingshighway toward the road we took out to the Circle.

When I made my big play, running from second to third, I had been conscious of the faces of spectators along the bank at the side of the field. A gallery of rounded pale shapes framed the action in my peripheral vision. Some people were cheering various players, while a few who had turned toward each other may have been talking about other matters entirely. For one moment I imagined my grandfather's calm face watching with interest.

We left Kingshighway onto Black Street, an old road with small frame houses. The Circle was a later development and had slightly larger homes, bigger yards. I saw faint outlines beneath spreading trees. In my mind I relived the dash for third.

"I'm worn out," said my father in the front seat. "I guess we all are." There was a chorus of agreement. The three men had played hard, and Beth got into a long game of "freeze tag" after the meal.

"We all did well, though," observed my mother. "And no lasting injuries." She looked back at me again.

Surprise was the biggest factor, I think: it hadn't occurred to anyone that I might try to steal. My Dad had to yell--"He's going, he's going!" But the catcher was playing well behind the plate, often letting pitches bounce off the fence before fielding them.

Although this had made it hard to stop people stealing second, no one had tried going to third. That throw was pretty short, and the runner couldn't take an early lead off the base. Anyway, most people weren't playing the game so seriously that they pounced on every chance to score.

"It's a great game," observed my father in the car. "America's game."

"How about the apple pie?" asked my mom.

"Oh, great as always," he responded, probably a little embarrassed that he hadn't praised her specialty earlier. "America's dessert!"

"Um-hm."

"What a cook too. Everyone was jealous. And not only for the pie."

"Oh?" She looked across at him, an eyebrow raised.

I did like the way I stood on the base nonchalantly before making my move. Out of the corner of my eye I checked my father, the shortstop, who might be the one to cover third. He was bubbling with infield chatter, ribbing the hitter. I didn't think he was considering the man on second. The third baseman, for some reason, expected a bunt and was creeping down the line. I figured the catcher would be watching for that too, so this would be the pitch.

The more I drifted off into my recollection, savoring the moment, the less exactly I heard the conversation in the front seat. I picked up only isolated bits and pieces, not their connecting terms or the larger structure.

" . . . pleased with..... play . . . "

"Oh, yes . . . . really..... good run."

The run was so good, I think, because I broke just as the pitch reached the plate, a streak toward third. Although I had never been the fastest in my neighborhood or at school, I did have good acceleration. And I seemed to reach my top speed almost immediately.

But it was really my slide that was special, something I hadn't even known I could do. Sometimes you just try to do what the situation calls for.

Now the talk in front was getting softer, gentler. My father's arm stretched across the back of the seat. He squeezed my mother's shoulder.

"Doesn't it . . . excite you..... big hitters."

"Mmm. . . . some . . . too old..... rest."

About ten feet from the base I launched myself head-first into the air. This was all pretty instinctive, since we didn't do any sliding back on Limestone Drive or on gravel playgrounds. I just let my body go.

"How about . . . ? . . . pie maker . . . quiet . . . ballplayer."

There was a throw from home, and accurate too. But I got there at almost exactly the same moment, and the tag would have had to have been perfect. In fact, a glove might have been necessary to snag the ball out in front and sweep back between the bag and me.

" . . .feel all right . . . sore?"

"No..... naturally you?"

"Hmm!..... OK . . . Yes!"

I may have been fooling myself, but I believe that in this remarkable flight toward third, myself absolutely horizontal above the ground, hurtling through space, that among the spectators one person, someone I thought I could really like, simultaneously stood up and clapped her hands together in spontaneous, exhilarated celebration. And in that vision I forgot, or at least pushed far from my conscious mind, Sam Blount's unsettling drawing in the dust.

Volume Two: Family

Part Three: Girls and Mothers

Chapter 1

My mother made the following surprise announcement one August morning at breakfast some ten months after I had played wiffleball with the men at the State Geological Survey's annual picnic: "Be home by 3:30 today because we're taking the train to Gr'om's this evening."

Gr'om (so nicknamed by the first grandchild) is her mother, who lives in New Jersey. We generally went back East to visit about every other summer as we were growing up. Most of the time we drove, a grueling two-and-a-half day trip each way. And this once we took trains, a California-Chicago one as far as St. Louis and then an overnight through Indianapolis, Pittsburgh, and on into Newark, the closest major stop to my grandmother's house.

"What, today?" I asked, for no one had told me anything about this summer's travel plans.

"That's right, Younger Brother," said Charles. He had known for some time, it turned out, and had arranged for two weeks off from his summer job at a downtown printer's. But neither Beth nor I had had even a hint of this plan.

"Gr'om's! Oh, boy," she exclaimed. Beth was, we believed, Gr'om's favorite grandchild, though we all enjoyed these visits.

"What about my yards?" I asked. I was mowing lawns for neighbors. I may have had twenty houses that summer. "I'll lose my customers!"

"I talked to Jack Rhodes last night," my father responded. "He said Billy would cover for you." Actually, by August, the Missouri heat had turned many yards brown, and they would probably hold until we returned.

While my father had resolved my most immediate fear, I was still angry at the fact that this trip, however appealing, was being sprung on me without warning. We were leaving today! I had no time to organize what toys or games I would take with me, no time to get excited about all the things I would do at my grandmother's, no time to tell friends I was going. No time, especially, to talk with Marcia.

Ever since Marcia Terrell had stood up to applaud during the annual Survey picnic as I slid into third, I felt we had moved closer together as neighborhood friends and perhaps more. (Actually, I never really learned for sure what her response had been to my heroics, though subsequent events suggest that she may well have applauded. I certainly maintained that image of her in my storeroom of fantasies.)

During that school year we found ourselves together a lot, although, since she was a year younger, we were in different buildings. We got along well in neighborhood play, for she was always a good athlete, holding her own at baseball and football while excelling in basketball. And we often fell in with each other outside the Circle as known and comfortable companions.

I began that year, in fact, to appreciate Marcia once more in a way that recalled our more innocent friendship before the Great Expedition beyond Springers' Pond. For months after that incident, when she and Archie Baker had stumbled upon the body of a man drowned in a shallow ditch by the railroad tracks, I had associated her with unpleasantness, with fear and guilt. This wasn't fair, of course, for she was not to blame for anything that had happened. But it took both the passing of time and seeing her in new contexts for me to get beyond this feeling.

I wouldn't have thought of it then, but perhaps Marcia connected me in a similar manner with that difficult moment in her life, an event that increased her mother's overprotectiveness and kept her almost always at home. It might have taken Marcia many months to reestablish a sense of me as the simple boy on the other side of the backyard fence, a fellow traveler on the journey through childhood. We were both also older now, more developed physically. And there was a strong, new attraction between us, soon, in fact, to be acted upon.

In this year of a restored relationship with Marcia Terrell I also gained a new appreciation for a whole class of people I had formerly tended to discount: those people who generally stayed at home.

I guess this was a reversal or qualification of the assumption I had picked up somewhere that only by going out into the world is anything worth doing accomplished. Beyond the Circle, into town, along Route 66, these were the ways of gaining distinction, of carving out a private and public identity for oneself.

Red-haired and beautiful Cathy Williams, for instance, was already at work making a name for herself singing at parties and starring in local dance recitals or play productions. And the Bell sisters, both outgoing and energetic, had won recognition as leaders (Tricia, as a cheerleader in high school; Susan as class president). For a good while, however, I grouped Marcia Terrell with her retiring mother and those who could not or would not take the chance to engage the world beyond the boundaries of their own neighborhood.

I suspect as well that I linked such apparently unassuming personalities with all the mothers, my own included, who stayed home every day on the Circle. In fact, I have a mental image of my mother, which isn't at all complete, that has persisted in my memory as a representation of individuals contained by their houses.

In this picture she stands, as she so often did in reality, in her kitchen, a small room facing the street between dining room and attached garage in our standard frame house on Limestone Drive. This room is so small that she really doesn't need to step so much as swivel to change the site of her operations from sink (washing dishes or peeling vegetables) to stove (cooking a pot roast or making her famous apple pie) to refrigerator (storing leftovers or taking inventory for the week's grocery shopping). From this position she even commands farther reaches of the house.

Right now, for instance, that summer day about a year after the Survey picnic, she has called down the stairs to the basement bedroom of my brother Charles and me that it is time to get up: "Time to get uh-UH-up!" Those stairs descend from a landing off one corner of the kitchen, a step down. A door to the garage opens off the other side.

Is it possible, as I now remember it, that my mother says exactly the same thing every morning and with precisely the same intonation in an identical rhythm? "Time to get uh-UH-up!" Surely she varies this wake-up call ("Boys, get up!" "It's 7:15--hurry Charles, Mark." "What would you like for breakfast?"). But try as I can to recall her using variations, this one repeated cry sounds in my memory: "Time to get uh-UH-up!"

My mother must step through the dining room (also small, perhaps 10 by 12 feet) to the hall in order to rouse Beth from the smaller upstairs bedroom. My father, organized and punctual, is already up, sitting at the dining room table reading, from cover to cover, the morning paper (the *St. Louis Globe-Democrat*).

But if Mom stepped out of her kitchen to wake Beth, it must be before I am upstairs. For when I arrive on the landing, she is back in place by sink, stove, and refrigerator. And I go on to sit in my accustomed place at the rectangular dining room table, in the corner by the window, my back to the kitchen, where I eat my standard breakfast of orange juice, dry cereal (Wheaties, I think, for most of these years, though, once in a while, Cheerios), and jellied toast. Thus begins, it seems to me, every day of my youth.

This stationary figure, my mother, cannot remain fixed in the kitchen all day, of course. She will move around the house, straightening and cleaning, making beds and doing laundry, mending broken or worn items, paying attention in more relaxed moments to the aesthetic character of this home by hanging pictures, replacing or moving furniture, adjusting her environment to fit the growing personalities of her children.

But there are qualities beyond efficiency or responsibility in my mother that made themselves felt by me and became linked to other stay-at-homes like Marcia Terrell. The time I became most aware of them--though it would be years before I could find appropriate names for her gifts--began with this day of her surprise announcement of a trip to New Jersey.

By the way, this totally unanticipated announcement fits with the way my parents usually operated: they conceived, developed, and fixed plans without consulting the children. I guess because Charles was old enough to be working full time in the summer, they had made an exception in his case. But when I think about it, all of our trips were announced the day of or the day before they began.

Children, it was assumed in those days, were not sufficiently mature to need involvement in such planning. They could be packed up like the luggage and placed where they would be convenient or useful to the adults. Given the extremes to which society has gone with the next generation, letting toddlers shop for their own clothes, for instance, I suppose this was just one swing of the pendulum.

In the particular instance of this train trip to New Jersey, however, there were other reasons Beth and I had not been consulted. And, again, I was not to learn about these additional circumstances until much later.

My father had decided back in June, at the end of the school year, that we could not make a major trip this summer because of several special projects at work he was determined to finish before September. He was in charge of creating an accurate record of water flow at the state's major springs. And he wanted to complete a reorganization of field supervision. My mother, however, felt it was time to see her family, many of whom still lived near her mother in New Jersey. She had accepted her husband's decision at first, but then she had had second thoughts.

Was there a scene? Did she make threats, an ultimatum? Were there tears and recriminations, ugly accusations? I don't know for sure. Whatever discussions there were went on behind the closed door of my parents' bedroom, a place we children almost never entered and from which we heard only muffled talk, nothing above a murmur. (Their room was, like all the house, small. With double bed, two chests of drawers, nightstand, and a dressing table there was hardly room for extra bodies.)

I stayed out of this small space also because of what I'd learned husbands and wives did together in bed. Especially after seeing Sam Blount's graphic representation in the Survey dirt of a man and a woman in physical union, I felt my parents' bedroom was not a place I should be. Not that I had any evidence (other than three children!) my parents had ever had (or were still having) sex. They were, like most of their generation, amazingly discreet.

On one of the last days of our surprise vacation, however, I would find out why my father reversed himself and agreed to make this trip. At the same time I would learn, or believe I had learned, about the circumstances of my very conception. I even rescued my naive understanding of sex from the crude picture drawn by a junior high school classmate.

II

Two encounters with strangers dominate my memory of our travel from Missouri to New Jersey, one on each of the two trains we took. The first was the Frontiersman on a Chicago-Los Angeles line parallel to the famous Route 66 through Illinois, Missouri, Oklahoma, Texas, New Mexico, Arizona, and California. We were, of course, going the other way when we boarded a coach car in Fairfield for the two-hour ride into St. Louis. There we would transfer to the eastbound Martha Washington.

St. Louis's Union Station was a major Midwestern intersection in those days. Some passengers changing trains there were headed north or south, traveling basically up or down the ancient connections established by the Mississippi River from Minneapolis to New Orleans. Others were, like us, going east, some toward New York and New England, while still more would angle South toward Washington or even Atlanta and Florida. Travelers in the other direction might not have gone southwest through Fairfield but west along the Missouri River through Kansas City, on to Denver, Salt Lake City, and beyond. So moving around the great polished floor of Union Station probably would have been representatives from most of the great regions of the country, all crossing boundaries into new or different territories.

I like to imagine now, in fact, from the perspective of many years later, that, on this August evening, walking near me among a great throng of people, carrying perhaps one large suitcase and a stuffed rabbit under an arm, was a young girl who would become, more than a decade later, my wife. It's remotely possible, you see, since she did take a trip through St. Louis with her family at about this same time.

She doesn't recall seeing anyone who might have been a young me that evening. Nor do I remember being intrigued by an alluring passerby in that short time, just over an hour, that we were changing trains. Still, it suits my sense of the ultimate order of the universe that we could have been in that central meeting place together

75

for one brief moment, that two people destined to grow old together would have had an early, special connection, a crossing of paths that foreshadowed their future together.

Although I did not see a strikingly beautiful young girl at Union Station, I did have, as I said, a memorable encounter with someone of the opposite sex in the coach car of the train coming into the city from Fairfield.

My family was sitting in two pairs of seats across the aisle and one additional seat a row ahead. My father took that extra spot, while my mother and Beth, Charles and I sat side by side. With a boy's natural desire to see and try out the train's special features, I made my way soon after we were underway (between Bourbon and Sullivan, I would guess) to the restroom at the back of the car. The train's wobbly motion as its speed increased and its course wound through rolling hills created the conditions for a slight mishap.

I wanted, of course, to look as if I took such train trips regularly and knew how to handle myself. So walking away from my family I planted each foot solidly in the aisle and avoided grabbing the backs of seats for support. Still, some steps found me leaning precipitously to one side or the other. A particularly sharp turn made the car lurch just as I neared the restroom. And, already leaning in that direction, I was thrown forward and to my right onto an upright aisle seat back, fortunately unoccupied.

While I was lucky not to have landed directly on top of some grandmother or an infant, I did not escape embarrassment. Directly behind the empty seat was a beautiful young lady, perhaps a college student or someone slightly older. She was wearing a dark suit, sat in a most proper, elegant manner, and was scanning the fashion section of the *St. Louis Post-Dispatch*. She looked up over the edge of the paper just as I flew onto the seat in front of her. The impact of my fall knocked the breath out of me, so I hung momentarily over the seat back, mouth open and teary-eyed.

I'm sure some of you, older and wiser, could have thought of something to do here, some way to pretend that what had happened was intentional, part of a larger, meaningful plan. There might be something to say--"The train's a little late, I observe"; "I like your hair done that way"; "Force equals mass times acceleration." But my brain was as stunned as my body. And, had I the physical capacity to speak, I lacked the mental means to frame a sentence.

I've always thought the young lady herself might have said something here, something not unkind, perhaps recognizing the dangers universally facing humankind: "Whoa! That could happen to anyone!"; "Whoops! Good thing you caught yourself!"; "Wow! Thanks for warning me about those sudden stops and starts!"

But she did not. She looked at and then through me without expression, unless the turning down of her mouth at the corners ever so slightly could have been construed as a frown. She held that look until, mercifully, I was able to roll off the seat back, gasp, and stagger on toward the back of the car.

I did my best to forget the whole incident, of course. And fortunately no one in my family, especially Charles, had witnessed my mishap. So, after a helpful extra pause in the restroom, I resumed my seat for the rest of the ride into St. Louis.

The other new person I met (if that's the right word) during this trip was on that second train as it labored through the mountains separating the Midwest from the East Coast. In the club car Charles and I sat with an attractive woman in her 40s who had volunteered to play cards with us. She was such an amusing companion, such a joyful game player, that she made a lasting impression on me. Before I relate how the three of us came to be together, however, I must explain why we boys were in the club car in the first place.

While the Landons rode coach into St. Louis, they had a sleeping compartment on the night train across Illinois and Indiana and into Pennsylvania. It was a tight fit for the five of us, but I have always admired such economically designed and functional quarters. In a tiny space there were: one easy chair bolted to the floor by the lone window; along the front wall a thin bathroom with shower stall and an even narrower closet between the chair and the compartment's door; a couch along the back wall by day (a double or single-and-a-half bed at night for my parents); and an even smaller fold-down upper berth for Charles and me. My mom would spread some blankets on the floor by her side and partially under the chair to make a pallet for Beth.

There wasn't any room for variation, then. But, once settled that night, we all experienced a deep relaxation from the hurried events of the day. It was nearly midnight, and my day had begun, remember, with no knowledge that we were going to take this trip. Too, there is always that reassuring clackety-clack, clackety-clack of wheels on rails, the gentle rocking, rocking of cars over uneven tracks, the evocative distant whistle from engines far up front. Speeding across the flat plains east of St. Louis, we were all, I think, asleep within an hour.

Although there was room to sleep five of us, the compartment made close quarters during the day. And by mid-morning the cramped conditions seemed to irritate my father.

We did, by the way, have a great time eating breakfast together in the dining car. We had to negotiate, both coming and going, the many doors at the ends of cars, which swung back at a touch, and the unnerving steps between cars. We understood that beneath us for a dizzying moment were the devices, huge metal fists, that linked cars together. For me at least, there was always an irrational fear that the cars would break loose just at the moment I put my weight on the platform above, the coupling tongue of one car slipping out of the grasp of the other's jaw and the plates beneath my feet dropping me down into darkness.

In the dining car we had to squeeze again--three children on one side of a booth, the parents on the other--but the novelty of a cooked breakfast (pancakes and sausage, French toast and bacon, perhaps?) and exciting views of the mountains in western Pennsylvania kept us all in a good mood. (Was it here that we saw the famous "horseshoe curve," the bend of tracks rimming a huge valley in the Alleghenies? No, that must have come later.)

Back in our compartment, the upper berth had been locked back against the wall by the porters, the double bed turned into a couch. Beth soon fell asleep again with her head in my mother's lap. My dad was sitting in the one chair by the window, reading the paper left for us while we were at breakfast. Charles and I, excited by all these new experiences, were too much for the small space. With no place to sit and desperate for something to do, we quickly got on my father's nerves.

"Let's see how close we can come to the engines," suggested Charles.

"You're not allowed up there," growled Dad.

"Is there a caboose?" I asked.

"You can't go back there either," my mother whispered and, pointing to the sleeping Beth, urged us to be quieter.

"Go to the club car," my father offered, suddenly pleased at his own suggestion.

We didn't know what it was, but this sounded promising. "What's that?" I asked.

"A place where you can sit and talk, play games. They have booths there," responded my father.

This sounded great to us, and we started off immediately. The club car, we learned from the porter, was behind us (the dining car was in front), so we took several more of those scary steps between cars, barely letting a foot rest on the shifting metal platform just above the coupling device. And within a half hour we were learning a new game ("Hearts") from a new acquaintance.

Who was this engaging woman who entertained us so well for the rest of the trip to New Jersey? Who was the carefree, relaxed person who pointed out places we were passing, bought us candy bars and sodas, laughed with us when, giddy with new delight, we said foolish things, ruffled our hair as we said we hoped this trip would never end? Why, it was our mother.

III

But the woman on the train wasn't our mother as she usually appeared. She seemed to have been transformed when she joined Charles and me in the club car on that memorable summer vacation.

Of course, part of this effect came from the fact that I was seeing her in a new context, in a situation where her domestic energy was not necessary to the regular family operations of eating, staying clean, sustaining shelter. In leaving Beth with my father, making him for a short time the parent looking after a young child, she had escaped her usual role.

In the club car, in fact, we could all be different from our usual selves. Although I had revealed my lack of experience on the earlier train, when I'd almost fallen into the lap of a stranger, here I'd been able to walk down aisles and across couplings with the appearance at least of a veteran, if young, traveler. Charles and I found an unoccupied booth in one corner of the club car and took seats there as if this was something we did routinely.

He even noticed that he could buy a deck of cards at the snack bar, and we began a game of "War," though we were generally just as interested in watching who came into the car and what flashed by the window at our side. So when our mother suddenly slid in beside Charles at our booth, this new context made for new persons all around. But I have also since come to realize that she changed herself on the trip from sleeping car to club car.

This alteration was not inspired just by these particular circumstances of a journey, the sleeping daughter, our father's desire to be alone. Whenever our mother left the Midwest to visit the area where she had grown up, she fell back into a character I almost never saw around home. Mrs. Richard Landon became Susan Williams (Williams, of course, was her maiden name).

Something of her girlhood returned when she approached the old home, an innocence and freshness lost in the hurry and effort of running a household. About the time we left Ohio, an East Coast identity could surface, and attitudes appropriate to a responsible citizen of Fairfield might for a time disappear. By the end of the entire vacation I had learned some things about who I, a child of this woman, might become, even as I began to recognize the frustrations she felt in her marriage.

The woman who joined Charles and Mark Landon that day had grown up the youngest of three Williams sisters in a rambling frame house on a stately boulevard in Paterson, New Jersey, across the river from New York City. Her father was a banker who had left the upstate New York family farm early in the century to make his fortune. For decades he commuted daily into the city but always dreamed of retiring to the country. And he found ways for the family to spend much of their summers on Greenwood Lake, an hour from Paterson.

Susan's mother, the former Rebecca Wohm, who had been raised on a farm in north Jersey not far from their summer campsite, kept house for her husband and three daughters, but also was able to write some remarkably good poetry in her spare time.

Thomas Williams was a grandfather I never knew, for he had died before I was born. During my mother's first year at college he caught a cold one winter day just before a planned business trip to Cleveland. Pneumonia set in, and he was gone in less than a week. There just weren't medicines for it at the time. The family grieved terribly, but endured. And the picture I inherited of this grandfather featured him at the center of many happy family occasions and steady, patient love.

Twenty-some years later we journeyed on the Martha Washington to see his widow. Rebecca Williams had had some difficult years, to be sure, accepting at age fifty an unexpected responsibility for herself. The large house in Paterson came to seem empty with the girls gone except for vacations, and within a few years she moved to a quaint cottage in the more rural part of New Jersey west of Paterson where she had spent her youth.

Her daughter, Susan, bloomed now before us, her sons, as she realigned herself with that old story, those different persons, that other place. Sitting down, taking up and shuffling our deck of cards, she didn't give us too much time to wonder why she was here.

"What're you playing? 'War'? That's a dull game. Do you know 'Hearts'? Let me show you." Before we could even respond, cards flew out of her hands into little piles in front of us, and she began explaining that the high card in the suit led would win each trick, that we didn't want to take hearts or the jinx unless we took them all, that we would play to 100. Pushing her hair back behind one ear, she picked up her cards and fanned them out in one hand.

At the same time she began to reminisce about playing cards with her sisters when she was young. "We would play canasta for whole weekends. With Marge, your aunts' friend, next door. And sometimes Gr'om would sit in if one of us had to do something."

"Was this in the Paterson house?" Charles asked.

"Yes. Father would be at work in the city until late. And sometimes our Grandmother would play, and my aunt Sarah." A number of her mother's relatives stayed with the family at various times, and many lived close enough for regular visits. This was unlike our situation in Fairfield, with my father an only child and our uncles and aunts on our mother's side all living more than a thousand miles away.

The three sisters were close in age, too: Margaret was two years older than my mother; and Elizabeth was eighteen months my mom's junior. More than neighborhood friends, the sisters, with their cousins and aunts, provided the Paterson house with its social life. And even more in the summers camping at Greenwood Lake, the girls learned to be their own entertainment.

A few years after this visit I saw the region where the Williams family had spent several months each summer.

Then, of course, the lakeshore was dotted with weekend cottages, craft shops, fishing piers, small swimming areas. In my mother's youth it had been almost wild, and the Williams took up residence first in tents, then, gradually, in a cabin that my grandfather built a section at a time. It lay at the foot of a small mountain on the lake's pebbly shore.

As is so often the case, the greatest family times seemed to have been enjoyed in this primitive setting, with the fewest of modern conveniences. They cooked on a camp stove, read by kerosene lamps, lived without heat. Recreation was simple, swimming and hiking by day, games and song at night. Gr'om organized most of the activity, for my grandfather had to spend some nights in the city or take two hours to get home by train.

And now I must admit that I have, however illogically, a sharp mental picture of my grandfather at Greenwood Lake. I couldn't ever have seen him, of course, but family lore so often described him that I can call up by myself the image of him swimming.

When he was at the campsite, everyone told us, Thomas Williams would get up at some unbelievable hour--5:00 am? 4:30?--in all weather except thunderstorms and take a swim in the lake. It was calm then, and he felt he had the world to himself. About fifty yards out he swam a steady breaststroke parallel to the shore, head always out of the water. He went back and forth a dozen times "the length of a good field of corn," he used to say. Then he came in for breakfast before hiking over a mile to catch the train into the city, or to begin a day in the woods.

When any of his daughters woke up early enough to look out through the tent flaps--or, later, to crack the heavy front door of the cabin--they would see their father's upright head almost magically moving across the clear plane of the water, a ripple of wake spreading its arms out behind him on the smooth surface. And I can see him right now too, as clearly in my own way, perhaps, as my mother does in hers. I have his name by the way (it's Mark Thomas Landon; have I mentioned that?), so maybe it's a part of myself I see out there in the first light of dawn.

As the only man in the family, my grandfather apparently could do anything he wanted, but he must have been gentle, the way my mother always talks of him. Now, on the train a generation later, she slides from talking about playing canasta on the lake to learning bridge at college. And then on to other occasions for train travel, this time in getting to and from school.

"You know what we used to do?" said my mother at one point, her eyes turned to the window. We were moving slowly through a pass in the mountains. Dark trees and rocky cliffs were close to the tracks.

"What?" Charles asked.

"When we were taking the train back to school in Ithaca, me, my sister Elizabeth, and some other girls from Paterson, we would all be together in one car, but not sitting right next to each other. Sort of spread out. On one of the cars like the one we took into St. Louis."

"Yeah?" I said, looking around at the people in booths, others standing down by the snack bar. The train had moved into a valley and begun to pick up speed at the head of a long straight stretch.

"We would hum," she said. She smiled and looked right at us. "It would be some popular song, a love song, or something from a musical we might have seen in New York. Very quietly, without moving our lips. So that the other passengers couldn't tell if they were hearing something or not." She hummed softly a few lines of "My Old Flame."

"Why did you do that?" asked Charles.

"Oh, it was something to do, to break up the boredom of the trip. See, we'd get louder and louder, but the noise of the train, the tracks, the talking, people would stop, listen, try to figure out if they were hearing something."

The train was really rolling down the valley now, not far from a stream racing over rocks.

"One time," continued Mom but suddenly stopped. "We'd better go see about your father."

So we started back toward our compartment, where we would find that Beth was still sleeping and that my father, having had several hours of peaceful time alone with his newspaper, had assumed a more cheerful demeanor. On the way, as we stepped over sliding, scraping platforms between cars and bumped along narrow passageways, did I hear, ever so softly, in front or behind me, now high, now low, to one side or the other, someone humming? A love song?

IV

In moving backward through time on this summer vacation to discover the young Susan Williams, I was also revising my own notion of who I was, of where I'd come from and where I might be headed. By the time I returned to Fairfield, in fact, I had added a surprising hint of the daredevil to my character, as you will see.

In the car with my Aunt Margaret leaving Newark I was already looking at the New Jersey countryside as territory ready to receive a new Mark Landon. The scenes flashing past the window, which I had encountered a number of times in my life, represented a mirror image of my own changing. I could recall many distinct features (a giant billboard advertising Singer sewing machines, for instance). Yet new buildings and repaired or altered structures added enough strangeness to make this world different for me (the hairstyle and clothes of the woman sewing had changed with the times).

My Aunt Margaret, as I said, picked us up at the train station. Although Gr'om still drove, she preferred not to take her car out at night and she feared the difficult route and heavy traffic going into and out of the city. Aunt Margaret's two boys, Bill (thirteen) and John (fifteen), were away most of the year at a private school in Connecticut. She was often the one to help out in this way when our family came east to visit.

Her husband was a successful Wall Street financier who seldom got home before 8:00 in the evenings, often worked Saturdays, and also traveled extensively. Aunt Margaret's silver Cadillac had plenty of room for us and our luggage. Even with three passengers in the back seat, there was space to spread out and sink back into the soft cushions.

This sense of comfort inspired me to continue my speculation about a personal metamorphosis in New Jersey. I would not become a totally new person, of course, but one altered in subtle ways. My new self would probably not even figure too much inside Gr'om's house, but on ventures out to the tiny village where she did her shopping and where her church was.

I didn't want to change in this house because it was, I still believe, the finest grandmother's house imaginable, and I did not want to lose my customary place in it. As we left the last signs of the greater metropolitan New York area, I warmed once more to the idea of this house.

The wide, busy roads we had been on--with puzzling traffic circles my Midwestern parents had great trouble negotiating when we came by car--had narrowed to two lanes. And the view from my seat was more and more of green woods and steep hills. Factories and industrial areas were no longer visible along the roadside. Now single homes were set on large tracts of land.

As we passed through the village of Maryville, I began to spot more familiar landmarks--a store, the lane that turned off to Gr'om's church, a pond with a section roped off for swimming (skating in the winter). And I tried to see my new self out there in new surroundings.

I sampled a few standard boyhood fantasies of me as knight in shining armor--saving a drowning child, wrestling a black bear who was terrorizing a pretty girl, luring a gang of bank robbers into a police trap--but they seemed too farfetched. I wanted something still heroic but a little more within reach. Perhaps I could be the first one to figure out a mystery no one had even recognized as needing an explanation.

Gr'om's house rested on a thin, deep lot, reaching several hundred yards back from the road. There were no houses immediately on either side, as in this rural area homes were scattered among small fields and untended woods in an almost random pattern. She lived about two thirds of a mile beyond Maryville, which was really just a tiny cluster of homes with a couple of churches, a general store (post office included), and a small firehouse. In the summer, though, this area could be busy with vacationers camping or staying in cottages on the many small lakes which dotted the area.

Gr'om's house, which we were now approaching, was not large, but it was, as I said, special. In the Circle back in Fairfield, all the houses were simple and functional structures, where the greatest variation was whether the standard two bedrooms filled one side or ran along the back.

When you stepped through Gr'om's front door, on the other hand, the living room stretched across two thirds of the main floor on your right and was open above to a cathedral ceiling perhaps twenty feet high at the peak. A stone fireplace and chimney filled much of the end wall (right) in this room. On the mantel was an ancient clock, which chimed the quarter hour, and a rich array of family pictures. Behind this great room was a dining room (right) and kitchen (left). A small sewing room and the bathroom were off the left side of the living room, reached from a door at the back.

That living room was the center of life in Gr'om's house, with all rooms except the kitchen and bathroom opening onto it. Even the upstairs bedrooms faced the living room, though from a height of about ten feet above the floor. To the left of the front entrance in the corner was a step up to a landing, and then a flight of stairs rose along the left wall. At the top of these steps a narrow balcony ran the length of the living room along the back. On that balcony were doors to two small bedrooms above the kitchen and dining room. And at the top of the stairs was a third bedroom, to the left, where Gr'om slept.

When they stayed here the Landons were distributed as follows: my parents had the little bedroom with no closets above the dining room, at the end of the slim balcony. There they had to balance suitcases on straightback chairs and squeeze themselves into a three-quarters bed, providing my father with a source of petty complaints for the length of any visit. The boys, who didn't mind sliding their suitcases under two single beds, had the middle room above the kitchen, where Charles slept by the window and I on the inside wall by the door. Beth had a nifty foldaway bed in Gr'om's room.

This arrangement, although it fixed everyone in a specific place, had worked in the past to break down the established divisions between children and adults. When Charles and I were younger and were sent to bed at an early hour, we could still keep our door slightly cracked and eavesdrop on conversations below. From the bed I slept in, I even had a direct line of sight to the living room couch, on which my mother and Gr'om would often be sitting, with old photograph albums or some kind of embroidery or stitching in hand. My father usually established himself in a wonderful wooden rocker by the fireplace on the end wall and read, or pretended to read, books about geology brought from home.

Only a few hours after arriving, I found myself one more time secure in that upstairs bedroom, tasting the special feeling of being in this house. We were all tired from the long journey, from being awakened occasionally on the train the night before, and from the excitement of getting here. My parents were still moving around downstairs as I felt myself sink toward sleep. And, peeking through the cracked door, I could see their shadows move on the front wall of the living room.

Lying in that bed I could also direct my attention over the heads of the adults, across the front yard out to the country road that ran past the house. Traffic at such times would be light, but occasionally cars did wind by, swinging their headlights around curves and brightening the front windows. On the Circle, with my bedroom downstairs, I had no sense of passing cars or pedestrians. At Gr'om's, the sounds of drivers climbing up hills and banking through turns inspired me to think that many remarkable people lived in this area, that they undertook night journeys for mysterious purposes, that the land was rich with adventure.

It was also possible for me to turn my attention out the window of the upstairs bedroom toward the back yard, where a small patio, a rope swing, a flower garden, and four ancient apple trees offered a variety of entertainments for boys during the day. The window was open, and a cool breeze swayed the curtains. At night I heard leaves rustling, perhaps a dog barking far in the distance. In the morning I would be awakened by song birds.

Beyond the rock wall fence at the end of Gr'om's lot were fields and small groves as yet unexplored by me, though Charles claimed to have found a dairy farm perhaps half a mile away. Cows mooing in the evening and early morning tended to confirm this account, but my imagination at night also found room in those woods for bobcats, a secret cave, jewels in a metal box at the foot of a large oak tree.

Finally, although less frequently, I thought about Gr'om's basement. Here were stored many of the family's keepsakes brought from Paterson. In the bedroom two floors above, I was inspired by these relics of my mother's family history to vague fantasies about the past. Perhaps my own future could be forecast in patterns established by my ancestors.

Also in this basement, on the left side under the sewing room, Gr'om had a garage where she kept her 1949 Plymouth sedan. And in the one room not crowded with unused furniture, packing crates, and gardening tools was a ping-pong table, yet another source of play at this fine grandmother's house.

This summer, fixed in this scene with a heightened sense of awareness, I found yard, house, and neighborhood to be ripe fields of potential. Something would happen, I told myself; something would happen. And, as I've said, something did happen to the new Mark Landon.

How wonderful the feeling years ago in that bed by the door, my ear turned to the crack through which muffled conversation rose, my eyes wide, as moonlight and dreams filled the bright square of the window! How wonderful the memory now of such moments in the past! The voices of Gr'om, my parents when young, the earth sweet with flower and song. May such moments stay with me in years to come, stars shining across the darkness of night sky!

V

This comfortable feeling of being at Gr'om's great house began to come undone the next day. "I want you boys to hike down to Ross Lake and see what it looks like," Gr'om said at breakfast. "See if you think it would be OK to take Beth there."

She was talking about a small lake just off the main road between her house and Maryville. Early in the summer a new owner had opened up one end for swimming, and Gr'om thought it would give us somewhere to be during the day.

"It's probably not going to get hot enough for pond swimming," noted my father. But we knew to ignore this comment. He was just asserting a Missouri set of values in alien territory.

There were, according to my father, a number of basic facts about the universe that Easterners tended to ignore. And he could not let certain of these assumptions pass unchallenged. This lake, for instance, was barely bigger than Springers' Pond at home, but people around here called such bodies of water "lakes." To my father, Greenwood Lake, some fourteen miles long and nearly a mile wide, was more than a pond, but not Ross Lake.

Second, to my father the weather never got "hot" in New Jersey. He judged by conditions on the summer plains of Kansas and in humid Missouri woods, so to him the air around New Jersey's northern hills and its deep bodies of water could never rise above "warm."

"You can go too, Dad," Charles stated. "A good morning walk."

"No, no. I have this report to work on." He had carried material from his office with him on the trip, a reminder that he felt he should have stayed in Missouri this summer to finish several key projects. But I thought I saw a troubled look flash across my mother's face when he said this. It turned out, of course, that he spent many days of the vacation in a hammock suspended between two apple trees, dozing and watching the clouds drift by.

"Beth and I are going to go through the trunk in my sitting room," said Gr'om with a smile. "There are some things she needs to learn about."

Beth was, as I've said, her favorite, one of only two granddaughters. Even at the age of six, Beth seemed to respond to Gr'om's special interests like the love of flowers, birds, the outdoors. Throughout this and subsequent summer visits, these two would often go off together to the sitting room or out in back. And, passing them along the paths of different projects, the rest of the family would hear conspiratorial whispers and giggles, see their heads close and their hands busy together.

"Peas in a pod," my mother often said of Beth and Gr'om. Grandparents, of course, can often be close to grandchildren when they are together infrequently and do not have to restrict each other's desire.

Beth had not learned to swim yet, and that was why we had to scout out the lake. If it had a large shallow area, it would be all right to take her. Mom was going shopping with Aunt Margaret, so Charles and I set off on our excursion at about midmorning. The sun was bright, the air cool, but the temperature rising. Charles soon complicated this simple adventure.

"Mom talk to you?" he asked as we hiked down the side of the narrow country road. There was a grassy shoulder between pavement and the woods that lined our way. Occasionally a lane or driveway turned off the road, but only a few houses were visible.

"About what?"

"Moving."

"Moving? Where?"

"Here?"

94

"What? We can't leave Fairfield." A small truck from a local nursery passed us, moving slowly with bushes and flowering shrubs reaching up over the cab.

"Um-hm."

"What makes you think we're thinking about moving?"

"You're probably right," Charles continued. "We're settled in school, we own our house, that's where our friends are."

"Yeah."

We passed a mailbox on a post in front of a lawn rising to a pretty house faced with stone. It was two stories, a kind I liked, with a separate one-car garage. A basketball goal had been put above the door.

"Except that Mom did mention it."

"Mentioned moving?"

"Yeah."

"Well, Dad has to have a job. What about Dad's job? He likes it at the Survey."

"OK. But it's just that Aunt Margaret wrote Mom about a job here, same thing, maybe better."

"In Maryville?"

"No, stupid. In Trenton. That's less than a hundred miles away. But Mom would like it. To be that close."

"What does Dad say?" I was staggered by Charles's information, by the sudden prospect of such a complete change.

"I don't know. Mom wouldn't go into that."

We had reached Ross Lake, which lay in a little valley on the right hand side of the road, the near shore perhaps fifty yards away. It would be a site of achievement for the new Mark Landon, but I didn't know that then.

The entrance to the swimming area was just ahead of us, and we could step across a ditch and lean on a wooden rail fence that followed the boundaries of the property. There were trees around most of the lake, but we could see from here to a section of shore. A white sign with blue letters gave the price of entrance, hours of operation, rules of behavior. (I wish, by the way, I could remember those instructions exactly, but I fear they have blended in with many other such notices from many different times and places.)

The lake itself was more tear-shaped than round. The narrow end, close to us, was where the swimming was. A lane branched ahead of us, one part going left up through woods to a house on a small hill, the other down to a newly graveled parking lot by the lake. We could see an area marked by red ropes held up on floats and a white platform out in the deep water.

"This looks good," said Charles. "Nice diving board even."

"It's bigger than the Fairfield pool," I admitted. Our municipal pool was tiny, but all the kids my age spent a lot of time there in the summers. Although it had two diving boards, a high and a low, there was always a danger of landing on someone below. I wondered if this meager facility had inhibited my development as an Olympic diver, my later Johnny Weismueller movie career.

"I wonder what the water's like," I mused.

"Cool but not cold," said a voice from behind the sign, startling both of us. We had not noticed anyone there. A freckle-faced boy about my age, wearing a New York Giants cap, poked his head around the edge of the sign and pointed a paint brush at us. "You'll like it."

"Oh," I said. Now I realized why we had not seen him: he was perched on a wooden ladder that blended with the posts down low, and his legs had been above the bottom of the sign. The rest of him now followed his head out from behind the sign. Apparently he had been work-ing on the lettering ("Ross Lake--Come Again").

"I'm Jerry," he said. "I help run the place. It's my par-ents'." He nodded toward the house.

"I see," said Charles.

"Me and my sister." Again he pointed, and we saw a dark-haired girl in jeans and sweatshirt on the far side of the lake, beyond the swimming area. She was pulling a canoe out from under low-hanging branches on the shore. She had a net on a pole, getting ready, I assumed, to fish some debris out of the water.

"Is it busy?" asked Charles.

"Not too busy. Weekends maybe. If you want to come this afternoon, you'll have a lot of room to yourself."

This sounded good, and we learned from Jerry that one whole side of the swimming area was only a couple of feet deep, good for nonswimmers. As we chatted, I found I couldn't get over a feeling I'd seen this kid somewhere.

Of course, you know how this works: whenever you go on a trip, you still have the feeling that you're going to bump into someone you know, someone from home. What is really happening is that you are so used to recog-nizing certain body shapes, hair styles, and characteristic gestures that you interpret people you see at a distance as familiar figures, known entities. You're subconsciously on the lookout for what you know how to look out for, and you see similar but not identical things.

The odds are, of course, overwhelmingly against run-ning into anyone you know, especially when you are, as I was, 1,000 miles from home. But you feel yourself tricked into it time and time again. This Jerry probably resem-bled someone I knew in Fairfield, triggering my sense that I had seen him before. He was, I'm sure, a complete stranger. I realized, however, that he might become a friend of the new Mark Landon during our week in the area.

Looking across the lake I also watched the girl in the canoe scooping leaves and sticks out of the water. After she dumped what she'd picked up into the bottom of the boat, she laid the net across her knees, took up a paddle, and moved on to other spots. Slowly she was working her way across the lake toward us.

If I was puzzling over who Jerry might be or be like, Charles, I knew, would be more interested in this girl. I could see that she was pretty, her motions controlling the canoe and net smooth and graceful. Charles would be willing to go swimming this and other afternoons.

Our report to Gr'om, then, was enthusiastic: Beth would have a place to play, I might have a companion (if Jerry didn't have to work while I was there), and Charles had at least a remote chance of summer love.

There was only one more troublesome moment for me at Gr'om's house that day: my father, almost in passing, mentioned that he and my mom were going to take a day-trip later in the week, probably Thursday. Although they claimed it was just sightseeing, I suspected that this was a trip to see about the job at New Jersey's geological survey.

This fear continued that evening as Mom and the children sat at the dining room table playing a new board game Aunt Margaret had brought over, "Careers." Dad was, as usual, reading, and Gr'om came in and out to kibbutz while she made jam in the kitchen. Although Beth had to have help, we were all enthusiastic, if not boisterous, in play

The goal of "Careers" was to reach a combination of financial success (gold bars), personal happiness (hearts), and fame (stars). Each player chose his or her own "Secret Success Formula," setting the amount needed in each category to reach a fixed total. There were dice to roll, cards to play, pieces to move around a general route and through special side paths that qualified you in the professions--law, medicine, the arts. The first to reach that personal goal was the winner. I was puzzled when

Mom fixed her "Success Formula" as all gold bars and stars, no hearts.

We played well past our usual bedtimes on this second night of our stay, enjoying the freedom. But the possible reasons for my parents' upcoming trip lay uneasily in the back of my mind. Much as I liked to visit here in the summers, and much as I was intrigued by the possibility of change in my own personality, I was not ready to leave everything I had ever known for a completely new life in a different environment.

Part Four: Up and Down

Chapter VI

We did not go swimming at Ross Lake on the next day of our vacation, for rain set in that night and continued on and off until the following evening. Here again, though, the special arrangement of Gr'om's house provided a varied theater for us to counter that childhood bane, the rainy day. And, while we were spending this time indoors, I moved closer to understanding my mother's frustration that summer, and to its resolution.

Charles and I spent a number of hours at ping-pong in the basement, where I was a consistent, though cheerful, loser. Beth continued to go off with Gr'om, this time in the storeroom where some family heirlooms needed rearranging. Everyone browsed through books in the sitting room, many of them beautiful editions with leather bindings and lush illustrations. My dad even found some old science textbooks worth reading. And the family picture albums unlocked stories about Williams ancestors living in England, others settling in early Massachusetts, and still others gravitating toward the commercial center of New York. And, of course, we continued to play games.

The design of Gr'om's house gave two of these games additional range and reward. One of my mom's childhood amusements became this year Beth's favorite, though she had to have help in playing. "Rooms" was a complex game in which players competed to build the biggest house.

Everyone started with a cash balance, earned more money by throwing dice to move around a board, and built a dream house according to a plan drawn up before play began. The object was twofold: to have at the end of the game the exact house you had proposed in your plan; and to have the largest house of those completed.

Players traveled around a fictional city to negotiate with real estate agents, construction companies, and bankers or savings-and-loan officers. The result of each venture was determined by spinning a pointer on a cardboard base. Rooms authorized for building were represented by cards awarded to the player. And tokens (little men with tiny briefcases, women in aprons) on a board (a map of the town, "Openville") showed where players were at any given moment.

You could begin building as soon as you had sufficient money for the down payment, though you had to keep up with construction costs and mortgage payments. Even after work on a basic design began, you were still allowed to add rooms as funds became available. Play stopped after a set number of turns, I think thirty, although I can't remember for sure. The completion of each round was noted by moving a plastic marker across a scale on the game board.

As you built your house, you also had to install plumbing, wiring, heating, and basic furnishings. These were represented by a second deck of smaller cards, which pictured the necessary items.

For some reason, either economy in production or simplicity in design, the equipment for this game was all black and white and the suites of furniture generic. Beth and Mom complained that this made things too easy because matching colors and styles was not necessary. The same drapes could go in the nursery as the library, for instance. But Charles and I probably would have followed the same strategies even if components clashed.

There were limits that everyone contended with. Your house had to go together within certain restrictions and in a fixed order. You could not dig out a basement once your basic house was constructed, nor could you have two kitchens. The house could be up to three stories tall, however, and nothing prevented you from having your dining room next to the attic, if you so desired.

Because you sometimes had to take whatever your token landed on--furniture, wiring, a bathtub--we sometimes ended up with rather strange combinations. If I had any special gift for this game, it was in blending unusual combinations into a reasonable whole.

Beth's special contribution to this game was to enlarge our playing space by putting cards all over the house. That is, the equipment cards were in Gr'om's dining room; the room cards were in the sitting room; and loan authorizations were on the balcony. This turned the living room area into a giant game board. And we had to move ourselves literally from place to place to pick up items.

All this slowed down play tremendously, as we carried the spinning arrow with us to determine the outcome of our negotiations. Still, at least as I remember it, these games were great fun no matter how long they went on.

Beth's extension of "Rooms" may well have been inspired by how Charles and I played another game in Gr'om's house. This was something that we had developed ourselves over the course of several summer vacations, a military adventure, "Bombs Away!"

Several of Gr'om's relatives had been in World War II. And her house became over the years a repository for model airplanes, battleships, aircraft carriers, and other military equipment left behind by visiting family members. Although they were stored in the basement, we were allowed to bring these gray plastic and metal bombers, cruisers, and patrol boats upstairs and play with them if we followed one restriction: we had to use books of military history to examine specific battles.

We would lay out a campaign--usually involving sea battles--around the living room, trying to keep all the pieces and the area of engagement roughly to scale. But because we had that upper level, the balcony, which could be used to enact related air campaigns, these mock battles developed along increasingly elaborate and intricate lines. We would move furniture back against the

103

walls in order to position whole fleets. Even Dad got involved, often sketching out the units and their positions on paper and then extending a retractable tape measure to check positions on the floor.

This year Charles added another element to "Bombs Away!" by using one specific unit of yet another game Gr'om had. This was a variation on darts, but players dropped rather than threw them, using a special launching device.

This launcher wasn't much more than a cigar box. Inside, a mirror was set at a 45-degree angle so that you could look in one end and see what lay below. Four torpedoes were loaded into the box and could be released by buttons along the side. There was also a playing board, which lay flat on the floor, featuring submarines. Players took turns trying to knock out the targets. Each ship was given a point value, and score was kept with each round of four torpedoes per person.

This, however, was the more benign version of the game, rendered obsolete by Charles's innovation. He took the bombing box upstairs onto the balcony and, leaning over the rail that ran the length of the living room, dropped ping-pong balls on the model ships laid out in battle formations. We modified the ping-pong balls with tape and cardboard, providing tails that could be placed inside the cigar box and released by the side buttons. As fleets moved in and out of the bombing corridor established by the balcony above, our bombers stationed in the different upstairs bedrooms flew out and made their aerial raids.

I too added to this principle by constructing a catapult we used to represent the firing of ships' guns. It was a simple design, activated by slapping the back of a tongue-depressor resting on a fulcrum. The ping-pong ball bomb then flew more or less at its target.

On rainy days like this one, we took over most of the house except the kitchen and the basement, moving ships and airplanes, calculating travel time and distance, dropping bombs and firing guns, discussing strategies and recording damage in an accountant's ledger. Sometimes, when noncombatants entered the theater of war, there was friction beyond such imagined military encounters.

Late that afternoon, Beth came out of the dining room just as Charles was piloting a giant bomber from our bedroom upstairs onto the balcony. Below, I had advanced a line of enemy tankers on route from the rug in front of the fireplace to the cherry sideboard on the back wall of the living room. Dad had called in the air strikes from his observation post on the sofa under the front windows. Mom and Gr'om were out of harm's way in the kitchen. Then there was the collision.

When we came to tell this story later, we always noted how fortunate it was that Charles had loaded the launching device with ping-pong balls rather than darts. Gr'om didn't like us dropping darts from the balcony at all, but we occasionally did anyway. Darts dropped from mere eye-level at the board on the floor sometimes failed to stick, leaning or even falling over completely. But missiles launched from sixteen feet made a satisfying thunk when they hit the board and stood up straight.

However, that day Charles let go only a fleet of four ping-pong ball bombs, hoping to blast the lead escort ship and still have time to rearm and drop another load before the convoy got out of range. Just as he released the bombs, Beth stepped through the dining room door.

Charles called out (as we always did in such operations) "Bombs Away!" and I shouted "Look out!" I could see not only that Beth might get hit but also that she might squash my ships. So I leaped up and pushed her back toward the dining room.

"Yeeeii!" Beth screamed, in exaggerated alarm, always her way of drawing attention to the fact that one (or both) of her big brothers was bullying her.

"Boys!" called my mother sharply from the kitchen, her habitual warning in domestic disputes.

Three ball bombs fell onto the ships, but one did bounce off Beth's nose before I had propelled her back out of range. She was not hurt at all, of course. But, startled by my cry and push, she dropped something from her hand that rolled over next to a Navy destroyer. It was a toy soldier, a pilot actually, with a tiny parachute unfurled from the harness and pack on his back.

"Hey! That's ours," claimed Charles from above. "It belongs with the war toys."

"No," explained Gr'om, who had been drawn from the kitchen by our shouts. "It's Beth's. Or, to be more precise, it's your mother's."

"What do you mean?" I asked. Mom had never had anything to do with our military games.

"It's hers," said Gr'om. "It's hers because she invented it."

VII

"Mom invented this toy soldier?" asked Charles, who was now coming down the stairs.

"No, not this toy," said Gr'om. "She designed a parachute harness like the one this model airman is wearing." She took the little figure and pointed. We could see that the harness was a separate item, although its olive drab color blended in with the rest of his outfit.

"Mom helped win the war," observed Beth matter-of-factly, taking the parachutist back from Gr'om.

"Wait a minute, wait a minute," I said. "When did Mom work for the Army?"

I was completely puzzled by what Gr'om was saying. I knew my mother had worked in New York's garment industry before she was married. She was a college graduate and had been out on her own when she met my father. And I seemed to remember, now that the subject was mentioned, that she had gone back to work for a short time after Charles was born, when my dad was away in the war. I came just as the war was ending.

"Oh, Gr'om is making too much out of one little incident," said Mom, now sitting on the sofa by Dad. "I worked at a clothing manufacturers for less than one year, doing contract work for the War Department. And I submitted a design for this thing." She gestured toward the figure. "Some of the things I suggested were incorporated into the final version."

"She got a medal," noted Beth. She had recovered the airman and was brushing his molded plastic hair with a fingertip.

"Where was this?" I asked. I didn't feel I was getting the full story here.

"Come out to the kitchen," Gr'om suggested. "I'll tell you all about it."

"We've got an aerial campaign to finish," objected Charles, picking up his ping-pong ball bombs.

"I'll take Mark's place directing the ships," offered Mom. She turned the pages of the military history book Dad had open before him on the coffee table. It contained a map of the battle we were re-creating. "Mark can help you make the pie." In the past year I had learned to peel apples for my mother's famous desert.

Leaning back, Mom continued, "I need a break from the kitchen anyway. And Beth needs to put away her things in the sitting room."

This arrangement seemed to please some of the family, and the rest of us, it turned out, had no choice. So before very long I was hearing the story of my mother's crucial role in the last world war as I peeled and sectioned half a dozen Golden Delicious apples.

Now I must confess that some of the pieces of my mother's story must have been in my possession before our summer vacation at Gr'om's house in New Jersey. I had been told, for instance, that, although all three of us children had been born in Missouri, Charles was the only one to have lived in another state, if only for some months. And I also knew that my parents had had enough money after the war to put a down payment on a house and to buy a new car, not only because of my father's Army pay but also because my mother had set some money aside from her own wages while he was gone.

Still, a coherent narrative of events did not take shape for me until Gr'om linked most of them together while she was preparing dinner. And, of course, over the years additional shadings, connecting links, and lines of influence would be put into the story, some accurately by people who knew, and some more conjectural, the products of my own intuitive sense of how it must have happened.

Susan had been considered the brightest of the three Williams sisters, though also the quietest. Active and interested in sports, she still disappeared regularly to read in the bedroom she shared with Elizabeth. She read everything, but history was her primary interest.

So when she went off to a small college for women in upstate New York, no one in the family was surprised that she planned to be a teacher and that she quickly earned a reputation for high marks and a distinctive intensity. Her mother assumed she would return to Paterson after graduation to teach, but a summer job in the City temporarily changed their daughter's ideas about the future.

"You're doing nicely there, Mark," observed Gr'om at one point in her narrative, looking into my bowl of sliced apples.

"Thanks." I was slow, but I valued precision, feeling that each slice should be the same size and shape. And I liked to see how long I could make a single spiral of peel. Some day I would get the entire peel in one continuous strip.

Gr'om bit off one piece of peel from my latest carving. "Do you make the crust too?"

I shook my head. "No. You'll have to do that."

Making crust didn't seem hard, if you looked at a recipe. But everyone talked about how Mom's always "turned out," that some people had "a gift." And I had tasted other mothers' inferior pastry. So I hadn't sought promotion to that task.

"Did Mom work at college?" I asked Gr'om, trying to trace the course of my mother's employment. I recalled that Charles already earning his own spending money at the printer's.

"Oh, no. Her father didn't believe that young ladies should work. He approved of her becoming a teacher; but that was all."

"Then how did she end up at the clothing place?"

"As much by accident as anything else, I guess. In her second year of college, it must have been, she suddenly took up knitting, something she would not do when she was little. I could never get her to try anything."

"Um-hm." I was working my way through the rest of the sack, picking up at this point apple number four. Gr'om had put a casserole into the oven and turned now to making the crust.

Pie crust is really just flour, a little salt, shortening, and water, a simple combination. But things have to go together correctly to avoid a gummy texture and flat taste. When it's done by a skilled artisan, and fresh fruit added, the result is, to my thinking, profound.

Flour, by the way, makes a number of basic childhood substances. (I'm not counting how it figures as the foundation in so many foods--biscuits, cookies, pancakes, etc.) Flour-and-water paste, for instance, was a staple on the Circle, providing a homemade glue for school assignments and rainy day projects. And, as amateur dishwashers like myself at this time learned, this paste often hardens into rock when pie making pots and pans are poorly cleaned. That's also how we made papier-mache, spreading paste over newspaper and letting it set.

"It was one of the girls in her dormitory," Gr'om continued. "Betty Armstrong, whose father owned a clothing factory in New York. She was a knitter and was always trying out her own ideas for sweaters, mittens. Your Mom got interested and began designing odd things."

"What do you mean, odd things?"

"Oh, purses, unusual hats, a backpack. Things you wouldn't think would be knitted."

Gr'om was getting some pie dough out of the refrigerator, where it had cooled before she would roll it out. The lower temperature makes the dough easier to handle. I guess the flour and shortening hold together better.

"So she knitted a parachute harness?"

"Oh, no. That came later. Her friend from school got her a summer job at her father's business. And, over Grandfather's objections, that's where her experience came in."

"As a designer?"

"As a machine operator. But she learned a lot about how clothes are cut, shaped, put together. She did it for only that one summer. The pay was good, but the work was exhausting. Give me that pie plate." She gestured toward the counter by the sink. I got up to reach it.

"Sprinkle some orange juice on those apples," Gr'om suggested.

"I know. They'll turn brown if you don't." I was down to my last apple now. Gr'om had rolled the flattened dough onto the rolling pin, then shifted it into the pie plate. And she was working on the top crust. "So Mom worked there summers?"

"Not after that. It was too much for her. She took one summer to help me move up here, from Paterson. After your grandfather passed away."

"Oh."

"She didn't stop knitting, though. She began to experiment with different kinds of yarn, inventing new stitches, making stranger and stranger things. The second time she stayed with me, she read all sorts of books about the clothing industry." That would have been the summer after she had finished college.

"Was that with the war on?"

"No, before that. We could all see it coming, of course. Your mom even thought about enlisting."

"She did?"

"She had this idea that she could work in communications, radio. She was reading about how women in England were working on the ground, directing air traffic in and out of bases, the fighters and bombers going off to engage the Luftwaffe. She wanted to do that."

I was finished with the apples now. Gr'om took the bowl up with her floured hands and scooped the slices into the bottom crust. As always, we had more than would fit easily in the pan and had to pile them up carefully in the middle. She poured a mixture of sugar, nutmeg, and cinnamon over the mound and then turned to get the top crust off the bread board. Her powdered white hands, though soft and a bit fleshy like most grandmothers' hands, moved quickly and surely.

One other thing you can do with flour, by the way: it can be an explosive. My father told stories about men lighting matches in grain elevators out in Kansas-- barroom! And some kids on the Circle, Roger Peterson, for instance, had found ways to aerate flour with a straw, shooting it into a flame. It would go in a flash. If you contain the mixture, I suppose, you would have a homemade bomb.

"But she didn't enlist?"

"No. Until the war actually started, after Pearl Harbor, it wasn't so easy for women to get into the military, except in certain areas, like nursing. It was especially hard in electronics. And then, remember, she took the teaching job out in Kansas City."

I knew about this. My mother had decided after college to see the world, or at least other parts of this country. She applied for positions in a number of Midwestern states and ended up as the tenth grade history teacher in Independence, Missouri.

"What about when the war did begin?"

"Well, by that time, of course, she had met your father."

VIII

I already knew a fair amount about my mother and father's first meeting. That was in Kansas City, when Mom was teaching high school and Dad had his first job with the highway department. But here again, all the pieces of this event were not given to me at any one time, in any one place. And the lines of causality behind my parents' separate journeys were made murky both by the scattered nature in which the facts were delivered to me and the different states of understanding at which I stood for each stage of learning.

But here I was, getting closer to a rather crucial historical event for me, my own coming into the world. Woman meets man; a first son comes along, then a second. Who is that second son? If he learned how he'd come into the world, would it change what he was?

I did not put together all the factors in my arrival in the universe during that afternoon while I peeled and pared apples in Gr'om's kitchen, however. As dinner approached, Mom came in to help, and I was sent back to the living room to put away the scattered forces of our mock battle. I picked up an additional key item of information about my parents' history, though, at Gr'om's church the next morning, before we went to swim at Ross Lake.

When I say "Gr'om's church," by the way, I mean the phrase more literally than you might think. At the time she had moved to her country house from Paterson, Gr'om could not find a congregation she liked. Membership in the church of her childhood had dwindled over the years. And Gr'om used her energy to inspire a number of people dissatisfied with the local country churches to begin anew.

She, a handful of old family friends, and some newcomers to the area established the Maryville Bible Congregation. It met first in an old house, just filling the long living room for its Sunday morning and Wednesday evening services. But within five years the growing family of believers had raised enough money for their own small building, about a tenth of a mile off the road between Gr'om's house and the village of Maryville. Gr'om apparently had a lot to do with the functional design of that chapel.

Maryville Bible Congregation's building was a simple rectangle with one main level over a half-basement. There were pews on each side of a central aisle. In front stood a slim pulpit. Three rows of pews for the choir faced the congregation beneath a traditional picture of the young Jesus in flowing robes. Down each sidewall were small arched windows with tinted illustrations from familiar Bible stories: Jonah and the whale, Mary and Martha serving Jesus, Christ feeding the multitudes. In the finished half-basement below, reached by a set of stairs in one back corner, were a storeroom and a small office for the part time minister. Much of the operation of the church was taken care of by active members like Gr'om.

In Fairfield, by the way, we attended the First Methodist Church, but with little enthusiasm or regularity. In fact, I never did feel my parents were doing much more than go through the motions, maintaining social form and providing their children with one more facet of a traditional upbringing. We were certainly not a family that prayed at home, beyond saying a perfunctory grace at the dinner table: "For what we are about to receive, make us truly grateful." Nor did any of us complain about our casual stepping through fields of orthodoxy.

Charles stopped attending Sunday school in ninth grade, though he accompanied us on those occasional times when we all went to the 11:00 service. I was still going at 9:30 each Sunday, but primarily, with Circle friends like Billy Rhodes and school buddies like Jimmy Donaldson, to tease girls and irritate poor Mr. Samuelson. He was the inarticulate insurance agent who had been unable to refuse the minister's plea to teach the difficult seventh, eighth, and ninth-graders.

I never said this to Gr'om, of course, but I could not see any reason for anyone to attend church. Sitting through irrelevant lessons in Sunday school, singing the meaningless lyrics of ancient hymns, listening to prayers that surely were never answered, enduring sermons in which even faithful parishioners dozed--this was a place where only subversion made sense. So when we made our obligatory visits to Maryville Bible Congregation, I had to put on a mask, pretend both belief and interest. (Why I am today an active churchgoer is another story.)

My imitations of a devout young person weren't so hard to perform once or twice every two or three years when we visited Gr'om. My greatest fear was that, having paid so little attention to the principles of faith or the practice of worship, I would not know what to do or when or how.

Fortunately, our sweet grandmother assumed any such difficulties were the products of variations in liturgy between different denominations, between the traditional rites of our Fairfield Methodist Church and the more individualized rituals of Maryville Bible Congregation.

Still, I feared there was one thing she wouldn't tolerate, one violation of belief into which I would stumble. So as the three of Gr'om's grandchildren stood in the sanctuary of this little church and watched her arrange flowers around the altar, I at least tried not to do or say anything that might prove an affront.

This was a Wednesday, and there would be a service that evening. Our parents had gone out on their own for the day, "visiting museums in the city" we had been told. Charles and I assumed, however, that they were driving down to Trenton for Dad's job interview. In any case, Gr'om had us for the day. We were helping her with errands in the morning but had been promised swimming that afternoon, weather permitting.

The knowledge that a major change in my life might be occurring at this very moment leant an air of additional uncertainty to the feeling I always had in Gr'om's church

115

of not knowing what to do, what to say, even what to think. A more innocent Beth was happily helping her grandmother in the front of the church. She chattered about what was in the flower baskets, arranging things at Gr'om's direction. But Charles and I stood back by the double-doored entrance and let our hands hang at our sides. (Was it wrong to cross them? Could you put your hands in your pockets? Should you stand feet together or slightly apart?)

I was particularly unsure about myself here because at home I never was in a church except for planned events, Sunday school or the 11:00 service. And such scheduled occurrences defined my actions in general, even though there were sometimes individual points of confusion (can you look over your shoulder if you hear a loud noise during the sermon? when you're standing in silent prayer, can you lean back against the pew to rest your legs?). Being in Gr'om's church in the middle of a week-day morning was a little like trying to stand naturally when naked or in a swimsuit.

I'd tried the former occasionally, by the way, in front of the mirror in my bedroom back home. Charles, of course, was not there at the time. I can't remember for sure now what inspired the idea, perhaps Archie Baker's claiming he'd been to a nudist camp (not true, of course).

More likely, this was about the time Billy and I had found a discarded girlie magazine by the railroad tracks. Such things were rare, and we pored over every picture of nude figures in a variety of poses. There was in particular a spread of several pages about a beach on the French Riviera where the women went topless. The women's faces had been partially hidden by black rectangles stamped across the eyes.

"Let's spread these lilies out a bit," Gr'om said to Beth. She knelt down and pulled the stems up higher in the vase. "They're your mother's favorite."

Hmm, I thought. Something to remember, perhaps. Mom likes lilies.

All I had discovered about standing naked, by the way, was that the issue was complex. I couldn't figure if it would be comfortable for someone without clothes on to stand up very straight, or would a more relaxed pose, one hip cocked, be appropriate? When you were married, did you walk around your bedroom naked?

"Did she have lilies at her wedding?" asked Beth.

"She certainly did. I had almost two dozen from the back yard." They grew in profusion along the stone wall at the edge of Gr'om's lot. Our parents had been married in Gr'om's house, as the church building we stood in right now hadn't been built at that time.

Lying down naked was something I could imagine. That was almost like being in bed in pajamas or underwear. But sitting? Can you do that in a relaxed manner?

"Did Daddy give her flowers when he proposed to her?"

"Yes, he did. At least, in the end."

Suppose you were coming to your bride's bed, having removed your pajamas, folded them and laid them on a chair. Would you stand one foot out in front of the other as your wife gazed (admiringly? curiously? puzzled?) from the bed? Or would both feet be in line, shoulders squared? Hands at sides or crossed in front? Clasped behind?

'In the end'? Wait a minute: I seemed to have missed something here.

"What do you mean, Gr'om, Dad gave Mom flowers 'in the end'?"

Gr'om had walked back to where Charles and I stood, looking toward the altar and making a final review of her arrangements. As she turned to us and smiled, she seemed especially satisfied.

"What do you mean, 'eventually'?"

Opening the door and ushering us out, Gr'om explained: "Oh! When your dad first proposed, your Mother said 'no.'"

IX

Driving home from church, Gr'om explained how our mother had turned our father down when he proposed marriage. Her reasons had nothing to do with how she felt about him. Susan Williams loved Richard Landon and knew it within the first month of their meeting, but she wasn't sure marriage was right for them at the time.

She had become excited by teaching. Students liked her, and she realized that in the classroom she would keep on learning herself. History was a love, and even her flirtation with a career in the garment business had been in part an exploration of the industry and its development in the twentieth century. She wanted to teach three years in one school in order to establish herself.

Richard, however, had only a temporary position with the highway department and was ready to move on to some place where he could function more clearly as a geologist. There were signs that he would receive an appointment in Jefferson City soon. So she said "no" to marriage right then, though she agreed to keep seeing this young man. He was, however, shocked at a refusal, especially a refusal on the grounds that she was pursuing a career. This just wasn't something many women did in those days.

Things might have become confused indeed if war had not broken out. Already in the reserves, Richard had known he would go on active duty almost immediately. Susan's sense of history made her feel that she should support a man serving his country under arms. And she would not have to leave her school, since his assignment was expected to be overseas.

They had less than six months together in the States, but in that time Susan became pregnant. She later worked briefly, as I've said, for the war effort, but I followed Charles into the world while our father was in Italy, the result, I have calculated, of a brief furlough he enjoyed in 1944. It occurred to me now, on the way from Gr'om's church to Ross Lake, that my coming might well have ended the work which had earned my mother a medal.

Susan Williams Landon did not return to teaching until Beth was in high school, Charles and I off at college. And at the time of this return to her old stomping grounds in northern New Jersey, it was still her husband's career that determined where she lived. But now I wondered if, by being born, I had blocked the career of a great inventor!

All the new information I now had about my parents' past was enough to keep my mind busy that day with Gr'om. Any knowledge that they might be starting a new life in Trenton--and taking me with them!--would have been more than I wanted to confront. Still, I kept trying out the notion that here in a new territory I might be more daring, more accomplished, more appreciated than at home.

When we hiked down to the lake after lunch, I teamed up pretty quickly with Jerry; and Charles stayed near the shallow end with Beth. It was easy to understand Charles's attention to his younger sister: the lifeguard perched atop a platform next to the wading area was Jerry's very attractive sister, Carol. As Jerry and I traded stories about life in Midwestern and Eastern schools, Charles leaned on the platform's corner post and revealed an intense new interest in lifesaving techniques.

In the water Jerry and I dove for coins in the deepest part, raced from buoy to buoy with different strokes, and tried to outboast each other on every front. The lake was great for swimming, cool but not cold, plenty of space (perhaps two dozen people came all day, and less than half of them were usually in the water). Jerry and I found we were pretty evenly matched as swimmers, and we enjoyed a spirited rivalry.

For a good while during this competition, I was eyeing the diving platform fifty feet past the shallow area, considering the perfection of a maneuver we called back home a "flip."

This flip I wanted to do was not really that difficult. Many kids younger than I back in the Fairfield pool could catapult themselves off the end of the board, make a complete forward revolution of feet over head, and splash into the water more or less upright. However, I hadn't been able to perform this aerial somersault consistently.

I think my problem was more mental than physical, imagining disasters that were not actually very likely. I would see my head banging into the board as I was half-way through a spin. "We'd be slipping on your brains," Billy would say from his position behind me on the board.

Or I felt I might come around more than 360 degrees to slap my face flat onto the water. Archie said one guy popped his eyeball out doing that. So most of the time when I bounced down on the board to attempt a flip, I would panic at the end, jumping straight up rather than tucking my head and starting the rotation. I came in feet first, arms flailing, legs splayed, but at least without injury.

I made one mistake at Ross Lake, however: I told Jerry I could do a flip. Did I forget to mention that? Perhaps I did. Anyway, it just slipped out that first day we were looking into the swimming possibilities for Beth.

Jerry had asked if we had a diving board back home where we swam, and I said sure. When I listed all the dives I could do--a cannon ball (knees drawn up, wrapped in arms), the jackknife (hands to feet at the top of a jump ending in a dive), a swan dive (arms wide until the point of entry), the can opener (one leg pulled up, that knee held in clasped hands)--I just added the flip without thinking.

Sure, I could do one! Not a one-and-a-half (a flip plus another half-turn, ending in a dive), but definitely a flip. Now I knew I would have to show this newfound friend in New Jersey how it was done. When the diving platform became the site for our friendly competition, the reputation of the entire middle of the country would be resting on me.

Still, I put off the moment of testing for some time, making sure we ran through our entire repertoire of strokes (crawl, back-, breast-, and side-strokes) and the possible courses in the lake. I also got lucky when Charles demanded I take Beth for a snack and then play with her for a while. Jerry seemed content to throw a beach ball around with us in the shallow end, and then he had to go take care of several chores up at the house. But all through the middle of the afternoon I had flashes of myself not only spinning into disaster but doing it in front of my siblings and these friendly locals.

Late in the day all prevarication had come to an end. A tired Beth was content to rest on a towel in a grassy area, and Charles told me to go on, "have fun." A second lifeguard had taken Carol's place as she was going to swim some by herself. Jerry was ready for one more round of competition.

By getting out in front of him in challenges on the diving platform ("Can you do a twisting cannonball? a jackknife swan? a sideways dive?"), I delayed trying the flip for perhaps one last half-hour. But I knew it was coming. And I was getting more nervous every second about what would happen when it did. Just as I had run out of things to try, Jerry reminded me of my boast.

"Hey, let's do the flip." We were in the water at this point, near the ladder on the side of the platform.

"Right," I responded. "I'd almost forgotten that one!" Then in a moment of feeble inspiration, I added, "You go first. I need to catch my breath."

Jerry didn't hesitate. We climbed onto the platform, and he shook water from his ear by hopping up and down on one foot. I stood behind the board, shaking water off my arms and legs to disguise the possibility that I might be beginning to shiver. It was cooler in the late afternoon, the sun going down, but that was not the only reason for my shaking.

Jerry skipped down the board, gave one big jump, rose, flipped, splashed in feet first.

As Jerry performed this trick, I had noticed Carol finishing her swim and coming up to the bottom of the ladder. Her crawl was strong and steady, tanned arms arching over and through the water. She pulled herself easily up onto the deck.

"Your turn," called Jerry. He was treading water out beyond the area where he had landed.

"OK," I called, but there must have been a catch in my voice; or I might have lost color a bit; or perhaps there was some body language that showed my uneasiness. I felt that Carol, watching me, saw through my charade of fearlessness.

All of a sudden I had two things to worry about: standing still and going forward.

I was worried about the flip, to be sure. But I had also a feeling similar to the one I'd had at church earlier in the day. How was I supposed to hold myself here in front of a girl when I had only a swimming suit on? I felt naked and awkward, exposed and observed, alone and surrounded. I couldn't stay, and I couldn't go.

The sun must have been dipping beneath the horizon to the west, sending shafts of light through trees across the lake. It made the surface glitter with reflected light, Jerry's head and face shimmering in and out of shadow. Everyone else had left the lake, and I would have been outlined to Jerry by the fiery sunset behind me. Carol sat on the edge of the platform, her legs dangling in the water.

Just at the moment I thought I might give up, take a dive off the board and admit I couldn't do a flip, she looked back over her shoulder at me. I can see her face today. The sun lit it up at the moment of a pretty smile, and she said, "Just put your head down and everything else up. You'll come out all right."

Head down? Everything else up? It sounded so simple. What the heck!

I took off. Down the board, one hop up to come down on the end of the board, springing off--head down, everything else up. I flipped.

I flipped that time, and then five or six more times, just like that. Head down, everything else up. I entered the water upright every time.

Later, I found out that Jerry never suspected I hadn't done a thousand flips back in Missouri. Charles told me, in fact, that Jerry thought I was some kind of madman, the way I kept swimming different strokes and doing all sorts of crazy dives. I seemed to be tireless, a dynamo of activity and risk. He'd had to invent the excuse of chores up at the house to give himself a break, to recover from the frantic pace I was setting. Who, he'd asked, was this crazy kid from Missouri?

X

When did I figure out who Jerry reminded me of? That's another of those things I can't place exactly. It might have been in the same vacation week at Gr'om's. Or perhaps on the train ride back to Missouri. Or even later, in Fairfield. The clue was his sister Carol's face lit up by the late afternoon sunset.

Her image against the glittering surface of Ross Lake stayed in my mind for a long time after the occasion of my successful flip. And at some point I realized it was Carol, not Jerry, who resembled someone I knew. As her brother, of course, he shared the crucial features of high cheekbones, dark eyes, athleticism. But it was Carol Ross who reminded me of my childhood friend, Marcia Terrell.

When I began to suspect it was Carol's and not Jerry's looks that called up another's, I thought of the girl on the train we had taken into St. Louis, the Frontiersman. I had practically thrown myself at her, remember?

But that was one step short on the trail of associations leading back to Marcia. My neighbor's hair had darkened as she got old. And, leaving home more often, she was developing an independence and composure more fully realized by Carol.

Of course, it is also possible that I was just thinking a lot more about Marcia in these weeks. Absence sometimes does make the heart grow fonder. So any pretty girl might have triggered thoughts of her, making the girl on the train or the lifeguard at the lake a double in my yearning. I think there were physical resemblances among all three, but I also know that sometimes you find what you are looking for.

All these considerations were background, however, to my primary concern during the rest of the week at Gr'om's. I was pleased with my own appearance on this foreign turf. But I wondered how much that outgoing, active boy owed his nature to the frustrated inventor mother he hadn't really known until this trip.

I also needed to know if I would have to be this new person full time. That is, I wondered if my father was going to take a job in New Jersey and move his whole family halfway across the country. Fortunately, all these questions were resolved on the very night I perfected the flip.

We had stayed late at the lake, so late that Gr'om drove down to find out what was keeping us. She had been preparing a special meal, her own fried chicken and fresh corn on the cob and tomatoes grown by her friends in the church. We stuffed ourselves at dinner, made ravenous by exercise, the sun, and the water.

Mom and Dad didn't return until we had started our first game of Careers. Insisting we go on with our play, they spent a long time having coffee and the last slices of apple pie in the kitchen. And they gave no clues before bedtime about what might have happened on their trip. I overheard the facts of my own history by accident later that night.

I had been so busy all day--at church, swimming, with games--that when I went to bed my body felt as if it was continuing these same activities. You know how it is sometimes: life is so intense that you can't separate day from night, waking from sleeping, consciousness from unconsciousness.

Upstairs in bed, not yet asleep but dozing, I daydreamed one minute that I was placing flowers near the altar of Maryville Bible Congregation. Then I felt my feet hitting the diving board, myself splashing into the water. I rolled dice and drew the top card from a stack on the board. Perhaps about midnight I sat up suddenly in bed, alert and aware of my surroundings.

I knew that I was in my grandmother's house in New Jersey, not at home on Limestone Drive in Fairfield. We were on vacation. I saw a light from downstairs shining through a crack in the door. Someone was still up. And I heard conversation softly going on in the living room.

Just as the clackety-clack of train wheels on tracks still inspires restful sleep for me, the muffled talk of grownups provided a gentle, reassuring background to my childhood consciousness. I recognized in that hum the presence of adults who understand the world and who keep it under control.

Rather than just roll over and go back to sleep that night, however, I listened more closely for a minute. The sound, sprinkled through that soft talk, of laughter, made me get up on my knees at the head of my bed and peer over the balcony. I heard not just my father's low chuckle, but a light, almost teasing giggle from my Mom.

"It's a big organization," I heard my father observe.

"But that silly man with the thick glasses!" She laughed.

"And I'd have to start in public relations."

"That certainly wasn't clear from his letters."

"No, probably on purpose."

Peeking through the door, I could see Mom's head and shoulders below. She was sitting at the end of the living room sofa away from the fireplace. She pulled a strand of hair back behind one ear and gestured as she talked. I didn't see my father.

"I think we had to come," I heard her say.

"Yes," answered my father. "You can't tell from so far away."

"Sorry I was angry, at home."

"Oh, I should have understood. It's family."

I assumed my father was in the rocking chair he liked by the fireplace. But my mother seemed not to be looking in that direction. Her head was bowed. And the way she moved her hands, I thought she must be knitting or

127

sewing something in her lap. I stood all the way up on the bed in order to see.

"They have a large budget for research."

"And you would have had a pretty secretary."

"Well, I don't know if she came with the position."

"You would have had to fire her, of course."

I looked back at my brother, sleeping in the other bed. Through the window I saw the backyard in moonlight. Everything there was still.

"We had to make this trip," Mom continued.

"Oh, yes."

"Not just for the job. For me."

"Um-hm."

"If I had really wanted it, would you have taken it?"

"If you really wanted it, yes, I suppose I would."

I got out of bed, came around to the door. On hands and knees, I pushed the door open quietly and crawled out. Through the rails of the balcony I saw that my father was not sitting in the rocking chair. He lay on his back on the sofa, his head in my mother's lap. She was smoothing his hair as they talked.

"But what about the job for you?"

"Oh, Betty was just being nice. I don't think there was really anything there.

"If there was, it meant a lot more money."

"Didn't we have this discussion once before, years ago? I don't regret any of the choices I made."

I lay across a little throw rug on the balcony just outside the bedroom door. From this spot above the living room I could see the top of my mother's head, her shoulders covered by a light blue sweater.

My father, still in the white dress shirt he had worn on the trip, but with his tie removed and collar open, was stretched full length on the sofa. Shoes off, his feet turned out on the armrest at the far end. His left arm dangled on the floor, the right crossed his stomach. He seemed absolutely relaxed, as if he might never rise from this position. From where I lay, it looked almost as if he had fallen out of the sky and landed comfortably where he was.

"What about when I came back from Italy?"

"Yes, that time too. Especially that time."

"Now that was a good time."

"There was a war on!"

"I put it out of my mind for those ten days."

The clock on the mantle chimed once, a clear note. Was it one o'clock in the morning? Was it a quarter after or a quarter before another hour?

"Those ten days," repeated my mother. Dad hummed a tune softly.

"That's why I stopped working. The furlough miracle."

"Ah, yes. Kept you busy."

"Busy and happy while you left town. Left the country!" They both giggled.

There was some shifting of positions on the sofa. And suddenly I began to feel very sleepy. Cool air was now drifting in the bedroom window and through the door on its way downstairs. My warm bed seemed just the place I wanted to be.

I backed into the room, pushed the door closed again, though still leaving a slight opening. I could hear my parents talking, but now in whispers. There was some

129

chuckling and again someone humming. Was it "My Old Flame"?

Did I dream as I fell asleep that night years ago in my grandmother's wonderful house? Or did I overhear a memory, pieces of a vision floating up from the sofa in the living room? Or did I make it up in response to some inner need I did not recognize?

I had one of those dreams of flying. It began on the ground, as I climbed from the field behind Gr'om's house over the rock wall into her backyard. Where I'd been, I don't know. I had a sense that I'd been gone a long time. After a moment's satisfied survey of the grounds, I took off from under the largest of the apple trees.

In a graceful, turning spiral I floated over the flower garden, across the patio, and past the window of the room in which I had been sleeping. (When I fly in dreams, by the way, it is never fast like Superman. Instead I am more like a balloon, gently motoring over the landscape.) Beneath that bedroom, I knew, was Gr'om's kitchen, and beneath that the basement in which so many family memories were stored.

My flying occurs in the early morning of a beautiful summer day, the sunshine brilliant, the birds singing. My sense of time is odd, for I feel that what I am seeing belongs in the past. Perhaps it comes from a 1940s movie scene.

Although I do not see them as I drift higher with the rooftop below me, I am aware of a couple lying in each other's arms in the bedroom at the end of the balcony. I realize also in this dream that the man and woman are making love, although this is something I could not at all put into words if I were conscious.

Then as I mount even higher and turn away from the rising sun, I find that I am no longer in New Jersey but back in Missouri. My house on Limestone Drive is just behind me. And I cruise easily across our backyard and past Marcia Terrell's house toward the top of the Circle.

Then I turn more directly west, the sun behind me streaking rays across the land. When I crest the hill above Springers' Pond, I see a train winding down toward the distant Gasconade River, Route 66 running parallel but less direct. It snakes around hills, across valleys, through the trees. The world seems immense as I hover, taking in that grand prospect.

Interlude: Watermarks

Sometimes the places that mark one's journey through life are not those where the most time is spent. It's not the home or the office that measures the end of one phase--say, young adulthood--or the beginning of another--for instance, middle age. Instead another, less intimate location figures as the place where you recognize how you or your view of the world has altered.

For me, one place that stands for the end of childhood is Meramec Spring, a 100-acre recreational site less than an hour's drive from Fairfield. Meramec Spring, where pioneers built the first successful iron works west of the Mississippi, was the location for every annual school picnic I attended after elementary school.

Most Midwestern communities have such a site, a place to which on separate days near the end of the school year grades seven through twelve travel by bus for an afternoon of games (softball, volleyball, capture the flag), educational opportunities (a nature walk, museum display, a crafts demonstration), and outdoor eating (hot dogs, cold soda, ice cream in little paper cups). And going there in successive years underscores the passing of time, the stepping stones beyond a life of play and away from the primary environment of the family.

At Meramec Spring one bright summer day very close to my sixteenth birthday I began to suspect that the story of my earliest years had probably concluded. That simple tale had been spun out, as you know, mostly within the confines of a quiet neighborhood on the edge of Fairfield, the Circle. I had come to understand how I was a recognizable product of my mother and father. However, key aspects of their lives had long been hidden from me, and my identity as their offspring could not be used to predict precisely my future.

As I think about it now, the central feature of this little park where I began to be aware of my own progress in life, the spring itself, embodies the dual qualities of all such landmarks (or, um, watermarks): stability and change.

The bubbling pool of cold, clear water, stationary at the foot of an Ozark tree-covered bluff, informed me, each time I followed the dirt path along its rim, that it was a fixed reference point in my journey through youth, a center to the circles of growth visible in a tree's trunk. And the river rising from deep underground in that spring, then cascading away over rocks toward the distant Mississippi River, showed, as I gazed at its rushing current, the race of time carrying me into the future.

There are many legends about Meramec Spring, stories of famous people who came there and myths inspired by properties of the place itself. Water rises in the spring, according to some, from as far away as Hannibal, Missouri, Mark Twain's boyhood home. Scientists like my father, who worked for the state geological survey, had reportedly put radioactive tracers into ground water hundreds of miles from Fairfield, finding the telltale element rising weeks afterward at Meramec Spring.

The limestone characteristic of this region dissolves relatively easily in rainwater, making south central Missouri a honeycomb of underground channels. Feeding these waterways is, of course, rainwater. But there are also whole rivers which, running straight into rocky hillsides or fields of giant boulders, dive underground and then surface in other counties as large springs with prodigious output.

Intricate, unmapped caves also characterize the Missouri terrain, caverns famous in outlaw stories as hideouts and treasure caches. And mammoth sinkholes can be found in many areas, depressions where the land has dropped in neat circles above subterranean cave-ins. Such features are linked in the popular mind with earthquakes like the famous one of 1811-12 centered in New

Madrid. They too are reminders of the many passageways beneath the surface in the southern third of the state.

From Meramec Spring flow millions of gallons of water every day, joining a stream a few hundred yards away to create the Meramec River, which runs toward St. Louis a hundred miles to the east. (The water itself, of course, travels many more miles in its circuitous course toward the Mississippi.) The river's twisting route lies across mineral-rich hill country that remains today nearly as wild as when this territory saw its first towns established in the last century.

The lack of major roads and few inhabitants made this region a haven for the bank robbing Jesse James of the 1870s. His gang's chief hideout was Meramec Caverns, some thirty miles from the springs and still a favorite stopping point for tourists following old Route 66 from the East toward California.

For many years I was convinced that the famous pioneer Daniel Boone had also visited these scenes near my home. Eventually, I learned that, though he did settle in what was originally Spanish territory in Missouri, that area was north of Fairfield, near the center of the state. Perhaps the many signs directing travelers to this American hero's final home inspired kids around the Circle to claim we were walking down paths in our neighborhood woods on which Boone himself once traveled. Certainly the popular television show made us all want to believe we had some connection to this legendary figure.

Though this region around Fairfield and Meramec Spring had beckoned to early settlers fleeing the constraints of civilization or seeking a chance to begin again, it was hardly a paradise. It has taken a hearty breed to homestead this cold in winter and hot in the summer northernmost reach of the Ozark Mountains.

One set of rumors about Meramec Spring underscored the difficulties of exploring and settling this area: rumors of men drowned in those waters. We Fairfield school children had all heard how efforts, both amateur and professional, to determine how deep the spring is ended in tragedy. Trained underwater experts, linked to the surface by ropes and breathing through hoses, went down, down, down. The cables and gear rose to the surface, so say the stories; but bodies were never found.

As a native, however, I generally felt comfortable in this environment, assuming, as children do, that other places were not much different in the essentials and that our region of the country was certainly adequate to the immediate goal of me and my friends--that is, our growing up.

Though the Meramec Spring water is crystal clear, its great depth creates a green cast at the center, perhaps reflecting the leafy overhang from the bluff on the south and east rims but also deriving from the volume of water through which light is passing. At the edge of the spring you can see far down, past ledges jutting out from the walls, around turns, and to descending spirals. But looking into the heart of the springs, everything becomes hazy, cloudy in the uncertainty of distance.

At different school visits to this spot I had seen or imagined a number of figures through the rippling waters of Meramec Spring and Meramec River: the Olympic swimmer I had pretended to be when visiting my maternal grandmother in New Jersey; the fabulous baseball player I, fulfilling my father's dreams, would one day become; an American traveler headed west along Route 66 toward a new destiny.

In that hypnotizing pool on one summer day I even saw, or believed I saw, the silver-clad body of an astronaut. The space program was at that time in its infant stages. The United States had successfully launched its first satellite in 1958, but the idea of space travel was still more science fiction than government program. Yet there was a timetable to put men into space, and early television and lushly illustrated magazine articles gave me images with which to project the future.

I saw, or imagined I saw, deep down in the heart of Meramec Spring not the explorer of stars but the settler of open space, someone who, coming after the first wave of pioneers had charted the frontier, brings meaning and order to new territories. Floating in zero gravity, arms and legs spread to push off nearby objects, the man in a puffy uniform and glass helmet seemed poised to perform some vital task. (In another, darker version from my imagination, he drifted lifeless after some terrible breakdown in the system designed to support his mission.)

I have not become an astronaut, far from it, in fact. Still, in the years that followed, the heroic figure of a man in space continued to hover in the background of my consciousness, generally just out of sight in the shadows of my dreams. I know now that it was a self I wanted to be, traveling along with the person I did become. The two are not completely disconnected, I hope, though my accomplishments have come on earth (and under the earth) rather than among the stars.

Other images hovered in and around Meramec Spring in those years, including the faces of girls like Marcia Terrell I felt were intimately involved in my destiny. Most of these womanly figures were grown-up versions of my playmates in the Circle, the charmed world of childhood.

Some, like Cathy Williams, with her eyes on distant horizons, were even then blurring the boundaries between innocence and experience. By this time I had also seen and admired the fabulous couple, Linda Roper and Martin Pruitt. And I wanted my future to include a romance as idyllic, as fine, as complete as theirs seemed to be. How, with Marcia Terrell, I very nearly achieved that goal is to be one of the key subjects in the next sections of this account.

But while I struggled to shape the outward me, I began to realize there was also an inner me, a hidden self I hadn't fully known to this point in my life. I had seen the water but not the sources of that water, nor its depth. I was a child of more things than I knew then or perhaps even know now. The effort to define them inspires this continuing account.

Volume Three: Forces of Destruction

Part Five: Soldier Boys

Chapter I

I suspect that it's not reasonable to assert that any girl's breasts are "perky." A whole person can, I think, be perky. Or some actions might reveal perkiness. But breasts, which have no muscle tissue, can't on their own exhibit qualities like perkiness, determination, vigor.

Still, no high school male in Fairfield would have argued for a moment against the assertion that slim Patricia Stewart had "perky" breasts. This undeniable fact made our new classmate an immediate topic of conversation and a common object of desire.

Patty's family had moved to Fairfield from Texas, and her appearance at the high school caused a stir, both among the boys (whose eyes widened in wonder) and among the girls (whose eyes narrowed in suspicion.)

This budding woman's ample bosom rode high on her chest. And unlike many girls' breasts--and certainly most women's--hers seemed to resist gravity, jutting straight forward and arriving at small but definite points. They were, to use a military expression, always "at attention" when the breasts of so many others were "at ease."

The question about those unusually erect breasts, of course, rose as directly as they did: were they supported

139

by more than a conventional bra? Did she have wires, a rigid undercup, even some kind of conical frame? Since we would learn in the following months that she never allowed her dates to fondle above the waist--though rumors about what she permitted below her waist were tantalizing--the issue was not quickly resolved. (No one, by the way, would have predicted that I would be the boy to solve the mystery of her breasts' perkiness.)

My involvement with Patricia Stewart's chest started one Saturday in my junior year, though she, I'm sure, did not mark that date (December 19) on her calendar. I was pretty well known as Marcia Terrell's steady at this time, and I shouldn't even have been excited by Patty's perky breasts. But I was.

That fall I had begun working part time at Gunn's Drug Store, a standard smalltown establishment. Because it featured a soda fountain, Gunn's was one of the regular gathering places for Fairfield teenagers.

It wasn't the premier hang-out in those days before fast food and drive-throughs. That title was owned by Dixon's Drug Store, a block and a half south. Still, many of my peers envied my position behind the counter because members of the opposite sex regularly came to perch on the twelve stools lined in an L-shape around the counter or seated themselves in the four booths that continued the long arm of the L.

These beauties regularly required my attention. And with such interaction came yet more breakthroughs in my exploration of the forces that bring together boys and girls, the powers that shape such raw material as we were then into the future's men and women.

"What would you like?" I asked the girl with the perky breasts as she hoisted one hip onto a counter stool, scooted the rest of her slim derriere into place, and scanned the menu posted above the mirror behind me. That menu, by the way, was constructed of white plastic letters with tabs on the back pushed into horizontal seams on a black felt board. The task of mounting the letters to reflect daily changes in our fare had become for some reason a specialty of mine.

"Oh, I don't know. What do you recommend . . . Mark." I would like to say Patricia knew who I was here. But, following the gaze of her eyes, I could tell she had simply read my name, stitched in red above the pocket of the white jacket worn by all Gunn's employees. Perhaps, I thought, she is just reminding herself of my name.

"Well, do you just want a dessert, ice cream or something? We also have sandwiches."

"I want something . . . " She hesitated. "I want something unusual, not the regular."

"Ah, something special." I mused.

"Yes," she countered. "Something with a bit of . . . a bang." And when she said that, she did something herself that I certainly found unusual: she snapped off a salute.

Up until recently, salutes were things that I knew about only from movies, those World War II classics my generation had been raised on. And salutes were executed, of course, primarily by men. Patty's thin hand shooting out from her forehead crossed a boundary into strange new territory, a place where women's desire, customarily hidden, became visible. Snap!

"There's . . . um . . . a vanilla cream root beer," I suggested without much confidence. This was, remember, the era of cherry cokes and their variations: sodas to which a squirt of fruit syrup (cherry, pineapple, apricot) is added. Vanilla cream root beer, my favorite, included two extras.

"Oooh, that sounds better than anything else," Patty smiled. Then she leaned closer to me and said softly, "Unless you can give me a rum and coke."

I was, I now know, a bit more innocent about the subject of alcohol than many of my generation. Some in my class had begun sampling 3.2 beer and cheap wine at weekend parties long before I was aware of the fact. And a few even got into the hard stuff. But, since my parents didn't drink at all, the closest I had ever come to real liquor was the stray empty whiskey bottle thrown aside along railroad tracks by hoboes passing through town. The stale smell of cheap bourbon never encouraged me even to taste.

Surely Patty was joking, then, about having a drink. So I chuckled and turned to make her a vanilla cream root beer. As I mixed these three elements over ice in a standard coke glass, I tried to untangle in my own mind the associations Patty's odd behavior had elicited.

War--especially "The Big One," "Double-U, Double-U Two"--provided the broad background for my generation's beginning. Yet we seldom saw its details accurately.

Our childhood understanding of the Second World War came almost exclusively from the black-and-white movies that celebrated Allied heroism and enemy evil. All the ships torpedoed, the tanks exploded, and the planes brought down by anti-aircraft guns were idealized graphic pictures stored in our memory banks, a record of survival and triumph. The reality from which they diverged was seldom if ever glimpsed directly. Even the men in our town who'd fought in World War II were not seen as soldiers, now that they had put on civilian clothes, taken on routine jobs, and moved on to postwar prosperity.

During this year in my life, however, some of the underlying facts of war began to push through the masks which had hidden them from me in my growing up. Patty's salute triggered the first of these emerging subjects, the individual soldier.

When I began working at Gunn's I had been surprised to find that, on Friday and Saturday nights, downtown Fairfield street corners featured little knots of off-duty enlisted men from nearby Fort Leonard Wood. These eighteen-, nineteen-, twenty-year-olds were looking for places to drink, of course, and hoping somehow to find female companionship for a few hours, or, if they were very lucky, the night. Most were in boot camp, though a few were taking advanced training as Army engineers.

These uniformed men had probably been on Fairfield's downtown street corners long before I first realized they were there. Earlier in my life, when enlisted men were prowling the streets, I had been at home in the Circle. And, if I happened to ride through town with my parents on a weekend evening, it's unlikely that I paid much attention to the details of a scene in which I had no potential role. My parents, you can be assured, never alluded to the grittier elements of Fairfield life in front of "the children."

Those military figures "appeared" before me at a particular stage in my growing up, a stage when the concept of warfare was becoming newly important to boys my age. While the U.S. had only a few military advisers in Vietnam at this time, the call for troops there would pick up in the next few years. And the nation already had a general sense that another line (like the 38th parallel in Korea) would have to be drawn somewhere else in Asia to "stop the spread of Communism." We boys in smalltown America could sense that we would become the men who fought in this next war.

Patricia Stewart's salute at Gunn's soda fountain resonated with a new awareness of the military context which had always surrounded me. I didn't know what to make of it at the time, of course, and simply tried to think of what to say to a girl whose masculine gesture didn't match her feminine appearance and who joked about wanting a drink.

"There you go," I said cheerfully, as I placed the cold drink glass on a paper coaster before her. "One special."

Patty smiled back at me, leaned forward again, and said, "Thanks, troop." Then she spun around on her stool and surveyed the rest of the store.

"Troop?" That was an odd appellation. Whatever did she mean?

Before I could think of a way to question her, another customer called me back to one of the booths for more coffee. And because Patty had leaned forward to speak to me, my attention strayed from her use of the word "troop" and wandered back to those perky breasts. She was wearing a tight blouse that buttoned snugly down the middle. And her breasts rested on her forearm, which stretched across the counter top. They were pushed up, but they remained firm, conical. What marvels!

I thought about Marcia Terrell's average breasts. With my childhood pal I had gone beyond the accidental contact inspired by a game of Kick the Can when we were several years younger. Then, bumping into each other on a run to base, we'd fallen together on the soft grass of a neighbor's yard and my hand ended up on one breast. We'd both been so shocked at this contact that we leapt away, not even daring to let the sensation of touching and being touched register in our memories.

Now, in irregular petting sessions I had charted every feature of her young bosom. She had fine breasts, though of only medium size. And the question of size mattered, I must admit, to me and my pals. (I didn't realize it at the time, of course, but the shape of my legs mattered in the same way to girls like Marcia.)

No matter the exact size of Marcia's breasts, her flesh was soft, flexible, squeezeable, even in her bra. The incredible apparent firmness of Patty's breasts made Marcia seem less exciting, more ordinary. What would it feel like to cup one of Patty's erect twins? I wondered.

Did I, by the way, ever notice any women with those soldiers on Fairfield's street corners? Or is my memory up to one of its usual tricks, borrowing brightly colored images from movies and television to populate the black-and-white pictures my mind has processed of the past?

144

I seem now to see a particular female figure in one snapshot of recollection, a slender, elegant form in red outlined by the darkened plate glass store window behind her. Who she is and what she's doing there is another subject of this portion of my memoirs.

Soldiers with a weekend pass, by the way, are not always, I'm afraid, a town's best visitors. I can say this in part because I became a "soldier boy" myself. And there are moments in that role I will probably choose to omit from this account of my life's journey.

At any rate, one eye-opening weekend of my junior year at Fairfield High I saw, thanks to one of these visiting soldiers, the human capacity for violence on a scale sufficient to change forever my concept of the human species--and of myself. And it was all connected to thoughts about perky breasts.

II

My attraction to Patty Stewart's bosom drew me no closer to the secret of perkiness at that first encounter. By the time I had a few moments free in my duties as soda jerk, she had finished her drink and walked out the door. I had seen her swivel around on her stool and survey the rest of the store as if she might be looking for something or someone. But then, while I was frying a burger at the grill, she must have hopped down and walked away. She did leave a dime (the correct price) for the vanilla cream root beer.

I wasn't sure that I would have much to do with such a prominent figure in our high school anyway, so I didn't regret her departure right then. I needed time to think about topics of conversation--as well as about my relationship to Marcia--if I was going to have more to say to Perky . . . er, Patty.

Fortunately, my work at Gunn's was not boring. While I know now it was mostly the people I worked with that made this job enjoyable, at the time I also reveled in the material of a drugstore soda fountain. Perhaps this American institution's demise with the advent of fast-food restaurants in the 1960s adds to my nostalgic feeling about it now.

Arranged in orderly fashion behind the L-shaped counter with four booths and before a mirror which ran the length of the "L" were:

soft drink dispensers, which mixed carbon dioxide, water, and syrup for Coke, Seven-up, and Hires Root Beer;

cardboard tubs of ice cream in the row of freezers under the counter, featuring your basic flavors of this pre-Baskin-Robbins era--vanilla, chocolate, strawberry;

on a shelf above the freezers, the quart-sized metal containers of toppings for sundaes (cherry, pineapple, butterscotch, hot fudge, marshmallow, nuts, whipped cream);

on the counter under the mirror, cream-colored milk shake mixer with three steel blending stems ending in those little rippled disks that cut the ice cream into the milk;

coldcuts and condiments for sandwiches in a small refrigerator, with white bread and buns in cellophane bags beneath the counter;

and a grill for burgers, grilled cheese, and fried egg sandwiches next to the deepfat cooker for fries.

The food and drink produced here brought together the citizens of Fairfield and their children for refreshment of the body and the spirit. And I was one of the people who managed the operation.

There were always two full time workers at Gunn's (taking 9:00-6:00 shifts daily with an hour for lunch) and about half a dozen high schoolers, two of whom came in each evening at 5:00 and stayed on for an evening shift until 9:00. Skinny Howard Bend and I were the only boys, as Max, our boss, liked to hire small brunettes.

These were the days, of course, before any government regulations controlled hiring. Personal preference was an established criterion for employers, and Max Gunn belonged to that class of men who enjoy having good-looking "girls" working for him. Fortunately, he didn't abuse that privilege, though the privilege itself now has moved into the category of abusive relationships in a politically correct world.

Generally, the regulars at Gunn's were recent graduates of Fairfield High School who were waiting for Mr. Right to take them away from all this. Many stayed for years before they did get asked to marry, and, more often than not, it was by Mr. OK.

The young woman I had come to enjoy working with most was not a local girl, but someone from, of all places, Fargo, North Dakota. Ruth Simms, a slim, brown haired-woman with a rosebud mouth that swallowed the "o" in "root" beer, had followed her boyfriend from their home-town when he enlisted out of high school.

"Who was that?" she asked me as I watched Patty push open the glass door and step out into the bright December sun. "A new girlfriend?"

Ruth's boyfriend had done basic at Fort Polk, Louisiana (she'd stayed in Fargo for those two months), then was sent up to Fort Wood for training as an "automotive engineer"--that is, a jeep mechanic. I couldn't get over her having followed a sweetheart that far and to this out-of-the-way place.

"Nah," I replied quickly. My burger was done, so I slid it between the two halves of a bun (warmed on the grill), added a handful of potato chips from a giant plastic bag under the counter and a trio of pickle slices from the little refrigerator. "You know I date Marcia. That's a new girl in school, too popular for the likes of me!"

Ruth and I had become friends working weekend hours together. Each regular had to take every other Saturday, getting assistance from two part timers in the morning and a different two in the afternoon.

"Still, Marcia wouldn't like the way you were looking her over."

I carried the plate to the booth and then busied myself with scraping the grill, afraid I might be blushing. I had been studying those breasts.

Why would I be studying those breasts if I had Marcia's to fondle? Well, the answer is simple for people of my generation: Marcia and I had reached another plateau in our physical relationships. And I was getting frustrated trying to get past it.

I know the present generation isn't going to believe that, though I had been dating Marcia Terrell on and off for several years, we still hadn't had sex. This makes no sense in an age where birth control is available and effective and when the facts of life are understood by children in elementary school. But this was another time. This was the era of elaborate, prolonged, incrementally increasing petting.

True, many a young man of my time regrettably discovered he'd impregnated his girlfriend. And others enjoyed sex throughout their teenage years, defying the odds of broken condoms, bad timing, and/or unrestrained impulse. Still, the great number of males and females went years doing everything short of intercourse. Marcia and I were such a couple.

Behind the counter with Ruth, I decided to change the subject. "Ron got a pass this weekend?" Ron was her boyfriend, a former high school hockey star (but not bright enough for college) whose gold tooth and handsomely scarred face made it look as if he were a veteran of the NHL.

"He's coming tonight," Ruth said brightly.

"Movies or bowling?" I asked, believing myself familiar with the nature of their dates. Of course, I only knew what she told me.

"Bowling. He says I can do better. He's going to keep working with me on my follow through."

"Ah. Marcia and I are taking in a movie. *Guns of Navarone*. Gregory Peck, David Niven. Seen it?"

I had never been bowling myself, by the way. The bowling alley had only recently converted to automated pin-setting, and before that I had been intimidated by the stark realities of manual pin-setting.

Before automation, pin-boys or "setters" crouched on little perches above the triangle-shaped arrangement of pins when balls careened down the alley. After collision and the scattering of pins, the boys dropped down from their invisible positions several feet above the alley, removed the fallen pins, and--if it was a second ball or a strike--set up the ten pins again in their triangle pattern.

150

My dad had often suggested I apply for work at the Pin-Up Club, but I'd always found a reason not to.

Pin-setting was hardly a risk-free operation. Men who threw hard or put plenty of spin on their balls could cause the pins to fly up as high as the setter's head. Barked shins were regular injuries. And sometimes over-eager bowlers sent balls down the alley while the boy was still at floor level. It was a little like being one of those moving targets at the carnival game, an upright turkey marching back and forth in front of the customer's gun sights. I didn't want any part of it.

But I did want parts of Patty Stewart. And, should I ever have a chance at them, I decided I would move quickly to those perky breasts.

Marcia and I had always followed a single path in petting. (This petting is "foreplay" that doesn't lead to "play," remember--unless you count what happens when I am alone in bed later that same night.) Everyone understood this procedure through the baseball game analogy: "What base did you get to?" Well, I had gotten to second base and even been given the "steal" sign for third. But my slide, so to speak, left me tantalizingly short.

Not that Marcia overtly stopped me. It's just that when my feet nearly reached the bag (my fingers the hot spot), other things happened.

Marcia's hands were roving too, you understand, all the time I groped and felt. And each time I nearly arrived at the heart of her warmth, she found mine. And I . . . um . . . well, I couldn't stop myself.

The first time this had happened--of all places, on a merry-go-round in Westlook Park--the explosions we both enjoyed were a complete and satisfying surprise. But now that Marcia knew where my vulnerability lay (or stood), she couldn't keep herself from setting it off. And that effectively put an end to my assault.

I had decided that the slow, cumulative buildup toward that point in our relationship was the problem. I simply couldn't hold back after 45 minutes of the escalating anticipation that had begun with lip contact and moved down bodies to that final destination.

Suppose I went out of the usual order, then: started low, worked my way up, then came back down again? Sort of a first base, third base, second base strategy.

If Marcia, like Patty Stewart, would save her breasts for a later petting achievement, I reasoned, perhaps I could get past my problem point when I wasn't at such a high level of combustion. After a cooling off period, I could resume play. That is, maybe I could stay perky long enough to return to the ultimate goal fully armed.

I came upon a way I could achieve my desire of altering our pattern of petting when Marcia and I were at the movies.

III

I had to finish my shift at Gunn's, of course, before I could get home, borrow my mom's car, and pick up Marcia. And I knew my shift wouldn't be over until I'd served coffee to Colonel Samuel Mack.

When I said earlier that I was surprised to find soldiers had always been on the streets of Fairfield, I should admit that I knew some representatives of the military other than these enlisted men with weekend passes from Ft. Leonard Wood. Some, in fact, I knew very well.

My father, like most of his generation, had served in World War II, but he seldom spoke of his time in Africa. And many of his fellow workers at the Missouri Geological Survey were former Marines, Navy seamen, Air Force pilots. I just didn't see them that way in their current lives. Dads in my set were men who went off to the office every day. They wore suits, worried about taxes, and rested on weekends. They weren't soldiers.

Perhaps the only man who represented the world of war to me was retired Colonel Samuel Mack. Though he didn't have on the uniform, he still looked the part of distinguished combat veteran. And his reputation preceded him.

"See that guy at the counter?" my boss, Max Gunn, asked me on one of my first days at the store. "Drinking coffee?"

"Yeah." I saw him. Not a tall man, but his form suggested compactness and strength. Close cut hair, upright posture, stern face.

"Retired Army. War hero."

"Uh-huh."

"Killed a dozen Japs with his bare hands."

"Oh!" I had heard such stories throughout my childhood, though more often in the movies than when seeing

153

someone first hand. I looked again at Colonel Mack. He sat still, with both hands on the counter beside his coffee cup, looking straight ahead. He didn't have the square jaw of legendary heroes, but somehow his more oval face showed the same strength.

"On solitary patrol, Pacific island. He fell into an enemy foxhole, dozen Japs."

"Wow!"

"When it was over, he was the only one standing. Got the Silver Star. 'Course he was cut up pretty bad himself, but he lived. Goddamn hero, that's what he is!"

You can guess how intimidating this was, to wait on someone so much larger than life. I was glad Ruth had already served him coffee on that day. It gave me time to prepare myself.

As Max then explained, Colonel Mack came in twice a day, mid-morning and late evening, to have exactly one cup of black coffee. He didn't say much and left quietly, but he was as regular as clockwork. Since he hadn't come in for the final time on the day I first met Patricia Stewart and her perky breasts, then, I knew my shift wasn't over.

I felt I had done well with Colonel Mack in the months I had been working at Gunn's. Whenever I saw him coming, I poured the coffee and set it out for him. He seldom said anything but nodded, I felt, appreciatively. He left the nickel and, every once in a while, a small tip.

Occasionally, we even talked. He knew who I was, that I was good in math at school, and that I planned to become an engineer. On the day I met Patty Stewart, I learned something more about Colonel Mack's military history.

"You have Alka-Seltzer?" he asked me as I passed by his customary counter stool.

"Alka-Seltzer? Sure." Max kept a box of standard medicines under the counter. The help knew to let regulars have anything they wanted, but refer others to the shelves. I slipped a package of two tablets and a glass of water next to the Colonel's coffee cup.

"Headache or upset stomach?" I asked. I knew about Alka-Seltzer from what became a classic TV commercial: "Pop-pop, fizz-fizz; Oh, what a relief it is!" The jingle went with pictures of two tablets dropping into water and bubbling energetically. The commercials often suggested people finding relief from hangovers, though the drinking itself was never shown. And, an innocent about alcohol, I hadn't made the connection.

Colonel Mack wasn't the typical Alka-Seltzer user, though. "Mm, not quite," he said, eliminating both upset stomach and headache as causes for his distress. "More the weather."

"Well, hope this does the trick."

I figured I had probably said enough and turned toward the grill. But he caught my eye and held it, so I hesitated.

"There's a change coming, possibly snow."

"Ah." Like most teenagers, I paid little attention to weather. My mother complained all winter that I didn't button my coat, got my feet wet walking through puddles, left my hat behind. "How can you tell?"

He chuckled softly. "I've got enough broken bones in here to build a small dog," he said, pointing to his body. "They let me know."

I understood: it was shrapnel, a war wound. Probably happened in that foxhole on Guam. I'd heard of men with metal plates in their heads, bullets lodged near the heart, pins permanently holding broken bones together. I shivered to think of the suffering this veteran must have had to undergo. I hoped I would never have to endure that kind of pain.

I haven't faced such physical pain, I'm happy to say, at least I didn't in my time as a soldier in Vietnam. I saw

155

enough of it in others, however, to be able to draw some conclusions about the effects of combat. Perhaps as depressing are the psychological effects of war, which, I fear, many in my generation have experienced. Of those I will one day have to speak.

While my insight about the Colonel's aching bones occupied my thoughts as I cleaned up at the end of my shift, it faded into the background the moment I picked up Marcia and we headed for the movies. The need to preserve my perkiness commanded all my attention. I was inspired toward a solution for this problem by the part Anthony Quinn plays in *Guns of Navarone*.

The movie's plot is, like many others of its time, pretty simple. The Germans have installed huge guns in caves above a mountainous coast along a strategic channel in the Aegean Sea, and Allied forces trying to free the Continent are blocked on this one front. A team of commandos takes on the seemingly impossible task of--at night--scaling the high cliffs, laying explosives to blow up the guns, and escaping back to their own forces.

The first hour of the movie is preparation, the gathering, testing, and packing of climbing ropes, explosives, fuses, weapons, maps, radios--the standard equipment. Then the ascent begins, and we moviegoers hold our breath as climbers struggle upwards (one falls, dangling on his rope, but is rescued), sentries fail to spot the commandos and are systematically taken out (our knives are silent and, in another movie convention of the times, bloodless), the team makes it inside enemy fortifications.

But, then, they are caught! Just like that, they walk into a room full of SS troops. Stunned, they drop their weapons, and we gasp in fearful anticipation. The mission is lost, the men will be tortured and die, the war will drag on for years.

Then Quinn's character performs an amazing feat. He turns on his comrades, says he didn't want to be part of the mission in the first place, throws himself on his knees in front of his captors and begs for mercy. He grovels, sheds tears, screams in fear.

It's a convincing scene. And it disgusts us patriotic moviegoers, who believe we'd never betray our fellow soldiers, our country, the cause. We put our hands to our foreheads in shock, shift uncomfortably in our seats, hiss our anger.

But we have been taken in just as the Nazis were. While the Germans are laughing together at this despicable American coward groveling before them, Quinn suddenly springs into action. He snatches one of the enemy's guns out of his hands and rapidly mows down three others. At the same moment his comrades, who knew to be ready, leap to the attack. In seconds, the room is full of dead Nazis, living commandos. The day is saved, the mission resumed.

It was Quinn's secret strong self inside the weak outer self that was my guide. I had been too passive with Marcia, letting her grab me when I should be in charge of the situation. All I had to do was be forceful at the right moment, take control when she thought she had everything (literally!) in hand. And I would do it with surprising energy.

Marcia and I had never declared that we were a couple, by the way. Her overly protective mother wouldn't have allowed it. And, I must confess, I liked the freedom this arrangement allowed me. I didn't want anyone else (say, my neighborhood best friend, Billy Rhodes) to date Marcia, but I didn't necessarily want to be tied to her.

Though we never said we were "going steady," we still tended to have dates at least every other weekend. And most dates end in heated make-out sessions.

That night I drove Marcia to my favorite petting site, the dark corner of the hospital parking lot, and began my work. Ignoring her breasts, I reached immediately for her rump. I was ready to be the steel willed commando on an ascent.

After a few moments, a breathless Marcia said, "Wasn't that a good movie?"

"Yes," I gasped. We were still in the front seat, but the temperature in the car had risen sufficiently to fog the windows. As my fingers had come around her hips to the front, her hand had slid from my waist to my belly. Thinking it might be wise to cool off for a moment, I said, "Those were sure big guns the Germans had. Unless they were taken out, no ships could have ever gotten into that port."

"Maybe they could have used the decoys." She shifted her position, and my hand fell naturally between her legs. "Let them waste their ammunition, then come with the big attack."

"Well, . . . " I had missed any reference to decoys. I was also a little confused now about my original petting plan. What was I supposed to be doing?

As I struggled to recall the advantages to scrambling the stages of foreplay, she noted, "The music was good. So ominous." Now her hand fell below my belt.

There had been music? All I'd heard were explosions. I guess we were seeing and hearing different parts of the movie. Her hand now found a different part of me, the perky one.

After a moment's pause, I congratulated myself on surviving initial contact. But my resistance to explosion was assisted more than I desired by one more question from my date. "What do you think of Patricia Stewart?" asked Marcia.

IV

I had nothing really to fear here. Sure, I'd ogled Patty's perky breasts, but that was all.

Still, a deflation occurred when Marcia brought up the subject of another girl, a girl with perky breasts. Perhaps it was Ruth's having caught me staring.

"Patty Stewart? I don't know. She's cute." I thought I might get away with that vague adjective.

"Cute, yes," agreed Marcia. "Have you heard anything else about her?"

"No. She's only been here since the summer. She was in the store today, though."

"Betty was telling me she dates boys from the college." Most parents in Fairfield wouldn't let their daughters go out with students at South Central Missouri State. Like other distinct elements of community life, high school girls and college men each belonged to their appropriate, well-defined sphere. The lines separating them were clear to all of us.

"She'll get in trouble with that," I noted. Nearly all of the students at this engineering campus were male. Because they worked hard at their studies during the week, they sometimes got a bit out of control on weekends.

"Well, Sally said she saw her . . . Uh-oh, what's that?" A car had come into the parking lot and didn't stop at the far end where visitors usually did. Marcia had seen the beam of headlights through our fogged window. I rubbed a spot on the windshield clear.

"Another couple?" Marcia asked, straightening her clothes. She looked in her purse for a comb.

I could see a car cruise to the middle of the lot and come to a stop perhaps thirty yards from us. There were no other cars anywhere near. The driver got out and walked unsteadily around to the passenger side.

"What are they doing?" whispered Marcia.

"He's helping someone out." A woman got out slowly. The man put an arm protectively around her shoulder, and they walked slowly toward the back entrance of the hospital. The light over the doorway illuminated the couple, and I realized I knew them. It was my co-worker and Ron, her Army boyfriend.

"Hey, that's Ruth. You know, works at Gunn's. I hope she's OK."

At the same time I recognized these two, I realized that snow was beginning to fall on the parking lot. Large flakes drifted through the glow that surrounded the light on the hospital wall. It occurred to me that Ron was not moving across the lot like the graceful ice skater he had been in high school.

Ruth had shown me her album of newspaper clippings. Ron had been the leading scorer in his junior and senior years and had even considered a pro hockey career. He was good, but not good enough to skip the exposure and refinement college would have given his game. There was a period of aimlessness, Ruth admitted. Then he enlisted.

I recalled a picture from the yearbook in which Ron was seen slicing between two opponents on his way to goal. His stick held low on the puck, legs bent into the turn, ice chips fly up from his skates. The pose shows skill, drive, power. They didn't wear face protection in those days, and a confident grin lit up a handsome youth.

A few years later Ron's gold tooth flashed in that smile. He'd lost the real one in a fight, not at the rink. But he still carried himself with the confidence of achievement. I admit to admiring this former athlete, now a rugged Army man.

What I had seen in the parking lot, though, was not the heroic figure on the rink. He leaned off balance and weaved, though no obstacles stood in his path.

"Maybe we should be heading home," said Marcia.

I looked at my watch and realized that my time to reorganize teenage petting sequences had gotten away from me. I was angry at myself, not Marcia, who seemed willing as usual. But Anthony Quinn wouldn't have been distracted from his mission the way I had been!

On the way home Marcia surprised me with a request: "Will you go bowling with me?"

"What?"

"Bowling. My parents have joined a league, and they want me to come. But I need a partner." This was odd because Marcia's mother seldom went out. She was shy and fearful by nature, and many in the Circle had puzzled at her partnership with a gregarious husband. But perhaps bowling was part of some new effort to strengthen the marriage, the family.

"I . . . I've never been bowling."

"Well, I've only been once. So we can learn together." I knew this was bad. If I was going to continue my petting campaign with Marcia, I couldn't very well refuse to see her in other contexts. And this wasn't even quite a date, just something we would do together. But I still had a phobia about the Pin-Up Club, those vulnerable pin setters I had such sympathy for.

"Sure," I finally agreed. "When do we do it?"

It turned out to be only once every other week, Tuesday nights. I figured I could schedule my work at Gunn's around it. And, who knew, it might give me more opportunity for physical contact with Marcia. Nothing too fresh, you understand, but the general plan to defamiliarize her body might give me the staying power I was seeking. And I arranged a date for next Saturday night.

I wondered if Ron, several years older, still bothered with petting or went right to the thing itself. I concluded he had sex whenever he wanted.

Ron had an intensity about him. And he was convincing me that real men didn't let anything get in the way of their desires.

"Let's say you're on guard duty in the Philippines," he told me once. Ruth was on break, and they had gone out the back door into the alley behind the store so he could smoke. "No one's alerted you, but gooks have infiltrated the base. One of those slant-eyed bastards gets you in a strangle hold from behind."

He demonstrates the hold on Ruth. His left forearm cuts across her neck as he pulls her chin up. She is actually lifted up on her toes.

"Ron," she giggles, but it might be a nervous giggle.

"What are you going to do?" he challenges me.

"Yell out? Pull a gun?"

"You've dropped your gun. And he's cutting your wind off." He pulls up a little harder on Ruth, whose face is getting red.

"I don't know. Hey, shouldn't you let her go, Ron?"

"Here, you jump me," he says, releasing Ruth, who rubs her throat. She maintains a weak smile, though, as Ron turns around. "Come on, put me in a strangle hold."

I do. While I'm as tall as Ron, he's much bulkier and I have trouble getting my arm around him. Already I feel my hold isn't as secure as it ought to be.

"It's all position," he says. "Leverage. Where I am, where you are."

He grabs my left forearm, the one across his neck, with his right hand and turns his shoulders swiftly down and to the right, pulling my arm at the same time. I am lifted up on his back and pulled forward.

Ron's left elbow bangs into my left temple and I let go. I'm actually dizzy for a moment.

162

"You see," he says. "There's always a counter, but you've got to know what it is. You've got to be ready."

It happened so fast, I had to get him to show me again. I understood it the second time, force and momentum. You have to reverse the situation, take power from your opponent.

He showed me a second maneuver, for when someone wraps his arms around you from behind, pinning your hands to your sides. He lets me grab him that way.

"You go into a sudden squat, like this," he says. "Then bring both arms straight up in front of you." His knees bend and his arms shoot out. The suddenness and the force break my hold on him.

"Then, without even looking, swing your left hand back and into his crotch." His fist goes right to the zipper of my jeans, but stops short of smacking me. I recoil, but it's too late. I would have been rolling on the ground clutching my privates.

I was impressed with this man of moves and counter moves, athlete and combat soldier. That's why the figure in the parking lot made me wonder. He didn't look like the same guy who could conquer all foes, no matter the odds.

I asked Ruth about their being at the hospital the next time I was in the store, I think a Thursday afternoon. I was just a customer getting a coke. She was working with Howard, who, a year younger than I, was still learning the ropes.

"The hospital?" she said, shaking her head. "I haven't ..."

"Ruth, I saw you." I leaned forward so Howie wouldn't hear me. "I was . . . um . . . parked in the lot, the dark far corner."

"You were with a girl, with Marcia? Or Patty?"

"Hey, I told you I date Marcia! Yeah, I was with her."

"Shame on you! And you just a boy."

"We were just talking. But what were you doing?"

I figured she was trying to change the subject here, but I didn't realize how intent she was on keeping whatever had happened a secret until I saw Ron enter the store.

"That's OK," I said, half teasing. " I'll ask Ron,"

"No, don't," she begged, her hand gripping my arm. Her voice was a strained whisper. "I'll tell you some other time. Please, please, don't say anything right now." Then she turned to greet her boyfriend with a smile.

"Hi, hon," Ruth said. "What are you doing here?" He seldom came into town on weekdays. Trainees had full schedules during the week, and Ruth used his car to get to and from work.

"I rode in with a buddy. Needed to tell you I've got special duty on Saturday." He didn't look that unhappy about it to me, not that I had anything to do with their affairs.

"We were going to Jefferson City, the capitol building!" Ruth complained.

"I know, babe. We'll have to do it the next weekend. Hey, Troop," he said, turning to me. "Why don't you amuse my girl Saturday night?" He knew I was fond of Ruth.

"I probably have a date already, Ron. I might go bowling."

"You can take Ruth too," he offered. "She needs the practice."

"You know I have to work the next weekend," said Ruth.

"Well, some time soon, then. Hey, I've got to go. Jimmy, he's my ride, I'm supposed to meet him at the Off-Duty Hall. Then we got to get back." The Off-Duty Hall was a greasy spoon two blocks north on Main Street, half a dozen tables and a short counter with a couple of pool tables at the back. Enlisted men often made it their base of operations when they had a 24-hour pass over Saturday night.

"I'm off in an hour," Ruth reminded him.

"Um, OK. Meet me there. No, wait a minute. Jimmy said we gotta be back by seven. There's not enough time. Hey, I'll call you later tonight, babe." He gave her a little pat on the rump and started out before she could stop him. I could tell she wasn't happy.

I also decided I'd better not press her about what she and Ron had been doing at the hospital the other night. There was something going on there I couldn't put my finger on. When I finally did, of course, I wish I'd never found out.

V

Since I had just stopped in at Gunn's on the way from school, I lingered a few minutes more and then left. I wanted to go by Ray's Racks, a benign smalltown pool hall. Billy Rhodes had recently introduced me to the game of snooker, and I found it an easy addiction

Something else had me going to Ray's, though--my increasing desire to be more like Ron. His quality of toughness wasn't being fostered by my current routine.

Much as I enjoyed it, working at a drug store wasn't developing my reputation as a man. I was a good soda jerk, true, but this skill often won me double-edged compliments: "That sandwich is as good as my mother makes." "You'll make someone a good housekeeper one day." "You sure do keep the place clean. Wish the old lady'd do as well at home." Since I figured I'd be in the military some day like Ron, I needed to think of myself as possessing other abilities. Pool halls, even reputable mainstreet institutions like Ray's, favored the development of the traditional masculine character.

Again, all the boys of my generation assumed we would do as our fathers had done, fight a major war. While it was OK to go to college, plan a career, anticipate having a family, you knew you had to fulfill your obligation to your country as well. And we weren't going to be clerks or medics, but infantrymen, hand-to-hand combat experts, battlefield heroes. I would have to have the strong grip and the steady aim of my Swedish grandfather.

Ray's was where the rougher high school crowd hung out: Gary Hamilton, Fairfield's hope for all-state fullback; Hugh Noone, a small but scrappy tennis player with a down-and-out father and a chip on his shoulder; Sam Blount, whose crooked smile seemed even more twisted after he'd hitchhiked into St. Louis to participate in several Golden Glove bouts.

I didn't fit in with those guys right away, of course, but I knew my old pal Billy Rhodes could be a transition figure.

He'd gotten in with a bunch of boys from shop class who were rebuilding old jalopies. They also spent time at Ray's, more often at the pinball machines in the back. Billy had obtained the wreck of a '49 Ford, and he could talk carburetors, ring jobs, and zero-to-sixty times with anyone at Ray's.

Just before I got to the pool hall, though, I saw something. Or at least I see it in my present re-creation of this key sequence of events in my life.

I said earlier that I have somewhere in my memory bank the image of a slender, elegant form in red outlined by the darkened plate glass store window behind her. Well, this is where I believe I saw it, sort of out of the corner of my eye just before going into Ray's. The woman was half a block away, and the light of a late winter afternoon was fading.

Memory further tells me that I probably didn't recognize the woman I caught a glimpse of at this time, so I didn't go back out to look more closely at her. The picture was just recorded in my mind's eye, to be brought out again later when what I saw then recalled it.

It may be, though, that at some much later point in life I took such an image--from a magazine, from a movie, from a cheap paperback book I saw during my work at Sam's Tire Shop/book distributorship--and inserted it into the order of that long ago day. Whether accurate or imagined, though, the picture fits with the discovery I was to make just before midnight on the following Saturday.

Directly inside the double front doors of Ray's Racks is a billiard table (no pockets, three balls), then the snooker table. Behind them, in two rows, stand eight regulation size pool tables. Four pinball machines, a pay phone, and rest rooms are along the back wall. We can play pool for a penny a minute here, not a high price for an hour's entertainment after school or a longer stretch on a Saturday afternoon.

To the left of the entrance of Ray's Racks, beside the bil-liard and snooker tables, is a bar behind which the owner and his wife (known only as "Mrs. Ray") keep the balls and chalk. You check them out there and are assigned one of the tables. They also sell soft drinks, candy, and various chips. The stools along the bar serve as spectator seats for the front tables and places to wait for those who don't come with a partner.

Across from the bar there's a side entrance into the al-ley, used by those boys who don't want to be seen going in and out of a pool hall or by those who don't want to be seen by anyone. The former are worried about their repu-tation, and the latter have already lost theirs.

I survey the crowd and realize Billy isn't there yet, so I settle in at the end of the bar.

Along the counter top and on benches that line the walls are back issues of standard fantasy and adventure magazines with stories like "Hunting Killer Animals," "Frozen but Alive in Siberia," "Hand-to-Hand Combat with Savages." The covers are frayed, the pages worn, and the content packed with illusion, but the needs of young boys are often eased in their perusal.

I have been drawn recently to a variation of standard war stories featured in many of these magazines, the "prisoner of war" genre. The twist involved the addition of not quite conventional sex to the adventure mode.

The cover of one I pick up that day pictured a battered and bloodied American soldier, his uniform ripped to al-low glimpses of a muscular frame. Our GI kneels on the ground following some kind of beating. And a female SS officer stands over him with a coiled whip, ready to break down the last of his resistance.

I look up to survey the crowd again, checking for Billy, but don't see him. So I open the magazine and search for the story--"Tortured by Female Nazi."

I think of Colonel Mack and wonder if he was a prisoner of war. No one has ever told me that, but it would account for his injuries, the pains he suffers.

How the soldier in my magazine, *Battlefield Heroes*, got into his present predicament is unclear. There's something about a screw-up at headquarters, and his platoon taken out by a tank. What matters is that now he's in the hands of the Nazi battalion's most effective interrogator, who wants to know how many divisions the Allies have committed to this campaign.

At this point, Billy showed up, and it was time for me to play snooker.

I probably didn't need to read the rest of the story anyway. I knew how it turned out. Our soldier--the only survivor from his unit, wounded and weak from loss of blood--never gives in to his captors, never spills secrets, never abandons his desire to escape. Kicked, drugged, threatened with death, he remains a hero, and his story fills us all with the hope that we too can be lucky enough to be tested under fire.

I am soon under fire from Billy, who has spent more time at this game than I have. Well, he may just be better at it.

Snooker differs from most traditional games of pool in that there are two kinds of balls: red balls and numbered balls. Many billiard games are played with fifteen numbered balls--seven striped and seven solids, plus the black eight ball. In most of those games (not nineball, however) the balls are to be knocked into pockets in some order, the first player to complete the process becoming the winner.

But in snooker you must sink a red ball (worth a single point) to have a shot at a numbered ball (worth its own number). The one with most points total wins. The victor here is usually the player who can make the high value numbered balls, not necessarily the most balls overall.

I was fascinated by the possibility of a different order of play, but I also feared that I wasn't a "money player," that is, someone who could make the big shots that won the big points, and thus the game.

While we're playing, I decide to ask Billy something. "Know Patty Stewart?"

"I know who she is. She doesn't know me."

"Yeah. Same here."

"Great tits, though."

"I'll say. Where's she live?"

"Got me."

"Who's she go out with?"

"No one more than twice, from what I hear. She hasn't been here that long."

"Yeah, but, those boobs, someone's got to be on to them."

"Roger Paterson tried. And Dennis McCutcheon. Nada. Though they say . . . "

"What?"

"They say third base is easy with her."

"But not second base?"

"Yeah. Weird, huh? I bet she dates college boys."

"That's what Marcia heard. You think it's true?"

"You know, her dad's dead. She lives with her mother."

"I didn't know that."

"Her mother works at the Catholic school." St. Christopher's went through grade eight. After that the Catholic children attended the one public high school in Fairfield.

I was raising more questions than getting answers here. Why did Patty and her mom come to Fairfield? Where did they live? What sort of social life did she have?

Of course, I got aroused at the idea she was Catholic. Protestant boys believed the stereotype: Catholic girls would put out because they could just make confession the next day. But that didn't throw any real light on Patty. When I got ready to leave Ray's I hadn't gotten any closer to what I wanted to know about perky breasts.

Oh, the female Nazi torturer. I forgot to mention what happens to her. Our GI is rescued, of course, but she's already realized he'd never give in to her. Though she's broken the wills of rivals in her own unit and a dozen other P.O.W.'s, this man defies her.

In the story's final scene she leans against a small wooden table, the whip fallen from her hand as she tries to envision another method of torture that will conquer this American's will. She's covered in sweat, limp from effort. The rescue party breaks through the door, and the GI, bloodied but still conscious, says simply, "Shoot her." They do.

I leave Ray's late that afternoon by the side entrance, alert, I believe, to my surroundings. But when I turn toward 9th Street, a powerful arm encircles my throat and I am lifted up onto my toes. My attacker says in a menacing growl, "Shake the change out of your pocket, boy, or you're dead!"

Chapter VI

Of course, my mind leaps to panic. I am so scared I can't tell my hands to take whatever money I have and surrender it.

Instinctively, I have grabbed the muscled forearm beneath my chin with both hands, but whoever has got me has locked his other hand on that wrist. I can only struggle frantically.

I want to beg for release, but my mouth is dry and my throat's constricted. I just sputter.

My attacker's breath is in my ear. "Never let your guard down, Troop," he whispers. "Jerry is waiting for you, and he only needs a second to take you out."

Jerry? Who is that? I don't know anyone named Jerry.

Holding on still with one hand, I try to find my billfold with the other. I'm ready to give up anything.

Suddenly I am thrown free, spun around to find Ruth's boyfriend Ron and another guy laughing at me.

"Hi, Troop, been playing some pool?" he says. That's Jimmy, I assume, a tall, skinny man with curly dark hair.

"Shit! Yeah," I gasp. What a relief to find I'm not in the hands of a crazed killer. "A little snooker," I manage to say. But then my real feeling erupts. "What's the matter with you!"

Jimmy has a cigarette dangling from one corner of his mouth, and his eyes don't seem to focus on anything. "We're just teaching you a lesson, Troop. Be ready."

"Ready? This isn't a war zone! I don't have to be ready in downtown Fairfield."

"You have to be ready everywhere," says Ron, ignoring my outrage and my surely too obvious fright. "You know," he continues, "snooker's not a man's game. Sometime you need to come shoot nineball with me at the Off-Duty."

"Well . . . " I realize he's giving me an excuse to pretend I knew all along he had jumped me in fun. I need to play along. "I could do that. One of these days."

I know full well that I shouldn't go there. While nothing says it's off limits to minors, the Off-Duty is definitely an adult establishment.

Before I really have time to respond, Ron slaps me on the shoulder. "Gotta go, Troop. Back on base by twenty-three hundred hours." He and Jimmy veer off across the street. I notice that he walks in the same uncertain way he had at the hospital the other night with Ruth. He swerves and jerks in changes of direction.

I rub my throat and look around, grateful to find there were no witnesses to my terror. It's embarrassing to think of all the times I've been roughhoused before, especially by my brother Charles and his buddies. But I couldn't keep my cool this time! It's clear I wasn't soldier material yet. I had the cowardice feigned by Anthony Quinn but not the composure of the American P.O.W.

At home that night I decide upon a training program. I will practice the two moves Ron had showed me earlier: pull your attacker's arm down and to the side, counter with the elbow to the head; squat, arms up, fist into the groin. It will have to become second nature to me, automatic response to external stimuli. No one's going to take me by surprise again.

Being taken by surprise reminded me of my campaign with Marcia and her roving hands. Saturday night I might have another chance to stay perky. I'd agreed to try bowling with her before we have to go with her family. It would take the pressure off us both the next time.

That week I went over my petting strategy frequently in my head: first base, third base, second base, third base again. I didn't really think of home plate, of course, as that came after marriage in the strict progression of correct relationships. Marcia had accepted enough of her mother's conservatism in this area to maintain proper order. Or at least it served her as a good excuse to do and not do whatever she wanted.

On the evening before that next date with Marcia, I found myself for a second time chatting with my inspiration for the unorthodox petting approach I hoped to employ. Sliding into the seat of the back booth Friday about 8:00 was the girl with the perky breasts. Ruth saw my obvious interest, grinned, and let me wait on Patty.

"Another vanilla cream root beer?" I offered pleasantly.

"Ah, no. No, I don't think so." Rubbing her temples, she scanned the specials menu over my head. Every weekend Max made sure he had one draw for customers: hamburger and fries for a quarter; ice cream floats a nickel; sundaes a dime. And, as I've mentioned, I usually was the one to fix the menu board.

Under the counter we had a tray full of white plastic letters, with 26 separate compartments for the letters, ten for numerals, and four for signs and symbols. They all had little tabs on the back that slipped into grooves in the black board.

I started with the letters already on the board, trying to leave as many from the previous weekend's listing in the same place for the present offering. It was the sort of challenge I enjoyed, seeing in my mind's eye the grid of spaces available overlaid by old and new lettering.

Of course, I always had to move some letters up or down, left or right, and then put letters back into the tray and get others out. But my goal was to make as few moves as possible while changing the message.

Today I had to go from "large order of onion rings, 15¢" to "two scoops of ice cream, 5¢." I'll let you figure out how to accomplish that change in the fewest number of moves (44), counting a move on the board as one, a move from the board to the tray (or the reverse) as two.

"Another vanilla cream root beer?"

"I don't think so . . . , um, Mark. I need something solid in my stomach."

Once again, this girl seemed to say the least expected things. I understood being "hungry," "wanting something to eat," even "feeling like a hamburger." But none of that is quite as elemental as downing something "solid."

"Well, we have lots of sandwiches: burgers, grilled cheese, egg sandwiches."

"Oh, I couldn't take egg salad."

"I can make one fried."

"OK, fried egg sandwich. No, give me two."

"Something to drink?"

"Coffee, black."

This wasn't hard, so off I went to fry the eggs. But coffee was certainly an odd drink for a teenager. Not that some parents didn't start offering their children coffee at breakfast when they were in high school, grudging recognition of their crossing over into adult territory. But the few I knew who took their folks up on the offer had to add plenty of milk and sugar. Patty was going to drink it straight.

I tried to think of some way to find out more about Patty while she was here in Gunn's. But I couldn't just demand to know where she lived, who she went out with, what she did for fun.

I thought of snapping off a salute for her, the way she'd done the first time she came in. But I didn't feel I'd earned the right to that military gesture yet, especially not after failing the test of Ron's sneak attack.

"Wonder if we'll win our opener?" I asked while the eggs cooked. The grill was right by the booth she was in.

"Our opener?"

"Basketball. Fairfield Bulldogs' first game of the season."

"Oh, I didn't know. Is it tonight?"

"Next weekend." I could see not being a big fan, but most students at least knew about the major sports. I had been hoping the topic might lead to who would bring her to the game.

"I wish I lived close enough to walk to the game, but I'm over on Limestone."

"Limestone?"

"My street, off Highway 00."

"Ah." She paused. "Where's my coffee?"

I could see this was getting nowhere, so I went back to just being the soda jerk who fills orders. I did keep an unobtrusive watch on her, of course, out of curiosity.

Oh, I might as well admit it: I had an eye on her for the other reason. Her sitting in the booth tempted me to look down her blouse from my standing position. While the blouse she wore fit snugly, the top two buttons were not fastened. And sometimes her movement widened the gap between blouse and bra, between bosom and fabric.

But I could see that Ruth was watching me watch Patty.

"Need some help with the back booth?" she teased.

"Uh, ah, no. She's fine. It's fine."

"Really, I don't have anything else to do right now." Then she added, less happily, "I don't have anything to do tomorrow, either."

I remembered that Ron wasn't coming in even though she had the day off.

"You can go bowling with me and Marcia."

She smiled and thanked me, but we both knew we were at divergent stages of going out. What would please Marcia and me would bore her; what might excite Ruth would seem strange to us. A night out for the three of us would never work.

Ruth's amusement at my adolescent efforts to look at Patty's breasts now underscores for me her more advanced position in the progression from very first date to marital tedium. Even though I sensed a cynical warning in her more experienced outlook, I couldn't help hoping that I would pass by the back booth just at the right moment to follow that firm line of bosom right out to a nipple. My, those things were perky!

Patty did eat her sandwiches, or most of them, scanning the rest of the store with a distracted gaze. But she got up without providing me the glimpse I desired.

She spoke to me when she was paying at the register, which sat at the end of the counter where the booths began.

"Your co-worker, there, she's not from here, right?"

"Ruth?" Ruth was looking through the magazine on her fifteen minute break. "She's from North Dakota."

"Yeah. I thought so. She have her own place, her own car?"

"She has an apartment near the campus, I think. She drives her boyfriend's car."

"Uh-huh."

"Why do you . . ., " I asked, but she cast one more quick glance at Ruth and left. She was, I concluded, as strange as her breasts were distinctive. I had no idea what she was thinking or doing.

She wasn't that strange, it turned out. But the next time I saw her, flat on her back and as if dead, she certainly left me with a vivid impression of her uniqueness.

VII

My first experience at bowling, I'm sorry to report, justified my earlier apprehensions. And, even more unfortunate, at the end of the night I found I would need another opportunity to complete a successful assault on Marcia.

I began the date full of false confidence inspired by a high ranking endorsement of my physical ability. Encouragement came from our regular Gunn's customer, Colonel Mack, who witnessed a little harmless scuffle between me and my boss on Saturday morning.

The owner and head pharmacist at this downtown drug store, Max Gunn, had been a quick, hard punching welterweight boxer in college. He still jumped rope to stay in shape and liked to entertain friends with displays of shadowboxing, slick footwork, the combination punching that was, he claimed, a trademark.

Max had put on a few pounds since his days as a Marine in Korea, but he was still trim. He probably would have moved up to the middleweight division had he been fighting professionally. His hair was cut short in the style of the times, and his white pharmacist's uniform gave a military air. He was a strict boss, but a good one.

This was an exciting time for boxing, because a brash young man from Louisville named Cassius Clay had been recognized by a few forward looking experts as a new kind of fighter, a man whose tongue was as much a weapon as his fists. Max was willing to take all bets that this young challenger would win the heavyweight crown from the formidable Sonny Liston.

When his buddies from neighboring downtown establishments came in for coffee, Max would often join them to talk over the sports scene, more than once predicting a changing of the guard in boxing. The traditionalists among them, like Mr. Simpson, owner of Fairfield's most fashionable clothing store, hated Clay and couldn't wait for his destruction.

"That boy's going to get clobbered. Anyone who doesn't keep his guard up is going to meet the champ's big right hand," said this high school and college football standout.

Clay seldom employed the customary boxer's stance, hands held high to block an opponent's punches. Instead he danced on his toes with his arms swinging freely. At first, his chin appeared vulnerable to the jab and the overhand right. But he was so quick, moving side to side, stepping up, leaning back, that Liston never even got close to his target.

"He's fast," countered Max. "And he hits hard. He'll keep out of range until Liston gets tired, then tag him."

In fact, that's exactly what happened. Rather than stand toe-to-toe with his opponent, trading haymakers as Rockie Marciano and Joe Lewis had done, Clay had reconfigured the space within a boxing ring. He was never where Liston thought he should be, and his punches came from all directions. The whole sport's never been the same, of course, since Mohammed Ali.

"Liston's too strong. Clay will go down with the first punch."

"I'll show you guys," said Max on that Saturday morning. "Come here, Mark."

Howie and I, Max's only male employees, knew to be ready for mock confrontations with our boss, fake punches, little lessons in self-defense. Max never hurt us, although, with his speed and experience, he certainly could have.

I came around to the front of the booths. Colonel Mack, who was not one of these sports fans, observed quietly from a counter stool.

"Take a swing at me, Mark," said Max. "Go right for the chin."

Ever the cooperative employee, I did. But I telegraphed the punch so that Max could look good to his pals. He pulled his head back, out of the way of my punch. And then he leaned forward to throw a stiff jab, deliberately aiming it a few inches to the side of my head.

Naturally, I anticipated Max's counterpunch. Sparring matches with Charles and my dad had taught me something. But Max wasn't thinking beyond his own demonstration, ducking a punch and then taking his own shot. So when I came forward rather than retreated from his jab, launching a hook toward his midsection, Max had to cover up quickly with his elbows.

I hadn't intended to follow through, of course, so neither of us touched each other. And Max threw a combination of shots that would have knocked me silly had just one of them landed. But he still took some ribbing.

"Hey, the kid mighta' taken you out there!"

"I thought you said you were fast like Clay. I guess this means Liston will go to the belly."

"It's the young fighters that win. You old guys have lost your punching power."

I, of course, was quite proud of my composure in this little exchange. I had applied Ron's lessons about force and momentum, position and reversal. And it had been in a relatively spontaneous situation. I reacted quickly, effectively. Maybe I was developing those very killer instincts every professional athlete needs to have. And every soldier.

"You've got good reflexes," Colonel Mack told me when I went to take his empty cup and the nickel that paid for it. "You'd make a good fencer or table tennis player."

"Ah, thank you, sir." I didn't think much of those sports, the first too aristocratic in its history and the second trivial (as its various names suggest). This was, of course, a few years before Richard Nixon's "ping pong diplomacy" changed forever U.S. policy with mainland China.

Still, I was warmed by the compliment and the genuine smile that accompanied it. And a new confidence stayed with me all the way to the Pin-Up Club with Marcia that evening.

How little I understood the fine sport of bowling, however, which consistently undermined my improved self-image. First, there was the question of shoes. Marcia informed me on the way there that I could not wear my own.

"You mean I have to put my feet where the sweaty feet of half of Fairfield's population have already been?"

"That's right, Mark. Of course, some people have their own shoes. They're the serious bowlers."

"And I have to pay for this?"

Then there was selecting a lane from the choices offered by a pimply, heavyset man at the shoe counter, whose speech came in fits and starts. "You can." We waited. "Have any lane." We watched. "But seven." We turned. "Or three." We hesitated. "Or four." We stopped. But he was done. I concluded that his limited intellect was the product of early years spent as a pin setter.

Most lanes were open, but I couldn't figure out whether I wanted to be next to a wall, on the right side of the ball return, or the left.

"What does it matter?" Marcia demanded. "All the lanes are the same width and length."

Finally, we settled on one lane in between the middle and the wall, not at the edge but not too conspicuous, lane nine of twelve.

"Which ball do you use?" I asked.

"Well, these light ones are for women. Those are children's. So, any of the others."

Here was a problem I had faced with other sports: the equipment I had to play with was often too big, too heavy, too long for my body and ability. From baseball bats with fat handles to heavy footballs that went through my fingers to golf clubs too long to control, everything seemed to be designed for kids two grades ahead of me.

I could barely hold the 16-pound men's bowling ball, but I refused to shame myself by choosing any other.

Naturally, the finger holes in the lighter balls, which I tested for Marcia, matched my hand. The larger balls had finger holes too large or too far apart for me. I finally found one man's ball I could hoist off the return rack, but I felt my elbow and shoulder strain as I swung it toward the pins.

Only the scoring system seemed appropriate to me. Marking numbers, slash marks, and X's on the sheet with large and small boxes made sense to me, an orderly grid, a space for everything.

Remember, now, that all this irritation was just what I was enduring so that I could make out with Marcia later that night. It was training in physical contact whereby I would learn to maintain my perkiness in the post-game rest and recuperation. At that time I would be the newly conditioned commando assaulting the guns of Navarone. I would exert a powerful control over myself and this girl.

If I lost track of my goal when a bowling ball crashed onto the alley at my feet, or when my thumb got pinched between two balls on the return rack, or when my feet in strange shoes slipped out from under me and I fell on my rump, wasn't it reasonable of me to conclude that the price for my sexual development was becoming excessive?

The final blow came when Marcia beat me for the third straight game and announced that she had to go home now.

"Now? I thought we might take a little ride . . . you know, a drive."

"I promised my mom I'd be in early tonight. The weather's supposed to be bad again."

"I know, but . . . "

"I want to too, but I just can't. Next weekend. We can say we're practicing bowling again. They'll like that."

Once again, the weak side of Anthony Quinn seemed to be ruling my personality. Or maybe the bruises on my backside and instep, the strained ligaments in elbow, wrist, and shoulder, the scraped extremities of fingers (wrong ball holes) and toes (misfitting shoes) discouraged me from more physical contact of any kind. At any rate, I took her home.

I was so frustrated, that I drove back downtown, thinking I might put in some time at Ray's, work on my snooker game. I had to figure out why Billy was beating me so consistently.

When I parked near Gunn's, though, and started out for the pool hall, a thought occurred to me: if I really was going to become a tough guy, a future soldier, why didn't I take up Ron's offer and stop by the Off-Duty?

I went past Ray's and kept heading up Main toward the college campus. The Off-Duty, a narrow building with darkened windows, was sandwiched between a barbershop and a gas station. Out in front was that group of soldiers hoping for any kind of action on a Saturday night off base I'd discovered to be a regular feature on a Fairfield weekend. A light snow began to drift through the streetlights.

The half-dozen uniformed men were smoking cigarettes, watching the late night traffic cruise the town. I know from later experiences that their laughing and joking was bragging about the sex that they would have if they just had some girls to have it with.

The scene was intimidating, and I turned down a crossing street to avoid coming right up to the GIs. I looked down the alley that went behind the buildings on that block. All was still in the semi-darkness of that corridor.

Summoning all the bravado I possessed, I decided to walk the length of the alley, past gas station, Off-Duty, barbershop, and furniture warehouse. This would be just as daring as coming up to the men on the sidewalk. Maybe then I would go around to the front and look for Ron.

By a group of trash cans, one turned on its side, I saw a half naked woman in a red dress lying on her back. Her breasts were exposed, and she lay perfectly still.

I stopped dumb. What should I do? Then, I recognized her. It was Patricia Stewart. Her perky breasts, their shape precisely visible, were recognizable even dusted with snow.

This is a terrible thing to say, I know, but before I could make myself think of what I should do to help, before my mind could take in the fact that a fellow human being was in great peril, I registered in my mind this observation: her erect breasts were saluting the sky.

VIII

Now I must make an even more embarrassing admission. Perhaps it's the most damning thing I've acknowledged so far about my teenage years. It's worse, I believe, than the window peeping Billy and I indulged in a year or so ago, marveling at Janet Master's superb young form in the bathtub. And it's nastier than any groping of Marcia I've been guilty of so far, particularly since she always could--and did--grope back.

I copped a feel of those perky breasts. I did.

I knelt down beside her, called her name, shook her shoulders. Then I looked at her body.

Well, they were standing there! Firm and pointed, not a bit of sag anywhere. It was too much to resist, and I planned to run for help immediately after I did it.

I did run for help. Before that, moving from the state of juvenile pervert to some semblance of responsible being, I draped my coat over her torso, embarrassed for her exposure and worried about her lying there in the cold.

People came out of the Off-Duty, and soon the police arrived with an ambulance. Patty had been unconscious, but not, thank goodness, dead as I had at first assumed. When I had shaken her shoulder, she had moaned. And I saw she was breathing. But she didn't wake up.

She was, in fact, dead drunk, passed out from downing half a fifth of vodka. The bottle was found under her coat, near where she lay, though it wasn't at all clear how she, underage, had obtained it.

We would learn later that she had been drinking since her early teenage years in Texas, beginning about the time of her father's death. Part of the reason for her mother's move was to start over and leave that problem behind. She'd chosen Fairfield because the family had lived here for a few years in happier times (before her breasts became perky). Sadly, the return didn't work.

There was more to what happened to Patty, but I wouldn't understand it for some time. Since all I had done was find her, the police turned to the question of how she'd gotten in the alley and to her physical condition.

While the temperature had dipped below freezing, it turned out she hadn't been outside very long. Exposure did not threaten her life, thanks to my chance trip down the alley.

As to other injuries, I can tell you that I did not see blood on or near Patty. And there were no obvious bruises or scrapes on any visible part of her. Frankly, I didn't try to figure out why she had taken off her coat, blouse, and bra. I had some fuzzy idea of a fight with a robber, who'd ripped her clothes while taking a purse. My innocence about all this amazes me now.

There was also something about her breasts I couldn't quite figure out, something odd, something not in the few *Playboy* pictures of boobs I'd been lucky enough to see. I wouldn't get an explanation of this feature, though, until I did some research in the town library.

One person who seemed intensely interested in what had happened to Patty was my coworker, Ruth. "You found that girl, from your school?" she asked me the next time I saw her. I think it was Tuesday night the week after.

"Yeah, I just happened by," I answered nervously. I still feared a witness would turn up, not a witness to a robbery but to my touching of Patty's breasts. "How did you know about it?"

The newspaper had buried the story, as they usually did in those days. No names, events, details were in the crime report, just terse notices that police were called for "a disturbance" or "to inspect the premises" or "to answer a complaint."

"Everyone's talking about it," said Ruth, though she seemed unsettled by my question. "I mean I heard about it at the hairdresser's."

"Well, I ran for help. I don't know any more than anyone else. Except that she'd been drinking vodka."

"Vodka? What brand?"

"Brand? I have no idea. I don't know anything about whiskey."

That was true. I had no idea how drink can turn someone into another person, release a hidden, often angry personality. I would learn, of course, like so many others, when I got to college.

Fortunately, my role in this episode faded fairly quickly, as Patty was reported to be recovering, first in the hospital and then at home. I was just the boy who had stumbled onto the scene (and I convinced my parents I had spotted her from the street, not in the alley). There was discussion about trying to identify her attacker, but that was kept pretty quiet by the authorities.

Words like "attacker," "assault," "robbery," were used in these days to mask all sorts of details now printed on the front pages of newspapers and discussed openly in other media. It would be another week before Marcia, of all people, opened my eyes to the full nature of Patty's ordeal.

Meanwhile, waiting for my next date, I practiced the art of self-defense and indulged in the pleasure of self-abuse. Work continued in its usual routine, though Ruth seemed moody and distracted. She didn't mention Ron, and he didn't come by.

I spent a lot of time playing snooker with Billy, struggling to be a good loser until I finally had a breakthrough. I realized I had imported from other pool games the wrong technique for snooker.

A key difference between snooker and more traditional games like eight-ball, call shot, rotation, is that the pockets on a snooker table are smaller and more rounded.

The regular billiard table has pockets with flat sides through which balls go into the hole. If the balls come in at an angle, they can bounce off either flat side and drop neatly into the pocket.

But the pockets of a snooker table are rounded, and the opening itself is narrower in relation to the width of the ball. To sink a snooker ball, you have to avoid hitting either side of the pocket. You have to go straight in. Any ball not hit precisely into the center of the pocket will bounce off the sides and, especially when hit hard, pop back out. For snooker you need soft strokes, great accuracy, impeccable control.

The model, however, of expertise in pool in those days--and probably still, at least for boys trying to be men--is the successful break. And the break is all about power.

Pool games begin with all balls except the cue ball racked together into a triangle or diamond shape at one end of the table. They are all touching, the whole is compact.

The goal of the break is, in a single shot with the cue ball, to scatter all the racked balls as far from their original position as possible, hoping that at least one drops into a pocket so that the shooter continues to play.

The person making the break is at the opposite end of the table from the rack, so it's a long shot across the full reach of green felt. And force is the key to success. You need to hit the racked balls with all the force you can.

The expert breaker bends over his cue stick, rocks his body backward and forward as he sights down the table, and takes several preliminary strokes to prepare for the shot itself. When he takes that shot, the weight of his entire body gets behind his arm and shoulder and into the stick and ball. Ker-blam! At the cue ball's impact, fifteen balls leap away from each other, caroming off cushions, colliding into each other, and--we hope--rattling into pockets.

Any boy learning to play pool naturally seeks the power and the effect of that stroke, an explosive break. And most continue to try to sink every ball they shoot with a similar force, ramming each one into the back of a pocket, producing a satisfying smack of impact between cue ball and numbered ball and the thump of the numbered ball's hitting the back of the pocket.

This was the strategy I naturally imported into snooker, and it led consistently to defeat.

Billy hadn't fully achieved the goal of precision in his game either, but he had figured out that finesse was the key to success. While I had been ramming balls into and out of corner and side pockets, he was trying for steadiness, pinpoint aim, a soft touch. I changed my strategy and began to lose less badly.

You might think I could make some connections here. Perhaps forceful collisions aren't the answer to all of life's difficulties. But I was slow to come to that conclusion.

In sharpening my combat readiness, I continued to believe power and its application were better than finesse. I even enlisted skinny Howie Bend, my co-worker at Gunn's, for the further demonstration of my skill.

"I'm giving you the authority to jump me anytime you think I've relaxed my guard," I told him. We were working the evening shift together.

"I don't know, Mark. I'm not much of a fighter."

"It's not a real fight. It's just practice, a run-through."

We were within an hour of closing, so the booths and counter were empty. Colonel Mack had been the last customer.

"I'd rather ride my bike for exercise," Howie explained. He was one of the few kids to own what we called an "English" bike, a ten-speed racer with thin wheels, a light frame. He could be seen on country roads far from town, pedaling intently up hill and down.

"I'll jump you too," I offered. "You can work on your countermoves."

Inwardly, I laughed at Howie and his bike. All the guys I knew owned one-speed, heavy framed bicycles, Schwinns or cheaper versions sold at places like Western Auto. They were slow and heavy, but tough, indestructible.

When I went to college a few years later, of course, I learned about the advantages of this different kind of bike, its popularity around the world. It was also, of course, the bike of the future, at least until advances in technology led to the current mountain bike, wide-tired and sturdy, but also lightweight and speedy.

Right now, of course, I wanted me and everything I owned to be tough, durable, powerful. I didn't see the consequences of such preferences, especially for the women I knew. Ruth, Patty, and Marcia, however, all suffered because of forces others, including me, couldn't control.

IX

So what was Patty Stewart doing out behind the Off-Duty late at night? According to my friend Billy she was meeting a man.

"You mean she was going out with soldiers?" I asked.

"Or trying to," said Billy. "I heard she'd been hanging around there."

This was unheard of in our circle, more shocking than a high school girl's dating college men. Maybe the fact that her father had been in the military gave her experience others didn't have. And her mother may have had a hard time controlling a daughter with no man in the house.

"She seemed like an ordinary girl," I said. "Except for those boobs."

"Yeah. And they may be what got her into trouble."

I should have gotten Billy to explain what he meant in more detail here, but I let the moment pass. At that period in my life I didn't fully understand the concept of sexual assault, its ubiquity in history or its prevalence in the modern world.

The social code of the time and the place--postwar smalltown middle America--employed a lot of ellipsis and euphemism. Terms like "sodomy" and "rape," for instance, were never publicly defined. Until recently, I had understood sodomy simply as some unspecified "unnatural" act. Rape meant "to beat up," and I wrongly believed men did it only to women.

Until Marcia and I had explored enough of each other's bodies to know all the parts, and until I had finally locked on to what went where in sexual union, I couldn't know what it meant for a man to force himself on a woman. And I wouldn't fully take in what it meant that Patty had been raped until I'd had one more date with Marcia.

Still, what Billy suggested caused a new idea of Patty Stewart and her perky breasts to take shape in my mind. There was another side to her I'd not seen. Or, perhaps, the side I saw of her--another pretty young girl in high school--was of my own creation.

I don't know now if drink caused her to take risks, or if a desire to break through limits led her to alcohol. Whichever it was, I had failed to recognize the little signs in her behavior that belonged to a person I wasn't seeing.

There are other less conspicuous things than drink that sometimes camouflage the true nature of others. Faulty perception can also lead one to the wrong idea about people close to you. Ruth Simms is another case in point.

Because she had only a high school education and was working in a menial position at Gunn's Drug Store, I had assumed that Ruth wasn't particularly smart. Still in school myself, and accepting the principle that qualities and abilities can be precisely identified and graded, I took a condescending attitude toward anyone not headed for college and beyond. Since Ruth had told me she had been a mediocre student and her goal was to be a housewife and mother, I concluded that, though older, she wasn't quite my equal.

I liked Ruth and enjoyed being with her when we were together behind the counter at Gunn's. We both were efficient workers. But whenever I was away from work, I'm afraid I put her into a class of people I would not expect to stay in contact with through the future.

A few years later, by the way, after my own days in the Army, I passed through Fargo, North Dakota, on a seeing-America trip. Ruth and I spent several happy hours reminiscing on her screened porch. And I regretted the fact that I hadn't appreciated her depth of perception and feeling when she lived in Fairfield.

But even that time after Patty Stewart's attack I began to realize that Ruth was capable of some reasoning and decisive action.

The first clue I had of her true character came when I saw her talking to two policemen outside the store. I was on the way into work, and she waved me on with a friendly look. So I figured she wasn't in any kind of trouble.

"Are you thinking of becoming a policeman?" I joked later. We were in a slow spell, and I was getting ready to clean up overflow from the grease trap behind the grill. This was one of the least pleasant regular tasks at the soda fountain. You had to get down on your hands and knees and reach back up under the grill to remove souring hamburger and bacon grease.

"No, no. They were just asking me some questions. Do you want me to hold the can?" We used old one gallon cans to hold the run-off from the grill.

"Yeah, OK. I don't have much room to operate here. Questions about what?"

"Mark, it doesn't concern you." Her voice was sharp here, and I could tell she didn't want me to push the matter. She went on, "Are you going out with Marcia tonight?"

"Um-hum. Where's Ron been lately?"

The grease I was scooping smelled terrible. That's how we knew it was time to clean the trap and the area below it, when something dead seemed to be hiding in the walls. Such an odor, of course, wasn't good for an eating establishment.

I could spoon up the gooey mess only for brief periods before my stomach reacted to the stench. And then I had to get out of there before I could resume. So at the same time I asked about Ron, I jerked back and up, inadvertently bumping Ruth in the ribs with my elbow as I did.

"Oooh," she cried out, much louder than I would have thought from what was really an indirect blow.

"Sorry. You OK?"

Her face had gone completely white and she hunched her shoulders in pain.

"Ruth . . . ," I said.

"No. No. I'm OK." Her voice was thin, reedy. But she gave me such a look that I backed off. Whatever was the problem, she didn't want to talk about it with me.

"She'll be OK," said a voice behind me. It was Colonel Mack.

Without my noticing, he had come behind the counter and now slipped past me to escort Ruth into a back booth. He eased her onto the seat in a grandfatherly manner.

My bumping into Ruth was unusual, despite the fact that we always worked in close quarters behind the counter and booths. Midwesterners in general--and me in particular--tend to avoid casual physical contact with the opposite sex. Men can shake hands with other men, and women can hug their female friends. But, as if equipped with special radar, men and women generally keep a respectful distance. That's one of the reasons I liked being on the same shift with Ruth: we managed to sidestep each other neatly while moving quickly at our separate tasks.

"She has, ah, bruised ribs," the Colonel informed me about Ruth. "She had a little tumble down her stairs the other night." He sat down opposite her, but motioned for me to remain with them. "I happen to know about it from some old friends at Ft. Wood."

I didn't say anything, as Ruth's bowed head didn't suggest she wanted the whole story told. Since Ruth lived in town, though, I didn't know what people at the fort had to do with her. Colonel Mack went on anyway.

"I know something about bruised ribs. When I was about your age, Mark, before I enlisted, I had a tendency to get into fights."

"Oh?" I kept on listening, but picked up a rag to continue my work. I wiped down the grill area and got ready to put the grease trap back in place.

"I was a bit of a hot head, in fact. I couldn't turn away from a dare, and I had a terrible chip on my shoulder. Most of the time I came out on top in any scrap."

He shrugged his shoulders, as if his ability to fight and win was an accident, something he couldn't control.

"I've been in some fights, too," I offered.

Colonel Mack went on. "But one time I got in for more than I could handle, a trio I thought I could take care of. They were college students, and I had contempt for that class of people. I figured they were soft, wouldn't even fight."

"What happened?" asked Ruth, who was sitting a little straighter and had regained some color.

"It turned out they were all on the college boxing team. They did a number on me. After the first couple of jabs, I was reeling. And they made me into a punching bag."

"Ouch!" I said.

"If I'd had any sense, I'd have gone down. But I refused to give in. They broke three ribs, my nose, my jaw, a cheekbone, an eye socket. I was lucky I wasn't dead."

"Why are you telling us all this?" I asked.

"Oh, I guess just letting Ruth know she'll get over this, this being black and blue. The body does heal, though the scars can run deep."

"Yeah," I agreed.

"It's the mind that takes longer to get right," said Colonel Mack. When he said that, his eyes took on a faraway look, as if he were seeing things we couldn't. I assumed he was reliving war experiences, events too horrible to convey.

Ruth gave a little sigh and said, "I think I'd better get back to work." The Colonel stood as she pushed herself up on the booth table. He gave her a little pat on the shoulder and then left.

Ruth didn't offer any more explanation of her injury, though I wanted to find out just how she'd managed to fall down steps, presumably in her own apartment. We had a little run of last minute customers, and then our shift was over.

And I was off to my date with Marcia. We'd told her parents we were going bowling, and we would spend some time at the Pin-up. But we knew we'd also find ourselves at the hospital parking lot by the night's end.

Earlier in the week I'd worried about whether I'd be in the mood for petting, after seeing (and feeling!) Patty Stewart's cold breasts. My curiosity had died with a shiver that night. But, those teenage male hormones had come through with their usual reliability. I was as horny as ever, the image of Patty's erect twins resuming their tantalizing encouragement despite her own misfortune.

As I stepped through the back door of Gunn's and into the alley, however, two strong arms encircled me and I knew I had been jumped again.

X

Let me pause a minute and confess what I had noticed about Patty in the alley behind the Off-Duty. I've told you that I knelt down to try to rouse her, and that, finding myself so near her perky breasts, I couldn't resist a closer examination.

It's true they were as erect as ever, though she lay on her back and gravity should have inspired some sagging. As I contemplated them, though, I noticed, even in the limited light of that scene, a white line running along the bottom of each breast.

She had had an operation, one of the earliest in the modern era of radical cosmetic surgery. I figured this out some months after these events, when I read in *Life* magazine about the first silicone breast implants. They were developed by two plastic surgeons in Texas, and Patty, I believe, was one of their first customers.

No wonder, then, her breasts were so firm, so erect, so perky. They weren't real.

If I have the story right, she had them undone a few years later, having concluded, perhaps, that male desire needs no additional encouragement. The surgery had come during a time of crisis for her, the loss of a doting father. And her conviction that she'd never be popular without a better figure overcame her mother's resistance.

I don't conclude that her breasts led to the attack that put her in the hospital. But she was playing with fire when, wearing a revealing red dress, she sought the company of soldiers.

I'm not sure why the whole concept of a surgically altered body upset me so much at the time, except that it seemed to violate the natural order. Patty's desire had been to conform to a cultural ideal that could be met by a favored few without artificial means. But would it all stop there?

We were, it's true, some years ahead of organ transplants and the even more complex processes of genetic engineering society is approaching now. But I sensed then that humankind was seeking the ability to rearrange the basic elements of its being into shapes never occurring in nature. Hyperbolically, I thought, some day we might create people with wings, women with the eyesight of eagles, men with the strength of elephants.

I don't think I made all the connections back to the philosophical model of Nietzsche's superman or to the Nazi war machine's goal of eliminating one race of people and perfecting another. But I knew I was unsettled in the end by the idea of . . . of, well, the idea of too perky breasts.

Who attacked Patty Stewart? You've probably already guessed, sadly, that it was Ron, Ruth's troubled boyfriend, former hockey star and now Army jeep mechanic. Ruth herself deduced his guilt from the changing nature of her own relationship to Ron and from the circumstances and timing of the deed.

He'd begun to drink more and more since he'd come to Ft. Wood, and not just when he was with Ruth on the weekends. He had been caught twice on base and faced demotion with any further offense.

He had also sometimes been violent when he was drinking. Ruth's own sore ribs, which I discovered by accident when cleaning the grill, came from the first time she asked if he knew Patty.

Ron had been seeing this thrill-seeking high school girl for several weeks. In fact, that's why Patty was stopping by Gunn's (not, of course, to have a vanilla cream root beer!). She knew he came there when he left the fort. Patty wasn't sure at first what his relationship to Ruth was, but she pieced together what she needed to know from him, from me, and from observation.

I don't know to this day what precipitated the attack that Saturday night, though both parties had been drinking. I'd like to think Ron told her he was not going to see her anymore, that he was going to be true to Ruth. But then things got out of control. I suspect, however, that this is just my own desire to place things into the least unpleasant arrangement.

As usual, the authorities in town and in the military kept this matter pretty well hushed up. Ron spent some time in the stockade before being transferred to another base. He lost rank and "military occupational specialty." Within a year he was serving somewhere overseas as a mortar man. Patty went away to a Catholic boarding school in St. Louis. And my friend Ruth, after a few months, returned to Fargo, where, as far as I know, she is today.

As for me, I too was changed by these events. With my second reaction to being jumped, this time behind Gunn's, I discovered a potential for violence in my own make-up. (I would learn a few years later in Vietnam that I was even more capable of destroying things.)

However, initially, I felt nothing but pride in the play of my lightning reflexes. I believed that the quickness of my reaction behind Gunn's exceeded the speed with which any account could be presented in words. It was all a single seamless event, from knowing I was being assaulted to felling my attacker.

Knee squat, arm thrust, shoulder turn, and hard blow to the groin, snap! Exactly as I'd practiced it. Down went my enemy with hands between the legs.

I can't tell you the instantaneous, rich pleasure I felt at this successful maneuver, especially after having been humiliated by Ron and Jimmy not many days earlier. In a flash I had defeated a dangerous opponent. He was down, I was the victor. The tentative, passive boy of the past had turned into a strong, decisive man. I was a man of war.

Unfortunately, my military skills had been terribly mis-applied. The alley attacker this time was my own girlfriend.

Marcia had wanted to surprise me with a plan whereby we'd end up at the hospital parking lot even earlier than I'd expected that Saturday night. Having waited outside the store until closing time, she'd thrown her arms around me in enthusiasm and desire. But I punched her in the very place I'd hoped to reach in the context of love.

"Oh, my gosh! Oh, gee! Marcia, I didn't mean to. I'm sorry."

She was rolling on the ground, moaning, clutching herself.

"What can I do?" I pleaded. What could I do! The injury was to a place I could contemplate touching only in one as yet unsuccessful scenario.

"I . . . I'll be all right in a minute," she managed to whis-per, but she hadn't tried to get up.

"Maybe we should go to the hospital?" I had an eerie feeling then, remembering Ron escorting Ruth along the same path just a few weeks ago.

"Maybe. I could have them arrest you for assault, for rape."

When she said this, the reality of sexual assault sud-denly became much clearer even in my dense boyish mentality. Before this moment I'd somehow concluded that women who were raped might not have wanted to have sex with a man, but, once everything began, it kind of went along as usual. What's that old joke popular in this pre-feminist era? "Know how to keep from being raped?" he asked. "No," she replied. "Relax." I had not pictured in my mind's eye the application of force.

Marcia had me take her home that night, rather than to the hospital. I tried to explain why it had happened, my whole desire to be a good soldier, Jimmy's taunting, my hanging out at Ray's Racks. But Marcia wasn't interested in my lengthy apology.

Needless to say, the plan to reorder the stages of petting--the age-old three bases and home--was put on hold. In fact, Marcia and I put our whole relationship on hold after this night's unfortunate events.

I don't think she was afraid of me after this. But when we went bowling with her parents, she announced we needed to take a break from each other. And we didn't date for over a year, a year, I'm unhappy to report, in which my sexual education did not advance a step.

Oh, I did eventually have success with my own perkiness, although it was a long time coming. I had to assimilate some new features into my picture of myself before that would come about. Still, I'll begin the next section of this account completely naked, a sign, I believe, of my acceptance of my own emerging sexuality, the reality of my body.

But I have one other thought with which to conclude this portion of my memoirs.

You see, all this struggle to come to terms with the units of my world wasn't over with mastery of any of the skills I attempted. Handling a rush of special orders at Gunn's or bringing a date to enjoy an ice cream soda together; bowling strikes or setting the pins afterwards; fine tuning the sometimes deadly moves of self defense or learning the necessity of restraint; smashing the break in eightball or running snooker's threeball ever so softly down the rail and into a corner pocket; unleashing destructive forces in your own psyche or building a sense of self that sustains an emotional balance--they're all part of a lifetime's project. You arrive at pauses along the way, not a complete structure.

Fairfield, like the small neighborhood of the Circle, was a relatively benevolent place for this enterprise of growing up. The great majority of the children in that town were, like me, granted the space and time to develop adult versions of ourselves. And we went off eventually to work or college nurtured by quiet forces of family and community.

Not all of us, of course. And latecomers to the cycle, viewed as outsiders, often had extra trouble. Patty didn't graduate with her class, and Ron carried a rage that destroyed any opportunity he encountered.

And I seem to have forgotten here Howie Bend, the only other boy working at Gunn's, whose story is an unhappy coda to this portion of my adventures. He hadn't wanted to indulge me in my hand-to-hand combat training, remember, preferring to tone his body by bicycling across the countryside.

I wish he'd gotten to do more of that in later years, as cross country biking has become a significant American pastime. Howie's racing bike, which the rest of us laughed at, surely reflects one of the important stages of development leading to the sleek, winning vehicles of the current Tour de France. He was ahead of the times, then, at least for this part of the country.

Howie died in Vietnam two years after these events, earning the Bronze Star with valor posthumously for assisting three comrades in an escape from a prisoner-of-war camp. May he rest in peace.

Volume Four: Constructive Acts

Part Seven: Building Blocks

Chapter I

If we could have gotten ourselves more under water, we would have done it. As it was, only the tops of our heads and our faces down to our noses appeared above the surface of the Banner Hotel's swimming pool.

It was 2:00 in the morning, and darkness was supposed to be our ally. The pool was officially closed, so ordinarily the primary illumination here would have been reflected rays from lamps above the hotel's doorways and roadside signs. But a Missouri state police car, with blue light turning on top, had pulled up alongside the pool. And we were afraid we were about to get caught.

We were not guests of the hotel, of course, but local teenagers who'd snuck out of our homes while our parents slept and hiked across town to skinnydip in this famous roadside establishment's expansive kidney shaped pool.

Our clothes were neatly folded and piled behind a tree fifty yards away, in the wooded grounds in front of the hotel beyond which a rich Missouri countryside spread itself out under a starlit July sky.

Billy Rhodes and I had been taking these midnight excursions for a month or more in this summer before I would leave Fairfield for college. It provided me with excitement after the routine of work and distraction from the apprehension I felt about being out on my own in the fall.

Billy needed nothing in the way of adventure, as he was always involved in multiple, generally unsuccessful schemes and enterprises: rebuilding his hot rod (a dilapidated '49 Ford, officially totaled some months ago in an encounter with a Missouri Pacific freight train), romancing famously well-built Karen Murphy (whom he would never win), and forming a farmworkers' union (in a county where ninety per cent of the workers were members of the family that owned the farm). Still, he could always be counted on for more fun.

Billy was the first to propose what he called "Bare-Ass Naked and Nude Swimming Parties," and his goal was to get some girls to come with us. He would succeed beyond his wildest dreams in a few weeks' time, but tonight it was just the two of us. Well, the two of us and whoever was seated in the idling squad car.

"How many of them are there?" I asked Billy in a whisper.

"I think it's just one," he answered. I thought I saw only one silhouette also and wondered why he was staying in the car. We'd been alerted by the beams of his headlights and had ducked down close to the edge of the pool. The car stopped, and nothing had happened for several minutes.

"What do we do?" I whispered with an increasing sense of urgency.

"Nothing, nothing. He might not have seen us."

"What the heck do you think he's here for, then? He's got us cornered."

This was true, for the Banner Hotel sat up on the highest point in Phipps County, where Route 66, coming west from St. Louis, swept over a rise and began its long, winding descent off the Fairfield plateau down to the Gasconade River. The police car had parked on the outside of the

208

pool. The logical route of flight was in the opposite direction, but that was away from our clothes and toward the front of the hotel itself.

"OK," said Billy. "This is what we do. We split and make a run for it. He can't go after both of us. Meet you back at the Circle."

The image of us racing across the lawn naked didn't encourage me. In addition to a culturally driven desire to remain clothed in public, I lacked physical self-confidence at this stage of my life.

On the other hand, we had to do something. The police car's idling motor and slowly turning light were adding to the tension. How had I gotten myself into this predicament?

I had to admit it was not just a new and crazy scheme from Billy, the co-ed skinnydip idea. I'd gotten interested in the Banner Hotel itself when our senior history teacher assigned each of us a monument or building in the area for research. The Banner was truly a landmark, and I'd been glad to accept the topic for study. Since I also hoped to study engineering at college, I wanted to learn more about how it had been built.

Now, months after I'd turned in my research paper, I also wanted to feel what it was like to be a guest at the hotel. But, given my limited capital, this was as close as I could get to the status of patron.

The Banner Hotel was a grand construction, especially for this relatively remote community. Built in the 1930s to host the more prosperous travelers sightseeing along fabled Route 66, the Banner Hotel had become a major stop between St. Louis on one side of the state and Joplin on the other.

Their advertising was meant to assert equality with more well known urban institutions: "Complete hotel and restaurant accommodations of the highest type, designed especially for motorists. Service and facilities unexcelled in metropolitan areas." Services were so good, in fact, that few citizens of Fairfield could afford to eat in their swank restaurant, let alone spend the night there.

The building's crescent shape followed the thin ridge of an Ozark hilltop, its two four-story wings like arms reaching out to embrace the landscape. The central unit, with entrance and registration desk in a spacious lobby, was open to the second floor and featured pairs of matched floorlength windows on each side of double entry doors. A four-column porch provided shelter at the entrance.

There were rooms on the third floor above this central part, and smaller rooms with dormer windows above that. The wings to each side came in two sections, the first four stories high like the central unit, the second a two-story extension.

Across the full reach of the Banner, then, were 36 rooms on the first two floors, twelve on the third, and ten on the fourth. Above them all was a banistered rooftop lookout and a huge pennant with the words "Banner Hotel" in red flying from a tall pole. The view from there would exceed, I imagined, the Circle's fabled spot, the Open Place, in the woods past Springers Pond.

That view was blocked at the ground and first floor levels, as houses, restaurants, and a few small businesses had been built to the west of the hotel. Once on the edge of town, the Banner was now half a mile from where Business Route 66 branched off from the main highway to come into Fairfield.

I loved this building's symmetrical structure, its paired sections and balanced architecture. But then I'd always been a sucker for design, especially after my imperfect attempt to construct a neighborhood store for kids in Old Man Simpson's garage. In fact, I was over my head in another attempt at construction this summer, though this wasn't one I'd taken on voluntarily.

Right now, with the state police about to nab me for trespassing and who knows what other offenses, I didn't have the leisure to contemplate the Banner Hotel's majestic appearance or my own challenging tasks. I had to make a run for it.

Billy slid down the pool's edge to the shallow end. And I inched myself along the rail to a point under the diving board. In another second, we would make our simultaneous attempts at escape.

In the best of scenarios, we'd grab the lip of the trough that drained splashes and overflow out of the pool, push off with our feet on the pool bottom, and rise like rockets straight up out of the water. One foot on the lip of the splash trough, the next on the cement walk at the pool's side, then fly.

There was no time for careful exit by the poolside ladder or deliberate walking between the lounge chairs (ignore those ubiquitous "No Running" signs!). Before the policeman could get out of his car and call "halt!" I'd be slipping between cars in the parking lot and Billy would have bolted around the north wing of the Banner.

I didn't relish having to sneak all the way back across town without any clothes on, even if it was the dark of night. But I didn't dare try to circle back and retrieve them, at least right then.

"Wait!" I hissed to Billy. "Our clothes, our things." I just realized we'd left our wallets in our pants pockets. We'd have to get them back or be tracked down and caught even if we escaped for the moment.

"On three," whispered Billy from the other end of the pool, ignoring my concern

"What?" I sucked in my breath, tensing my muscles for the spring from water to air. If he was going, I would go. Maybe he had a plan to retrieve our things?

In the last seconds of preparation I had a dismal image of myself and my life. It was as bad as when, years ago, I believed I had set fire to the woods west of the Circle and that my carelessness would cause the destruction of half the town.

In sneaking away from home and slipping into the Banner Hotel's pool, I had left behind the trappings of civilization--my clothes, my name, my social and familial identity. I was truly naked.

Perhaps I believed I could be again the combat ready young soldier, tapping hidden reserves of strength and daring to slip away into the night. I worried, though, that I might once more inadvertently injure an innocent bystander in my flight.

My parents believed that their son was sleeping peacefully in the room they'd made for him in the attic, just as their daughter Beth slept in her bedroom on the main floor. (My brother Charles was a junior at the University of Missouri in Columbia by this time.) All the items documenting Mark Landon's identity were either in that house or abandoned behind a maple tree on the grounds of a hotel patronized by travelers from other cities, other states. So this naked boy pretending to be a hotel guest couldn't be who I had always pretended to be.

This was also a time I was fantasizing that gypsies had stolen me at birth from my real parents, and I'd been raised by people who didn't know the real me, a "me" I myself had yet to understand. My idea of myself didn't seem to fit with a kid who grew up on Limestone Drive, child of the respected Assistant Director of the State Geological Survey and his New Jersey wife, a woman who'd had a role, albeit a small one, in winning the Second World War.

A slender boy nearly six feet tall racing between parked cars, hair flying wildly, leaving wet footprints on the pavement, ducking the spotlights of authorities--who was he, where was he heading, what would he do with himself?

Just then Billy and I heard the deep rumble of a truck engine and saw more lights coming from the back of the Banner.

"What now?" I whispered.

"Wait!" he answered, with a smile of confidence I couldn't fathom.

II

Still clinging to the splash trough, Billy and I watched a long semi-trailer come around the corner of the hotel and pull up alongside the police car. The truck driver gave the lightest of taps on his horn, then pulled on past.

The policeman cut off the light on top of the patrol car, waited a moment, then followed the truck out to Route 66.

"What?" I asked Billy, though any explanation didn't really matter so long as we'd escaped arrest.

"He was showing him how to get back on the right road. I've seen it before. Some big truck drivers miss the turn on Business 66, looking for highway 00. They can't get their big rigs turned around anywhere downtown, so the police route them on to the hotel. Then they can circle the building and be headed the right way. He was just parking here as a reference point."

"Wow! And I was sure he was after us."

"There you go, doubting your fearless leader again," said Billy, splashing water with the palm of his hand in my direction. "The Bare-Ass Naked and Nude Swimming Parties shall continue! And next time we'll have participants with titties."

I thought I knew who he meant: Sheila Knight, a luscious junior who lived down on Black Street. Billy had lusted after her forever, even when we were still technically short of our teenage years and she a prodigy of female development. Although he was officially dating Karen Murphy, I knew he occasionally took Sheila to the drive-in movies--not, of course, to watch any films.

The prospect of skinnydipping with an attractive girl reminded me of another reason I was haunting the Banner Hotel in the last summer of my Fairfield youth.

Marcia Terrell, my on-again, off-again highschool sweetheart, worked in the hotel's restaurant. Although she wouldn't have been there at this time of the night, I often passed by the Banner in hopes of exchanging a few words with her. We were officially "off" at this time, but I had had a few hints that we could be "on" again, if I played my cards right.

"You want to get an ice cream or something?" she'd asked me in front of her house one day recently. I was on my way to work the evening at Gunn's, she just coming back from the Banner.

"Sure. Not at the drug store, though. How about the Dairy Queen?" This was a block from the Banner. "I could meet you after your shift one afternoon." I happened to know that she finished each day around four o'clock.

"Friday? Good. I want to ask you something."

My campaign of two winters back to gain control of Marcia's and my relationship had, as you know, failed miserably. Not long after the debacle in the alley behind Gunn's, we'd decided to go our separate ways. I realize now she wasn't happy with the man I was trying to become, though at the time I attributed her lack of interest to female fickleness.

In the next year or so, I had a couple of dates with one girl, a few with another, and so forth. Sometimes I would even go out with Marcia. But nothing really went anywhere until recently. I had, almost as an afterthought, invited her to my senior prom, both of us wanting to go and me having no other potential partner.

During the course of her junior year at Fairfield High, tomboyish and athletic Marcia Terrell had grown taller and slimmer, transformed before the young male population of her generation into a willowy, brown haired-beauty. She also had just the round rump I'd discovered that I desired. I was once again crazy in love with her, or in love with the idea of being in love with her. As always in my case, sex had a lot to do with it.

I still held in my mind's eye pictures of the most famous pair of lovers in our high school years, Martin Pruitt and

Linda Roper. When Linda inadvertently popped Martin in the groin at a rehearsal for the junior class play, remember, I'd witnessed a physical intimacy I could not comprehend until years of my own experience had given me a broader and deeper frame of reference. Nevertheless, I wanted to substitute Marcia and me into that picture of carnal knowledge.

Sadly for me at least, Marcia had required that I go through the same old steps of sexual experimentation-- first base, second base, etc. It didn't matter that I'd nearly reached home over a year earlier. During that spring and summer I had been required to establish each stage in our petting relationship before I could attempt to move on to the next.

Mind you, she didn't announce this as a formal program, but in the kissing, holding, groping nature of teenage romance, I discovered that I was blocked at each level until it had become routine.

Eventually I concluded she was making me earn each right because I had dropped several pegs in her ranking of young men. She was spending time, you see, with people from out of town and from a higher class. She was serving the elite who cruised Route 66 in Lincolns and Cadillacs, the well dressed city dwellers whose clothes and manners naturally put my own smalltown, smalltime identity into unfavorable comparison.

That comparison would have been even sharper if I'd happened to be seen running from the Banner parking lot in my birthday suit. Had Marcia spotted me ducking behind trees and crouching beside cars on the way up Limestone, I would confirm a reputation in her mind as a boy who couldn't control himself.

My renewed campaign to regain petting rights seemed to get a boost in the topic she wanted to consider at the Dairy Queen. She wanted to learn about human reproduction.

"I don't know any more than you do," I protested immediately. Whatever I might know, of course, I would also have been embarrassed to admit. And I certainly didn't want to explain that, at one point in my life, I'd thought babies were produced when a man poked his index finger through a circle made by a woman's thumb and forefinger.

"But you told me you had seen a book your parents have. With drawings," Marcia went on. This was true. When it was time to have his talk with me about "the birds and the bees," my scientific father had produced a college anatomy textbook. I had alluded to that volume more than once in an effort to seem sophisticated.

"Yeah, but I don't know where it is. They don't keep it out on the coffee table, you know."

"Is there one in the library?"

"I suppose so. But you probably have to ask for it. It'll be kept behind the circulation desk." I had learned this on my own, pursuing the same topic for myself. The results of my research in books from the general collection were uninspiring, as what I wanted to learn about was not reproduction, but sex.

"Why, um, why do you need a book, anyway?" This question had considerable force for me. If she was seeking information for its own sake, well, OK. But was there more to this request? Was this the sign I had been looking for that all the stop signs on the road to my sexual initiation were being taken down?

"Well, I just want to . . . um . . . to be a little clearer on all the details."

I thought back to our own petting sessions in the hospital parking lot. We'd gone pretty far by touch, but it was always dark. I wondered myself what some parts of her anatomy looked like, what I would have been able to see in the light of day. Even when you have something in your hand or under your hand, it's not always easy to visualize it correctly.

"The details . . . ?" I offered and then stopped.

"Could you ask about it for me at the library?"

"Me? Why? I mean, couldn't you get it for yourself?"

"Mark, don't you think you could do this for me?" she asked. Then she added, "For us?" She put a hand on my arm and looked intently into my face.

And that did it, of course. To this day, when a woman combines a request with putting her hand on my arm, I can seldom resist. The gesture scrambles whatever relationship we'd had before--mother to son, wife to husband, daughter to father. I become a slave to a princess.

Completing this particular mission, though, was not going to be easy. I knew from my own experience I didn't have the courage to ask Mrs. Prism at the town library for any reference works on this topic. Sex education involving humans didn't exist in the schools of those days, remember, as this eternal human process was kept a mystery to all boys my age or younger. What we learned, we learned in the street or by extrapolation from animal life.

Whenever a forbidden topic arose in my life, however, I usually felt I could turn to Billy.

"Say, Billy," I asked as we walked along Kingshighway after our close encounter with the Missouri Highway Patrol. We'd retrieved our clothes without incident and now appeared as reputable citizens, though we were out later than any curfew our parents would have recognized. "You got any books on sex?"

"Books on sex? I got *Playboy*. That what you mean?"

"Well, not really. I guess I mean medical books, science maybe."

"Nah. Nobody wants that stuff. Of course, what you could do is break into the college library. They've got some weird things." And he launched into an account of how he'd done it himself, taping over the latch to a side door during the day so that the staff thought the door was locked when they left. But I'd finally learned to be careful about Billy's schemes, and this one put me off immediately.

Skinnydipping in the Banner Hotel pool would probably be considered a boyish prank. We'd get a lecture about safety if we were caught, perhaps have to do some work for the hotel as punishment. But breaking and entering a state owned building, taking books--that could lead to jail.

As it was, I was suffering some nervousness already about our midnight excursions. Whether it was the violation of property rights or the possibility of getting caught without my pants on, I'd begun to harbor a gnawing, nearly constant sense of guilt. A feeling that I'd done something terribly wrong inspired a recurring dream. In familiar everyday surroundings I would find myself without clothes.

The most frequent situation was a throwback to my paperboy days. I'd begin this dream happily striding down Fairfield's main street, a *Daily Mirror* paperbag at my hip, the strap crossing my chest. Glancing down at that strap, I'd realize I was wearing, not regular street clothes, but pajamas.

This was odd, but not, I thought in my dream, completely ridiculous. I was clothed at least, and--who knew?--many people might also wear pajamas, say, to work or school. Unfortunately, a disguisedly casual inspection of my surroundings revealed that no one else on the street had on nighttime wear. All I saw around me were pants and shirts, skirts and blouses.

My walk was certainly less jaunty now, though I tried to stay focused on the task at hand, delivering papers. Into Dents' Store, paper by register, out again. Through the door of Harry's Barbershop (he loved the pun), paper next to the coatrack, on my way.

I began, though, to think that I probably should slip into an alley or behind a phone booth and consider my situation. If I could just get out of the public eye, I might be able to devise a plan. I might run home, change clothes, return in proper attire.

Then, the worst thing happened. The next time I glanced down at my chest, I was not even wearing pajamas. I was naked except for a paperbag.

And then I met Marcia Terrell on a street corner.

Wake up! Wake up! And I would.

But these dreams left their mark on my daytime self. I feared I was committing an infraction of some fundamental social law. There was something I should do that I wasn't doing, or something I should not do that I was. I just didn't know what it was. And it hampered my ability to court Marcia.

In addition to my own unrecognized failings were Marcia's untold successes. Six nights a week the real version of my dream creature was inside a building I could only contemplate from the outside, achieving recognition and stature in the Banner's rarefied atmosphere of money and travel. My sense of the hotel's looming over me as I floated in the kidney shaped pool confirmed the feeling that Marcia had risen above me in wisdom and strength, in goodness and maturity. I wanted to climb up with her.

What I needed was a transformation. I needed to change from one of many guys finishing high school and heading off for college to someone distinctive, special, interesting. In the mythology of those days, I thought I could get all those things with an automobile.

III

Cars were the vehicle to any girl's heart, we believed. A new automobile was an impossibility, but many a secondhand car had its romantic aura. The 1957 Chevy was my personal choice, though a 1949 Ford was not without its charm.

As we walked down Kingshighway near the Holsom Bakery after escaping the state police, I asked, "Billy, tell me again how you got the Petting Machine." That was what he sometimes called the wreck that used to be a '49 Ford.

"You never get tired of that story, do you?" said Billy. "Let's stop at The DC. Besides, you know I found it parked in a barn along with three others."

The Dining Car--almost always shortened to "The DC" (and pronounced Thee Dee See)--was one of the few 24-hour establishments in Fairfield. It was a former railroad car turned restaurant. A single row of stools ran the length of the diner, and a single cook took orders and prepared food behind that counter.

It amuses me now to think that I didn't recognize The DC as a railroad car for a long time. It was just a long and thin building, I thought. The name (The DC) didn't give it away to me until my little sister Beth asked one day, "How'd they get that dining car from the railroad tracks to the side of the highway?" Fortunately, I was able to disguise the shock of this discovery from the rest of my family.

The diner was located about a mile from the Banner along Business Route 66. While 66 Bypass now passed north of town, truckers and people on night shifts knew where The DC was. And there were few hours of the night when it was completely empty.

We had taken to stopping there on the way back from our Bare-ass Naked and Nude Swimming Parties. We'd order eggs with toast and a cup of coffee, which was really more an excuse to smoke a cigarette afterwards as we hiked along the highway toward the Circle.

Neither of us was particularly good at smoking yet, and we pretended to inhale while taking only the lightest of drags from the cigarette. I still resented the fit of coughing that my first attempt produced instead of the sense of satisfaction and pleasure inspired by the sight of older men smoking. Still, Billy and I felt positively transformed standing outside The DC a few hours before dawn with the smoke of two Lucky Strikes curling around us.

There was only one more thing necessary to elevate us to the status of men. And it, too, could be found at The DC. Rubbers.

The diner's rest room, which you reached from a door outside the building, had a machine on the wall that would dispense a condom for a quarter. And it was the only place in Fairfield, so far as we knew, where you could buy one.

Condoms were another hidden element of the adult world to children in those hypocritical days. It was years, in fact, before I finally understood that their primary use was not "the prevention of disease," as was written on the machine.

I studied, by the way, every word printed on that two-foot-square metal box: "Trojan," "lubricated," "ribbed," "tipped," "scented." How evocative these words were to a boy who remained innocent of the physical sensations of intercourse!

The only public word used to hint at a rubber's existence in my youth was "prophylactic," and few kids knew what that meant. The term "condom" would wait another thirty years before AIDS provided it with respectability, even dignity. The more commonly used "rubber" was a four-letter word to polite society.

Most guys in high school, of course, carried a rubber in their wallet, many so old (passed down unused from one boy to another for a price) that they were no protection from disease or pregnancy. While I couldn't show any evidence that I would need one with Marcia or any other girl, I thought I was ready to buy a brand new one.

I'd had several hand-me-downs, the packages so worn and dirty that I knew they were good only for show. But I hadn't quite gotten up my nerve yet to buy one myself. I feared that as soon as that item slid from the chute of the vending machine into my hot sweaty palm, a police officer would open the door to the restroom and demand my reasons for needing such a thing.

Just as bad, I sometimes feared that merely turning the crank that delivered the goods would infect me with "V.D." (If mentioned in public, all venereal diseases were lumped together under the single category identified only by the initials.)

Billy and I finished our smokes and continued down the last leg of the walk home, following Black Street down from Kingshighway toward the Circle. I returned to my musings about automobiles and girls, jealous of my friend's good fortune in possessing his own car, even if it was in constant need of repair.

"The Petting Machine was in a barn?" I asked rhetorically.

"In what looked like a barn but was really a garage, a four car garage."

Billy had worked the past two summers bringing in hay for local farmers. He was one of a dozen kids from town who hired on with Mr. Martin. Martin owned several hundred acres of grassland north of Fairfield, but spent much of his summer helping other farmers harvest their crops.

Billy found his car before he started that ill-advised effort to unionize workers. He was bringing in hay on Samuel Billings' land.

"What do you mean, a 'garage barn'?"

"Well, tight old Mr. Billings liked his '49 Ford so much he decided he'd never need another kind of car."

"Yeah."

"But he thought it might wear out. So the old guy went into St. Louis and bought three more of them. Same color exactly. You couldn't tell one from the other."

"That meant he owned four cars, all the same!"

"That's right."

"Didn't his neighbors notice?"

"He told everyone he had old tractors in that barn. He claimed he was going to start a museum for restored, vintage farm machinery."

"OK, but get to how you ended up with one of the four."

"Well, two years ago the first car went over 200,000 miles and it was giving him trouble."

"And you'd found out about the other cars?"

"Completely by accident, mind. I was thinking about whether the hayloft of a barn would be a good movie theater. There's one down the road from the Banner I thought I could rent cheap. So on my lunch break out at Billings' farm I climbed up there to look around. And I found these cars."

"So to keep you quiet about his treasures, the back-up Fords, Billings sold you the Petting Machine?"

"Yeah, but I haven't been completely quiet about it." Billy laughed. People in the town and county knew about the Billings' Fords, though many thought it just a story. I kept thinking I ought to be so lucky, coming upon an underground cave full of '57 Chevys.

Instead of stumbling across a free car, however, I had been assigned the restoration of a ten-year-old blimp by my father. He had purchased a 1953 Buick Roadmaster Estate Wagon in nearly as bad a shape as the Petting

Machine. He was overhauling the engine, while I was to redo the interior.

This model was the last "woodie" to use the real thing on the exterior, though you could barely tell that with the mud and road tar that covered the car when I first saw it. Underneath all that crud, though, was genuine maple and oak, as I found over the course of my labors.

I'd already spent hours getting the road grime off the exterior wood and as many hours stripping corroded finish from the cargo area in back and the floorboards. The upholstery, though dirty, was salvageable, but I'd had to install new seat covers. That was a task, stretching the generic replacement set over the sad old cushions!

My dad explained that he wanted this Roadmaster for his personal rock collecting. In the last few years I'd been able to talk my way out of accompanying him on treks into the wilderness, up cliffsides, along creekbottoms, and over ridgetops. But he still took off about once a month, leaving before dawn on a Saturday and coming back with cardboard boxes full of dusty specimens to be stored in our basement. Now he wanted a vehicle specially equipped for these expeditions.

Until they emerged as ideal family vehicles in the 1950s, station wagons had actually been viewed as trucks by most drivers. Rather than cargo, they now hauled children, pets, and luggage down America's highways, like Route 66, as a post-war boom inspired extended family vacations. "See the U.S.A., in a Chevrolet," was a favorite slogan, and the car featured in radio and television ads was often a station wagon. But my dad was taking his Buick back to its earlier function.

The second seat had been removed from the Roadmaster, and he wanted me to build cabinets along both sides all the way to the back. The smaller, backward-facing third seat was retained, as it could fold down to provide more cargo space or be raised to carry passengers.

Some spaces along the sides were to have deep drawers for large rocks, others shallow beds for maps and charts, some with removable bins so that gravel and sand could be carried home for testing. There were also places to store tools, water, and food. In the end, this was to be a very utilitarian vehicle.

"But Dad, I have to work at Gunn's for my college money," I had complained when he first told me about this project at the beginning of the summer.

"Aren't you just working part time?" he countered.

"Yes, but I'm asking for more hours." Max typically gave his high school employees about thirty hours a week during summer vacation.

"Well, you give me a couple hours every day and a few Saturdays. I'll make it worth your while."

"Exactly how much money do you mean?" I thought perhaps if I demanded too much pay, I could get out of this job. But my dad was unyielding.

"You just do it. You're not out on your own yet, so you owe the family some time."

I hated this argument, though it allowed me to keep alive my half-hearted conviction that I'd been stolen by gypsies, that this man was not my real father.

Of course, now I can see a certain fairness in it. I didn't really want to be completely on my own. In fact, I was nervous about how I'd fare at Southwest Missouri State in Springfield come September. I hadn't, for instance, lost my virginity. Could I be ready for college?

I did have a genuine prospect for sexual initiation right now, as Marcia had seemed as eager as I in the hospital parking lot. We just hadn't taken the final step. I needed to get that book (or another like it) for her.

Actually, I reasoned, I had the opportunity to find the book, as I was now, once a week, tip-toeing through the house in the middle of the night on my way to the Bare-

Ass Naked and Nude Swimming Parties. Why not make a stop in Dad's study?

My father had taken over the room in the basement Charles and I used to share before we had bedrooms built into the attic. It was a bit damp and dark, but it was quiet. And those cold cement walls probably appealed to a geologist.

I wasn't eager to go rifling through drawers and book-cases down there, though, as my father was a private person about his work. He didn't even let my mom clean his study unless he was there to supervise. Still, this was surely where he'd keep such a book. And I began to think about how I could make an efficient, speedy search.

The next time I hunched on a stool with Billy Rhodes at The DC, however, another idea came to me about how I could satisfy Marcia's request. It seemed at the moment a brilliant inspiration, but only a few weeks later I could see that it had backfire written all over it.

IV

I saw Marcia in the Circle.

"I have something to show you," I offered.

"That book?"

"Well, not exactly. But it's along the same line."

"That's good. It turns out, I have something to show you, too."

"Oh?"

"Can you meet me one evening after work at the Banner fountain? It's being turned off at dusk this week, so we'll be alone."

Alone with Marcia was what I wanted to be. And the fountain was a romantic meeting place. So we agreed on Wednesday night at 9:30, half an hour after I finished at Gunn's.

"Is what you have to show me larger than a bread box?" I asked coyly as we were parting, willing to guess within the rules of familiar games.

"You'll see. Wednesday night?" According to my understanding of "Twenty Questions," she should have said either "yes" or "no." Clearly, she wanted to surprise me.

I recognize now that so many things were new for us, two people emerging into adulthood, that either of us could easily have been surprised by a number of novelties. And the times in which we lived, the 1950s, were, we would later understand, modern America's Age of Innocence. We stood on the threshold of individual and collective discovery. It turned out, however, that Marcia was farther along that road than I was.

As I hiked from Gunn's out toward the Banner (lamenting the fact, of course, that I had no car to drive), I got to thinking again about the man who built this icon on Route 66. The prospect from the swimming pool in front of the hotel was very much the same as the one we kids on the Circle saw from the Open Place out in our woods. The highway snaked off the Fairfield Plateau down toward the distant Gasconade River, railroad tracks running parallel to the thin ribbon of concrete out into the distance.

That's what Meriwether Clark wanted to offer highway travelers, the sense of open space free of the confines of an increasingly industrial and bureaucratic society. He'd grown up in St. Louis in the last century, when it was still primarily an agricultural center, transportation hub for grain and cattle raised on Midwest farms and headed for Eastern and world markets by rail and river barge. The fields themselves weren't that far from the Mississippi riverfront.

Clark, who made a fortune selling that new fangled machine, the automobile, understood the closing of the frontier not as a loss of nature but as the entrapment of the individual. In his old age he selected Fairfield as a jumping off place for wealthy Americans who would flee the restrictions of society for the freedom of the West. He purchased fifty acres and laid out ambitious plans for a luxury hotel perched along an Ozark ridge. The rooms were to be large, the furnishings elegant, the service first-class. High priced architects and experienced engineers were involved in design, and a veteran St. Louis firm handled construction.

In addition to the spacious kidney-shaped pool on the west side of the hotel, there was an impressive fountain on the south lawn which afternoon travelers from St. Louis could see against a backdrop of colorful sunsets. Clark thought it an appropriate symbol of unfettered power.

At the center of the shallow pool, a single powerful jet of water shot perhaps 25 feet into the air. On some nights red, blue, and yellow spotlights beamed through the splintering column to create moving shapes, even a rainbow. "It's a picture of the future," I thought to myself as I walked, imagining a rosy life at college with a girlfriend, Marcia, back home.

Tonight the lights around the pool and the fountain itself had been turned off, as Marcia predicted. All the better for some cosy togetherness, I thought. I wondered if Marcia, with connections to the Banner's management, had arranged the darkness.

"I wasn't sure you'd be here," I said, sitting down.

"Why is that?"

"Well, you've been kind of, um, stand-offish lately."

She ignored my complaint, which was unjustified anyway. "You remember that biology filmstrip Mr. Womack always shows in eleventh grade?" she asked.

The film, famous at Fairfield High, was announced as an overview of scientific research, some conducted at the University of Missouri, where Womack had done his graduate study. But the subject, animal reproduction, generated more student interest than far better filmstrips. There was always tittering at the rabbit pairs used in experiments.

"Sure. I like animals," I said pointlessly.

She recalled the men in white lab coats who studied new crops to be farmed on the oceans' floors, futuristic versions of the men whose harvests Mr. Martin and Billy brought in.

I tried to turn our conversation toward the direction I wanted to pursue. "Would you like to be one of those rabbits, cooped up and watched all the time?" In the film scientists in dark suits bred Asian predators that could be used to eliminate local pests on the other side of the globe.

"Maybe students at Fairfield High are the subjects of an experiment, the 'Show Me Laboratory,'" Marcia joked, using the Missouri state slogan.

"Well, for right now, at least, I think the two of us have escaped from our cages. We can do whatever we want."

This time her directness was the surprise. "What do you want to do?"

"What do you think I want?"

Marcia was looking off into the night, seemingly reviewing the filmstrip in memory. Perhaps she recalled men with stethoscopes manipulating hormones to amplify growth, strength, even intelligence in controlled populations.

"You want to push back the frontiers," she said slowly. Then she added, smiling: "Of science."

Reaching a hand into the spacious pocket of her sun dress, she pulled out a small plastic case. She gave a wry grin as her fingers curled around it.

"What's that?" I asked.

All of a sudden I thought of the legendary (perhaps apocryphal) story about how men tried to discourage women in medical school. Into the lab coat pocket of the class's one female student, male colleagues slipped a penis, callously obtained from one of the corpses used in anatomy. They assumed the discovery her hand would make during daily rounds sufficient to drive her from the profession.

Their assurance was strained, however, as she went several hours without a sign of discomfort. They saw a hand go deep into that pocket, but it came out again with only a pencil. There was no agitated reaction. And she continued to take rigorous notes on a clipboard.

Some of the men concluded silently that she had freaked out, been shocked into denial. But in the changing room, where lab coats were hung on wooden pegs, she threw out a question for the rest of them. Holding aloft the anonymous, inert manhood, she asked casually, "Did one of you boys lose something?"

Our nation's sexual mythology would take one more turn nearly a quarter of a century later when a Virginia housewife removed her husband's member with a kitchen knife, claiming later to be the victim of domestic abuse. In 1959 neither men nor women used the word "penis" in public.

I didn't think Marcia had a penis to show me. But she didn't answer my question

"What do you have to show me?" she asked instead.

I exhaled sharply, "Whff!" and reached for my billfold.

I had to be careful here to pull out the right item. Not the condom, which was tucked into the same pocket.

I held up a miniature book, a pamphlet really, and set my wallet on the rim of the fountain between us. The lettering was small and hard to read in the little light we had. But Marcia picked it up and deciphered the title: "Ancient Secrets of Sex?"

"I couldn't find my father's book," I explained. "I found this . . . um, I got this from a friend."

The truth was that I'd used the quarter I'd dedicated to buying a new condom for another option on The DC's rubber machine. In addition to a jell guaranteed to prevent premature ejaculation--"D-Lay" (pun intended)--and a supposed aphrodisiac--"X-tasty" (a picture on the cover showed a woman innocently swallowing the pill with a cup of soda)--the Trojan dispenser contained this tiny guide to pleasure. And, of course, I liked the abbreviated version of the title on the top of each little page: "A.S.S."

"It has pictures," I offered as a postscript. They were really drawings, hardly detailed, though they excited me. They showed positions I'd never imagined.

Here I should give my father some credit in his "birds and the bees" talk with me. He had identified the missionary position and suggested that there were alternatives. Sadly, he didn't detail them for me.

Of course, not that long ago I'd witnessed Slim and his girlfriend (whom I dubbed "Blossom") at work doggy style in the tire room at Sam's Garage. So I understood that two people didn't have to lie on a bed to have sex. But my literal-mindedness didn't encourage my imagination to take those hints and extrapolate: standing, sitting, woman on top, and more were sketched out in Ancient Secrets of Sex.

Marcia thumbed through the pages, and I was relieved to see that she was smiling.

"I know about all this," she said. "What I want to know about is contraception."

V

Surely, you are saying, this guy knows what "contraception" means. I wish it had been so.

Think about it, though: birth control was a secret of the upper classes through the nineteenth century and well into the twentieth. Condoms made of animal skin were expensive, and the education necessary to understand their use was limited to those with money enough to afford schooling.

Other methods--relying on a woman's cycle, for instance--were legendary in their unreliability, especially given the fundamentally impulsive nature of the sex act.

Too, the infant mortality rate was, until more recent times, so high that the laboring classes had as many children as the woman could bear (so to speak), hoping that a few would survive to adulthood.

At the middle of this century, though, as science was poised to made dramatic breakthroughs in controlling human reproduction, public education reached all but the most remote and most impoverished citizens in this country. And chemical contraception would inspire one of the most dramatic changes in human behavior in modern times.

I looked at the rectangular plastic case Marcia held on her palm. It was perhaps three inches wide by five inches long, only a quarter of an inch thick. She prized the top up to reveal a grid, five rows of seven circles, 35 little caps. Popping up one tiny lid, she pulled a single small pill, about half as large as an aspirin, out of a slight recess. She held the white dot up between thumb and forefinger, smiling. It stood out before me even in the dim light.

"What is this?" I asked.

"It's a birth control pill."

"What . . . ?"

"You take it, silly, to keep from getting pregnant."

"I . . . ?" I was, of course, completely in the dark here.

"Not you. Me. A girl. A woman."

"Take it!" I commanded immediately.

"Oh, they're not mine. Not for me. This is just to show you something you didn't know about."

"But what good is it tonight?"

Marcia's face showed a momentary flash of anger. But, after a brief hesitation, she explained how drug companies were taking great pains to make a new system simple for the women who would take this medication. Each pill rested in its own capped recess, labeled for the day of the month.

Marcia understood how it all worked, the hormones and responses. But I was conspicuously not interested in a scientific explanation.

"Why did you ask me to meet you here, if not . . . " I couldn't finish the question.

She shrugged, replaced the pill, closed the case, and slipped her surprise back into the sun dress pocket. Then she reached out to take up my wallet, which still lay on the fountain's rim.

"Maybe I wanted to see this," she offered and pulled my old condom out of its hiding place.

"Oh, you already know what that is."

"Open it."

"Open it? Well, I can. But it ought to be used, if I do."

I didn't think she'd fall for this old lie, of course, but I had to try. It was another of the miscellaneous pieces of advice Billy had offered for such situations. Her response, however, had not been anticipated in our rehearsals of hoped-for opportunities. "Well, I do want to see it on."

238

"On?"

"On."

"Well, OK. Fine. Let's find a place."

"No. Here."

"Here?"

"Here. We're alone. It's dark." Then, with a funny grin, she used the Missouri state slogan again: "Show me."

I glanced over her head to the looming structure of the Banner Hotel and thought how someone might be looking out into the darkness around the fountain. I thought about Meriwether Clark.

In my research at the town library and in the archives of the Fairfield *Mirror*, I'd developed a radical version of this visionary's history. There had been, I concluded, another woman in his life, another woman who might have had him doing what I was ready to do with Marcia.

Clark was respectably married, father of three children. Indeed, many of the accounts of his rise to fortune touted his civic standing, a proper Victorian family man. Church goer, Chamber of Commerce officer, public benefactor, his name was never touched by scandal.

Mrs. Clark too was an eminent figure in St. Louis society, and she was regularly mentioned as wife of the prominent businessman, organizer of charity benefits, and tireless campaigner for social reform. She'd never abandoned the fundamental ideas behind Prohibition, and she had special interest in the rights of women.

I had turned to Theresa Clark's story after uncovering the secret in her husband's life.

In all the pictures connected with the construction and opening of this grand hotel in Fairfield, I had discovered that there was always a young brunette among the party, seldom more than two people away from Clark himself. She was, I believed, his mistress.

In those pictures I was sure this mystery figure was looking at Clark as a woman looks at the love of her life. Mrs. Clark never appeared in any pictures, was not even mentioned by the Fairfield newspaper. And in one key photograph I was sure Clark was winking at his paramour even as he cut the ribbon stretched across the hotel's entrance at the grand opening.

Perhaps she was a Fairfield native, with whom the millionaire had an affair during the three years of planning and building the Banner. Or, if she'd been from St. Louis, they probably didn't take special precautions to keep their relationship hidden this far from his home town and the big city press. They didn't anticipate, however, a later day sleuth, perceptive Mark Landon, soon-to-be college student who had ferreted out the truth.

I interpreted the following paragraph from one *Mirror* story as evidence of their secret relationship. It reported the Banner's opening, a gala event which concluded with dancing in the hotel's spacious ballroom:

"Mr. Meriwether, however, was not in attendance during the late hours of the celebration. The Banner manager said his boss was touring the facilities.

"All hotel rooms were occupied, as representatives from the town, county, and state had been offered free accommodations. And representatives of national travel organizations had come to hear about the gem on Missouri's Route 66."

Old man Clark was shacked up with his sweetie, I believed, probably in the honeymoon suite.

When I checked out Clark's later career in old issues of the *St. Louis Post-Dispatch*, the mystery woman was nowhere to be seen. Instead, in all the public ceremonies Theresa again appeared at her husband's side.

The biggest force that pushed me to the conclusion that the famous builder of the Banner Hotel had had a torrid love affair, however, was not visible to me at the time. I can see it now, of course, from the vantage point of approaching middle age: I suffered profoundly under the adolescent obsession with sex.

Now that I had all the pieces of sexual union linked together in my mental construction, I pictured every couple I knew in physical intimacy and every single person as a potential bed partner of everyone else. What would Roger Peterson do in bed with Cathy Williams? I was pretty sure I knew: missionary position by candlelight. How did Linda Roper do Martin Pruitt? I knew she'd be hunched on top in the backseat of his VW Beetle.

These imaginings were fueled by another regular adolescent feeling, the terrible fear that I'd never live long enough to enjoy sex myself. Some unexpected catastrophe would cut me down just before that ultimate physical sensation was before me. Car wreck, unexplained heart attack, carbon monoxide poisoning while parking with my intended partner, Marcia Terrell.

Of course, this vision of the world as omnipresent pairs in union had its gaps: like many children, I couldn't imagine my parents having sex. And my imaging was exclusively heterosexual. Despite the rumors of homosexuality that occasionally attached themselves to a few individuals in our town, I couldn't picture that coupling. I was a child of my time.

Still, when Marcia took the foil packet in her fingers, deftly tore off one edge and returned it to me, I believed at that moment that my time had come at last.

Rising and putting one knee on the brick wall so that she was leaning over me, Marcia kissed me flush on the lips. One hand caressed my cheek, the other rested on my shoulder. I squirmed uncomfortably for a moment, but the pleasure was too much to resist.

"Mmmm," I said.

"Mmmm-mmmm!" confirmed Marcia.

Meanwhile I rattled the package, fumbling at zipper and clothes. Marcia stood up, keeping her two hands on

241

my shoulders. At first I wanted to stand up with her, to sustain the kiss. But my pants, the belt loosened and the zipper open, restricted me. So I remained sitting uncomfortably on the fountain's rim.

"Oh, oh, oh," I moaned imploringly.

"Hm, hm, hm," Marcia responded, admiring, I hoped, that part of me newly visible.

To this day, I have never come to a completely satisfactory explanation of what happened next. I considered it first an action of the gods, or destiny. But it might also have been simple chance. Later I concluded some testing of the Banner Hotel's electrical and hydraulic systems had been underway throughout that day.

Whatever the cause, at the precise moment I leaned back to look up at Marcia with a face openly desiring, and when Marcia stood looking down at my proud display, the fountain behind me and the lights around us suddenly cut on. There was a whoosh of water, a flash of bright, and boy and girl jumped in surprise.

Marcia's hop merely put her a few steps away from the fountain's two-foot-high brick wall. Hampered by my loosened clothes, I lost my balance, tottered, and then fell backward into the fountain's pool. The splash I made produced a miniature version of the fountain's rising structure of red, blue, and yellow shapes.

Marcia turned in time to see the column of water spread, peak, and return to the surface of the pool. Putting her hands comfortably back in the pockets of her summer sun dress, she smiled at the display.

"Mark," she asked. "Was that in the book?"

Part Eight: Creative Juices

Chapter VI

Believe it or not, some good things came of my water-soaked rendezvous with Marcia at the Banner fountain. For instance, I got to see more of the inside of this famous hotel.

Though Marcia couldn't help laughing at my dive into the water, she felt sorry for me when she saw hair plastered to my forehead and water pouring out of my shoes. She took me inside to get dried off. As a member of the restaurant staff, she knew where clean towels were stored.

I'd been in the Banner's registration lobby before, as part of my school research project. And the manager had shown me one of the rooms as it was being cleaned. But walking toward the laundry room with Marcia gave me the sense of being a Banner insider, of learning about the understructure of the whole establishment.

"So," I observed, "this is what it looks like to those in the know. I see, I see." We were following a single hallway that ran the length of the basement.

"What, the Banner?"

"Yeah, sure." I quoted from their roadside advertisements: "'Service and facilities unexcelled in metropolitan areas.' This is where it all happens, the ground floor."

"Well, I have seen some interesting things working here. Ah, we have towels." She stopped at a door marked "staff." Opening it, she studied the rows of shelves on each side of a deep closet.

"Give me a for example," I continued, curious about what odd event had occurred on the floors above me.

"I shouldn't," she said and frowned. "Here, take these and go in there to dry off." There was a restroom across the hall. It was, I calculated, right beneath the restaurant where Marcia worked, a large, open room decorated to emphasize harmony with Route 66. There were pictures of old cars on the walls--Packards, Hudsons, Cords--and vistas from famous spots on the highway like Devil's Elbow, only another thirty miles west from Fairfield.

When I came out of the restroom a few minutes later, tolerably restored, I pressed Marcia for more of the insider's view.

"OK." She brightened. "This is interesting. And I've never told anyone about it. Every Thursday night, these two women come to dinner at the restaurant. I don't know their names, though I've waited on them dozens of times."

We began walking slowly back down the hall. I was happy to prolong my time with her.

"Yeah?"

"Well, it's funny. They never say much to each other. They're polite to me, always leave me the same tip."

"What are they, old friends?"

"Hmm. I suppose so. Maybe they're sisters. I think they're about the same age, close to our parents probably. They dress well, but I've never seen them anywhere else in town."

"Maybe they're school teachers?"

"I don't think so, at least not in our schools." Rural schools had been closed over the last few decades; a single consolidated system in town now served the outlying districts as well as the town.

"What's so interesting about them, then?"

We'd reached a door marked "No Exit" at the east end of the building. Marcia swung open the heavy door and

244

paused to look out at the night, which was cloudy and dark. She chewed her lower lip. "They seem so . . . so peaceful."

Peaceful? I was lost here. I looked at Marcia, studying her. She glanced at her watch and said, "Oh! I should have been home by now. My mother will worry."

I took a last long look back down the hall, thinking of Marcia's connections to the guests who stayed there and my own status as outsider.

I've always been a sucker, by the way, for the view of a long hallway, what I was seeing as the hotel door swung closed behind us. It probably began with schools, where a familiar sight is the two rows of lockers which suddenly become visible when you open a door at one end of a building. Every child in America, I guess, has seen that view of the orderly arrangement into which society places each individual. Each student has a locker; groups of students belong in certain classrooms; the whole floor contains the school's population.

What also appeals to me in such hallway prospects of school and hotel is the limitless sense of possibility, door after door opening on both sides all the way to the end. There are places for everyone.

Though the hall appears to narrow the farther you look in front of you, it also seems that the doors in the distance are closer together, the places to turn more plentiful. You will never run out of options.

It's particularly inviting compared to where most boys of my set seemed to end each day of their limited existence: a little room at the end of a short hall in a small house.

Even though my brother was away at college and I had, in one sense, the entire second floor of the Landon household to myself, I didn't really go into Charles' room or make use of any extra space. I left the dinner table most nights, climbed the steep set of stairs built into a former closet, followed a narrow hall to my bedroom on the right.

I would read a lot--old issues of *Popular Mechanics* and biographies--or listen to the radio. So there were ways of seeing beyond my 12 X 14-foot refurbished attic space. And the double windows on one side overlooked other backyards--including Marcia's--so I was not completely contained in these walls. But the places I most dreamed of going felt inaccessible, too distant from where I was.

I wanted, for instance, to drive down Route 66 past Springfield, where I would attend Southwest Missouri State College in another month. I wanted to go on to the American West. I needed to feel that there was more than one stop on the road of my future, that there were as yet unseen opportunities more exciting than those on the path I saw laid out before me.

One small door, however, did swing open before me at the end of the evening and my rendezvous with Marcia: we set the time and place for another meeting. And this one had definite romantic possibilities.

"Would you like to see the tower?" Marcia asked me when we got back to the Circle. She was driving her family's second car, a Plymouth from the early 1950s.

"The tower?"

"On the roof of the hotel. Where the banner flies."

"Oh, I didn't know you called it 'the tower.' It looks more like a platform with a rail around it."

"Well, the tower, that's what everyone who works there calls it. It's neat at night. You can see the town, and the stars."

"You want to try the pool first?"

"The pool? You've already been in there," she laughed.

"Yeah, but I've been in there before this." Then I told her about the Bare-Ass Naked and Nude Swimming

246

Parties. She was surprised at our boldness--well, at my boldness, as Billy was well known for crazy stunts.

"Come on and go with us. It's great fun on a hot night." I pictured her trapped at home in her small bedroom. Wearing a filmy nightgown, she was standing beside an open window. She hoped for a breeze.

"You know how my mother is. If she ever found out . . ."

"Shoot, our parents sleep straight through the night. They don't hear anything. You should hear my father snore!"

"I don't know, my father is pretty restless." She chewed her lip. In my mind's eye I imagined that negligee stuck to her skin in the heat.

"I might come one night. But if I do, I'll be wearing my bathing suit!"

And then I had a vision, a vision of what Marcia and I, beginning in swimwear or nude, could do in the tower. It was a vision fueled, I now realize, not just by my fantasies of her in her bedroom but also by one of the pictures I had seen in Ancient Secrets of Sex.

As I've told you, my general image of coitus had featured man and woman in the missionary position, though I'd recognized intellectually that there were alternatives. Now I saw myself having sex with Marcia high atop the Banner Hotel.

After the obligatory caressing, she hoisted herself up on the wall that went around the platform, and I stepped between her knees. She wrapped her fine long legs around my waist, and we kissed long and sweet. Over her shoulder I saw the future gliding down Route 66 over a moonlit landscape.

The crude drawing in A.S.S. showed a man with his jaw set in determination, his legs taught and straight. The scene was a kitchen, and the woman sat perched on the counter. Her face was blurred, but I assumed she was consumed by ecstasy.

There was to be more excitement in my scenario, of course, after Marcia's and my initial engagement. But I could not picture that so precisely. I knew the final sensation from nights of what we called in those days "self-abuse." But the many pleasures of the whole act were no more within my grasp than the subjects I would one day be taking in college--hydrogeology, thermodynamics and statistical mechanics, topology.

I should have known, of course, that some other place would surely be the site of any coupling I would accomplish and that, if it ever occurred, the missionary position was far more likely to appeal to Marcia. Even if I had understood the craziness of my vision, however, I would not have missed the one chance I saw to be even better than a Banner guest. I would ride the hotel to ecstasy.

Suddenly dizzy at the prospect, I thought of the two of us up there doing it as the hotel's figurehead, the bride and bridegroom on a giant wedding cake!

VII

My tenuous sense of connection to the Banner Hotel's grandeur had faded completely by the time I reached the Landons' little house on Limestone Drive. I found the light on in the garage, and, inside, my father was working on his rock-collecting automobile, the Buick station wagon.

"Mark, just the person I was hoping to see," he said.

"Oh?" I held back in the darkness, not wanting him to pick up on the fact that my clothes were still damp.

"Yes, I've got some more drawer handles for the big cabinets. Now that you've got them finished, this is all you'll need."

Though I lagged behind my father's original schedule-- he had wanted all this done by the end of July--I had nearly finished refurbishing the inside of the station wagon.

"I should get to it this weekend," I offered.

"After that there's not much to do except recovering the floor."

"Yeah. You'll be set then." I still resented doing all this work just so he could have a more efficient utility vehicle. The gypsy boy's anger simmered at being put to work by his stern, adoptive parents.

"Did you see how I reversed the back seat?" He pulled it up from the folded position. Though still smaller than a conventional seat, it would allow the vehicle to carry four adults. "Now someone riding back here will look forward like everyone else."

I thought to myself that I would never again be riding there, facing forward down this man's path in life. My true destiny lay elsewhere. "You can take some students from the college, I bet." He often helped out the geology department at South Central Missouri State,

249

accompanying classes on field trips to caves and river beds.

By this time, I figured I'd had sufficient conversation to be appropriately filial, so I tried to end our exchange. "Well, I'm off to bed. It's gotten late."

"Were you working?" the family patriarch asked, closing the wagon's rear door.

"In the evening. Then I was out with friends." Of course, I had to work for spending money, as all allowances had stopped when I began high school. Oh, the injustice! At least I had found ways to be with my own set.

"You didn't happen by The DC, did you?"

I stiffened, though I shouldn't have been worried since Marcia and I had not stopped there. Still, the underlying guilt inspired by Billy's Bare-Ass Naked and Nude Swimming Parties set off an automatic worry alarm. And gypsy boys were falsely accused all the time. "The DC? No. I saw Marcia Terrell after her shift at the Banner. We rode home together."

"You know, The DC's not the kind of place you kids should be, especially late at night."

"Hey, I wasn't there. Didn't you hear me?" My voice rose, though I was just trying to be clear in my denial.

"I heard you." He came up close to me and pointed a finger. "Now you listen to me."

I hated it when he said this. As if his every word were voiced by an oracle!

"When I say you don't need to be at The DC, I mean you don't need to be at The DC."

Did he need to say it twice? 'You don't need to be at The DC.' Now I was really getting hot.

"When you see me there, let me know," I said and stepped away from him through the back door.

"Now just a minute," my father said, catching me by the arm. "Don't you speak to me in that tone."

"You're the one who's accusing . . . "

"Why is your sleeve so wet?"

"None of your business!" I'm afraid I shouted this last sentence. I guess I knew I couldn't explain everything. And then I bolted.

I raced through the kitchen, the dining room, and up the stairs toward my room. Although I was probably as much mad at myself as at my father, I exploded one more time in the middle of those steps. "Shit!" I said and took a swing at the wall.

I regretted it as soon as I'd done it.

In the first place, we just didn't say such things in front of our parents in those days. My father seldom swore, and, when he did, it was mild--"hell," "damn," "that son of a bitch!" I'd never heard my mother swear, ever. And in our family, who were casual about going to church but respectful of social etiquette, blurting out barnyard epithets would be more offensive than using the Lord's name in vain.

If Mom had heard me, I'd have a confrontation on my hands. In my room with the door shut, I hoped neither of them was following me up here.

The other part of my explosion guaranteed confrontation, whether it came immediately or was delayed even until the next day. I'd punched a hole in the wall.

In the houses of our neighborhood, all built in the post-war boom, walls were sheetrock hung on two-by-four frames, not plaster spread on slats. So, in one sense, I was quite lucky. My right cross landed squarely between two vertical frames, and the unsupported sheetrock broke neatly. If the wall had been plaster, or if my blow had landed on top of one of the supports, I probably would have broken my hand. As it was, I'd made a neat fist-sized hole chest high at about the eighth step on the stairway.

At first, I was actually a bit impressed with myself. Once again I was the trained jungle fighter I'd been under the tutelage of Ruth's Army boyfriend, Ron. Smash! there was a black space rimmed with powdered and bent sheetrock. I was a machine of destruction. Don't get me angry!

Before too long, though, I realized I'd made a mark that wouldn't disappear, that wouldn't be ignored. And, given the makeup of my father, there would have to be reprisals.

My father's strictness was legendary, at least in my view. The rigidity of his approach to life was forever represented in his instructions for assembling and flying a kite. Everything had to be done in a precise way, following a set order--sticks, paper, string, rag tail, all connected in an unchanging configuration. And the goal was to stabilize this kite against the backdrop of sky, an unmoving star below which more transitory forms came into being, passed through phases of existence, and then faded from the scene.

Like many sons, I am afraid, I forgot entirely the evidence I did have of a less unyielding man. Adept at baseball, he'd still loosened up amazingly for a recreational game of wiffleball on an office picnic. And he was, I now know, susceptible to sudden inspiration.

It's a strange thing, how children hear the stories of their parents' childhood but often make no connection to the adult personality. It's as if we can't believe the adults who dominate our lives once existed as kids.

My dad loved to the tell stories of how he and his fellow Kansas youths battled the fierce summer heat of the plains. But I saw those impulsive boys as characters in a story, figures unrelated to the man I knew as Assistant Director of the Missouri Geological Survey.

According to my father, he and his friends routinely had what they called "Hot Attacks" throughout the months when school was closed for summer vacation. At some point during their daily wanderings, when the 100-plus-degree heat went from oppressive to unbearable, one of the boys would call out, clutching his chest as if he were suffering heart failure, "Hot Attack."

And they would all race to the river, strip down to underwear, and leap in the water. The Arkansas River wound through my father's home town of Wichita, a thin brown ribbon in the dry months of summer, a rushing torrent at times of heavy rain in fall and spring.

In some versions of this story there were girls in Hot Attack episodes, but he never gave any details. And I didn't realize until years later, probably when a parent myself, that the grown man who determined and executed justice on Limestone Drive was in fact that same boy who dove into the Arkansas River leaving shirt and pants in a heap along the bank.

Later that night my mother knocked quietly at my bedroom door.

"Mark," she started cautiously. Then followed a mother's favorite question. "Are you OK?"

"OK? Sure."

Lying on my side in the bed, I pretended to be reading a history textbook. In fact, I'd once again been studying Ancient Secrets of Sex. Fortunately, I'd heard Mom on the way up the stairs and had had time to stuff A.S.S. under my pillow and prop *The Story of America: Pillar of the Free World* in front of my face.

"I guess you know what you did to the wall?" She sat on the edge of my bed, patting me on the hip.

"I think I dented it or something." I was already relieved that it was my mom, not my dad, I had to talk with about this. She could usually be counted on to be more lenient. On the other hand, what I was studying in my little book had created a bulging source of embarrassment not very far from where my mother's hand rested. So maybe it would have been better if my father'd come up the stairs.

"You knocked a hole in it!"

"Oh. Well, that's not going to bother anyone. Nobody comes up here, especially now that Charles is away."

The illustration I'd been studying in my little book had been of a man and a woman in the missionary position. But the woman wasn't lying passively under her partner. She'd locked her legs up around his waist and her fingers dug into his buttocks.

"It will have to be fixed. Your father and I," she hesitated. "We talked it over."

This was the part that could be bad, I realized. She'd been able to intervene on my behalf, but the punishment was still going to be a product of my father's strict code of discipline.

I was additionally uncomfortable at that moment because my state of arousal had not diminished. Any shifting of my position on the bed could make this fact conspicuous, so I had to stay frozen in a prone position.

"You'll have to repair the damage."

"Fix the hole?" This didn't sound too bad. I tried to focus my imagination on that effort rather than the intriguing realization that, even though he was on top, the man in A.S.S. was not necessarily in control of his destiny. . . .

"Yes, you can get the material at the lumber store. There's a patch kit."

"Ah."

"And Mark . . . " She paused again. I thought of the two lovers under my pillow, the man held in the scissors lock of the woman's legs.

"Yes."

"You're going to be just fine at college," she said.

"College?" I answered, wondering what in the world this had to do with anything. Then she walked out of my room.

256

VIII

I began work on my infamous "hole in the wall" the next day. The lumber store downtown did, in fact, have a kit for repairing such damage: rag stuffing to fill the hole and to brace the patch; a section of sheetrock, which you carved to fit the space; spackling to fill in around the edges and smooth the surface; sandpaper to prepare the area for paint. Before I filled the hole in the wall, however, it opened on another can of worms, so to speak, in my world of adolescent discovery.

I moved quickly on this repair job, hoping to forestall extended discussion with my parents of what had led up to it. Perhaps I also saw this as a way of delaying the final steps of reequipping the Buick Roadmaster Estate Wagon. There was no urgency, I thought to myself, in Dad's need for a better rockmobile or in my desire to provide it.

It would have been even better, as I said, if I'd completed the whole job of home repair in one day. When I was sneaking out of the house one more time, that hole in the wall provided some scary sights for the adopted gypsy boy of the Landon family .

Billy had called for another Bare-Ass Naked and Nude Swimming Party, and I considered it a point of honor not to decline.

"I'll be at your house at 1:15," I told him. While Billy generally organized our late hour expeditions, I was always the first one in motion. Billy had a habit of sleeping through the ring of the alarm clock he had wrapped inside a towel and left on his bedside table.

"OK, good. We've got titties coming this time, Mark." We were in front of Gunn's on my coffee break.

"Who?" I demanded. All I was thinking of these days was Marcia, so it didn't really matter to me. Still, any girl would make the whole enterprise more interesting.

"Sheila said she'd go with us once," Billy explained.

"Now that is a set of knockers. Are you sure she'll play by our rules?"

"You mean leave her clothes out under the trees? Sure, sure."

Well, I had my doubts that she'd agreed to this, but I wasn't going to object if it happened. While at one time all that drew Billy on to this beauty was her gorgeous auburn head of hair, I'd always admired her full figure. Her round hips filled out a pair of blue jeans better than anyone's I knew, including, I'm sorry to admit, Marcia Terrell's.

"What about Karen?"

"Karen's never going to go skinnydipping. She's worse than a Baptist." Billy was Catholic, so his ideas of Protestant morality were perhaps a bit severe.

"I'm not going to get Marcia to come either, but she's going to sneak me into the hotel later."

"Oooh, are you going to a room?"

"Maybe. We might."

Of course, I didn't think we'd do that. But boys have to exaggerate about conquests or possible conquests.

Billy, I know, would have loved to conquer Sheila Knight. She lived in a poor neighborhood between the Circle and Highway 00. She was in the "home economics" track at the high school, and most of us thought she'd marry, probably already pregnant, and drop out before graduation. Every boy in Fairfield, future BMOC or potential draftee, recognized her animal heat.

So, I had some rather intriguing possibilities opening up before me that weekend, skinnydipping with Sheila and taking Marcia to the Banner Hotel's famous tower. I likened myself, in moments of anticipation, to Meriwether Clark, famous builder of the Route 66 landmark roadside attraction.

Clark had, no doubt, visited the area before buying land and committing himself to construction. Perhaps he returned to Phipps County several times to survey potential sites, always looking into the future for the realization of his dream.

Billy and I had our aspirations. We pictured ourselves paddling around the Banner swimming pool with nude companions of the opposite sex. Just a glimpse of those nubile young forms sliding into the water was enough to make the risk worth taking. And, who knew, we might be even more lucky, copping in the dark a feel of warm floating flesh. "Whoops! Excuse me. Was that you?"

Meriwether Clark had ulterior motives, I was sure, behind his public-spirited development of Route 66 tourism. There was that mystery brunette he'd found somewhere in the line of business. And she was probably tucked away in the hotel's most expensive suite waiting for him as he closed a deal on longterm maintenance or agreed to a retirement plan for prospective employees. Would I have Marcia Terrell all to myself in a room officially listed as occupied?

On the way to this Bare-Ass Naked and Nude Swimming Party, however, I confronted, as I said, some things I hadn't foreseen.

I can't decide now if my procedure for slipping unseen and unheard from my attic bedroom through the hall, down the stairs, across the dining room, into the kitchen and out the backdoor was excessively elaborate or neatly appropriate. I do know it was rigorous in every detail.

It began with the muffled ringing of the travel alarm I had placed under my pillow, set for 12:45 in the morning. My folks were always asleep by 10:00, and I was confident they would have long been deep in dreamland by the time I slipped out of bed and got back into the clothes I'd worn that day.

I didn't put on any shoes, of course, as I had learned that I could avoid making noise most effectively in bare feet. I carried the shoes (a sock tucked into the toe of each) in one hand. In order to avoid bumping into anything at any point, I kept the other hand on the wall, the doorframe, the banister, the sideboard, the kitchen counter, the backdoor knob, the screen door. Of course, all lights were turned off and shades were drawn--it was the 1950s (which lingered well into the Sixties in the Midwest)! We were careful to keep our private lives absolutely secret.

In my memory of those days at least, no one had nightlights. As far as I understand American history, such things were not invented prior to the early 1970s, when my wife wanted to be sure we could see our way to the baby's room at 3:00 in the morning. Even if they had existed before that time, I'm confident the Assistant Director of the State Geological Survey would not have recognized a need for anyone to be up and about after 10:00 in the evening. And he would never have wasted so much electricity.

In the darkness that obscured my path that night I was guided almost exclusively by touch and by memory. I knew how many measured strides I needed to go from my room along the hall to the top of the stairs, the number of steps down to the first floor, the distance from hall to kitchen, and the obstacles past which I had to navigate through the entire journey. What I didn't remember on this occasion until I encountered it, however, was a hole in the wall.

My hand was trailing down that wall as I stepped with meticulous caution from the seventh to the sixth stair. Then, at the same moment, two fingers of my right hand slipped into a crack and I heard an odd, creaking sound coming from the hole itself, krrrrppp-krrrrppp.

That could not be me making a sound, I thought, though I froze instantly. I knew every step in this stairway, and only the third and ninth from the top, I believed, had the potential to creak when weight was put on them or taken off. I had not leaned against the wall where my hole was, so that could not be what jumped my heartrate from a slow thudding to rapid pounding. Krrrrppp-krrrrppp. What was that?

The two fingers of my right hand penetrated past the second knuckle into the wall, fitting snugly into a gap between the patch and the unbroken sheetrock around the hole. The stuffing I'd used hadn't quite filled the space of the hole, so there were several openings reaching all the way to the sheetrock on the other side of the wall. With my hand stuck in that gap, I contemplated the odd sound I heard: krrrrppp-krrrrppp.

I remembered reading Edgar Allen Poe's chilling story, "The Tell-tale Heart," in my eleventh grade English class. A guilty man hears--or believes he hears--the beating of the heart of his murder victim. It finally drives him mad--thump-thump, thump-thump, thump-thump. Was I hearing my own guilt for these late night escapades with Billy?

I thought of the rotating light on top of the police car that had scared Billy and me on our last cross-town outing. Parked beside the pool while waiting to redirect a confused truck driver, the officer's revolving beacon seemed to be counting off the seconds until we were caught--swish-swoosh, swish-swoosh, swish-swoosh.

I recalled my own labor on Dad's woodie, the Buick Roadmaster Estate Wagon. While paint remover had loosened the old finish on wood and metal, there were still hours of leaden-armed sanding and scraping to clean the grooves and corners. Grrrpp-grrrpp, Grrrpp-grrrpp, Grrrpp-grrrpp.

I suspect now, of course, that I knew instantly what that krrrrppp-krrrrppp sound was. But I repressed what it meant, repressed it until several days later when Marcia helped me graphically picture its source.

Those stairs I was descending, you might remember, had been put in through a coat closet on the first floor of our house. The closet was in the short hallway running from the dining room to the bathroom. On one side of

261

that hall, just past the closet, was my parents' bedroom. On the other was my little sister Beth's room.

The hall closet backed up on a double closet, turned ninety degrees to open into my parents' room. They lost a triangular portion in the top right corner of their storage area as the stairs continued on a slant from what had been the hall closet up to the floor above. In other words, the hole I knocked in the wall in a fit of teenage frustration was on the other side of my parents' bedroom wall.

And the sound I heard that night was the creaking of my parents' bed in what I came to understand was the rhythmically steady lovemaking of an organized scientist intent on finishing a necessary task--krrrrppp-krrrrppp, krrrrppp-krrrrppp, krrrrppp-krrrrppp.

IX

I pulled my fingers carefully from the hole. I took another step down the stairs, from the sixth to the fifth step. Then another, and another, and another, and another. Carefully, quietly, I completed my precisely scripted exit from the house.

In ten minutes Billy, Sheila, Marcia and I were all hiking along Kingshighway on our way to the Banner Hotel. It was a moonless night, but the sky was littered with stars.

"How do you know we won't be spotted?" asked Marcia of Billy. I, on the other hand, wondered how Billy and I were going to ogle one girl without getting spotted by another.

"Hey, the grown-up world is asleep at 10:00 p.m.," Billy countered. "Mark and I've been doing this for months and no one's seen us."

I was careful not to mention the police car, though technically, Billy was right: the officer hadn't seen us. In fact, the hotel had seemed deserted on most of our expeditions.

"Who watches our clothes?" asked Marcia.

"No one," Billy said. "I'm telling you, no one's awake. Mark?"

"We've been going all summer," I admitted. "We'll have the pool to ourselves."

"I'm just glad to be out of the house," said Sheila. None of us knew who was trying to keep her in the house. Belonging, really, to a completely different social class in Fairfield, she didn't come into our homes, and we'd never visited hers. We just ran into Sheila, either downtown or sometimes walking home. I don't know to this day how Billy got her to go with us on a Bare-Ass Naked and Nude Swimming Party.

"After, you know," said Billy. "we can stop at The D.C. and get something to eat. Have a smoke."

My hunger was not for food here, please understand. It was for what I'd see diving into that pool and what I might find high atop the Banner's tower.

Though the girls insisted that we look the other way when they ran up to the pool from the clump of trees where we'd stripped down for the swim, plenty of young beauty was, in fact, glimpsed later on the surface of that water. In an unanticipated, shocking burst of rebelliousness, Marcia had even foresworn her swimming suit!

The lights were off again in this area of the hotel grounds, though reflected light from street lights and parking areas prevented the scene from belonging to complete blackness. And the stars--well, the air was clearer in those pre-smog days, and my eyes sharper, so the visual feast, as I remember it, was abundant.

One might describe Billy's and my delight in terms of plump round shapes breaking the rippled surface of dark pool water. Breasts, calves, hips, shoulders, bottoms, knees, tummies bobbing and diving in a gentle dance.

Later my hands explored Marcia's fine form under the water, swiftly making my own excitement tangible. And her hands found my excitement enough times to make the evening rich for both of us. What Billy and Sheila were doing I didn't, after a while, see or care. Soon I only wanted to get my Banner Hotel employee alone up on the rooftop tower.

We had to dress for that short journey, leaving the other couple in the pool. Despite a reputation for confessing his worst desires and his greatest accomplishments, Billy kept to himself what happened between him and this beauty from outside our neighborhood. What I learned came to me indirectly, not from Billy.

I would do so much learning with Marcia that night it was quite some time before I even remembered to pump Billy about his adventures. Marcia started it all by looking

264

east from the tower, emitting a long sigh I took for satisfaction.

We could lean into the low wall that ran waist high around the tower, our thighs pressing the wood. A sturdy railing of metal pipe was attached to the wall's outer edge, preventing anyone from falling onto the slanted roof below. Above us the hotel's banner rustled now and then in a gentle breeze.

"See that darkness north of the highway?" Marcia asked me. She was gazing toward a large, relatively unpopulated area of south-central Missouri. The Ozark Mountains extend to their farthest point north in this region, and that rough country of small farms, dying villages, and eccentric loners retreating from modern civilization was accessible only by small twisting roads.

"Sure. Not much out there, though."

"Yes. An escape from the cares of this world."

"Now, back this way a little bit," I put an arm around her shoulders, pointed her due east. "That's the road to St. Louis, the city, where the action is. Lights, camera, action!"

"I'm not much for cities. I'm not even sure I'm good at smalltown life."

"You'll feel different next year, when it's time to start thinking about college."

I turned her another 180 degrees so we could look west, down Route 66 toward what I thought of as my future. Of course, I had another reason for putting her back to the railing that ran around the tower. I wanted to get her in the position I'd seen pictured in Ancient Secrets of Sex.

"Hop up here," I suggested, patting the top of the wall beside me. Placing her hands palms down on the rim, she did just that.

"Springfield's out there," I explained, pointing with one hand while the other went casually around her waist.

265

"Beyond those lights, of course." Although the Banner sat on the highest point around Fairfield, the town's growth had brought businesses right up to the hotel grounds-- gas stations, burger joints, the Dairy Queen. So it was hard to see much through the glow of town in that direction.

"You'll be there soon for college," Marcia agreed. "And then, who knows where you'll go. To California, maybe."

"Remember how we used to look out there from the park, and from the open space?"

"Sure. It was the future."

"Of course, you can't see things at night. In fact, I can't recognize much from here. Is that the courthouse?" I saw a large dark shape where I thought that building would be. "The hospital's there. And the Hotel Edwin Short here." Lights were on in some windows of the downtown hotel, once a rival to the Banner. With the building of Route 66 Bypass, however, business was drying up for the older establishments in town.

"I come up here for the stars," Marcia said. I stepped away from the wall and turned, facing her. I looked again at the canopy above us.

"You know, up here," she said. "above everything, you can be close to God."

Close to God? This was certainly not what I was think- ing about!

"Yes, it is inspiring. But there are some earthly things right here that could use your attention." I was ready to pick up where we'd left off underwater half an hour ago. I pushed my hips against her knees and leaned toward what I believed would be a long and satisfying kiss.

"You know, the Banner's not doing very well," said Marcia. Her knees hadn't come apart, and there was no kiss. "I wouldn't have a job here after high school."

"What? Of course you would, if you wanted. This is a famous roadside attraction."

"The owner tells me we're losing business. The interstate now makes the trip from St. Louis to Springfield or Tulsa so much faster. People don't stop. The cars are faster, plus gasoline's so cheap. People go right by us for bigger places."

I would later realize this was true not just for Fairfield but for the entire Midwest. Easterners and Californians led the nation in fashion, entertainment, popular culture. And the trend setters jetted from coast to coast over what they saw as a vast, empty wasteland, staid Middle America. Automobile travel down famous roads like Route 66 was dwindling, and the Banner's banner flew over less and less.

"Besides, you'll be gone in another year. You can come to S.M.S. with me."

"I'll be gone in another week. I have something to tell you, Mark."

"What?"

"You know those two women I told you about, who eat at the restaurant?"

"The ones who seem like sisters?"

"Yes. They are sisters. They're nuns."

"Nuns? Oh, OK. So?"

"They've been helping out this year at the Catholic school, St. Patrick's. And I've gotten to know them."

"You're not Catholic," I said, not really following her. I knew only a few Catholics in Fairfield, though those families, plus other people in the surrounding counties, were enough to maintain a school for grades 1-8. As many as one in ten households in Phipps County was Catholic, but I'd never particularly recognized their presence in the neighborhoods around me.

The Landons were, as I've said before, pretty casual about their religious life. And we didn't participate in the church rivalries that can consume a small town. In general, we shared a fundamental Protestant distrust of the Catholic Church, I suppose. I know there was concern about Kennedy being a Catholic President. But that a religious minority constituted a significant force in our community had never really occurred to me.

"Men," Marcia said suddenly, apparently changing the subject. "Men think women are only good for one thing--having sex."

"I don't think . . . " I couldn't really complete my objection to this statement. The statement was too direct, too radical for those times. At least it was too direct for me.

Nobody I knew talked about "having sex." We--that is, boys--thought about sex as something we did individually. We would be, if we were so lucky, "getting some." The girls/women necessary to the process for us were only incidental.

"No, it's true. They want us to have babies or to have fun with them without having babies. That's why I was studying up on contraception, birth control. I thought maybe I could have the fun and not worry about the babies."

I blushed, thinking about Ancient Secrets of Sex. She had been interested in the realities of reproduction, while all I wanted was a guide to what goes where and how.

"We were having fun a little while ago," I murmured. I almost said that we weren't thinking of having babies, but I knew this wouldn't please her. The cold logic of her argument was actually beginning to sink in with me, though it would be weeks before I followed the full reach of her thinking.

"Oh, it's fun, all right," she smiled. "But I've come to believe that the fun should belong only in holy matrimony. And maybe some of us girls aren't right for marriage. This, this was really my last fling, a one-more-time thing. If I've learned anything from my mother . . . "

She stopped there. I knew, of course, that her parents' marriage had always been fragile. Mrs. Terrell was shy, retiring, afraid; Marcia's father outgoing, lively, and good looking. There had always been rumors about his straying.

"I'm becoming a nun, Mark. In one week I'll enter a special order under the sponsorship of sisters Mary and Anne. This is a last night together for the two of us, or at least it is this side of heaven."

X

If there hadn't been that pipe railing around the tower, I would have fallen onto the roof down to the ground over three stories below me. Marcia a nun? Marcia a nun!

Somehow, surprising though it was at the moment, her retreat from a troubled world was something that I would gradually realize I could understand. She'd had shocks in life, more disappointments than the average child in America's age of post-war innocence. And, when I really thought about it, I was probably one of those disappointments.

After all, what had I ever wanted from her but the chance to experiment sexually? From inadvertently (but pleasurably) feeling her breast during a childhood game of Kick the Can, to bumping up against her on a merry-go-round as an adolescent, to fumbling under her clothes in the backseat of my parents' '52 Studebaker as a gypsy boy adopted by a conventional family, I was always just out to get some.

But what was "some"? I thought of one picture in our 12th grade biology book, *Plant and Animal Life*. It was a schematic diagram of a pregnant woman, the fetus silhouetted within an outline of the womb. (Other body parts, of course, were not represented.) It was what women did. It was where sex led.

Reproduction, I thought, going over in my mind Marcia's question to me some weeks earlier and considering the answer she'd found in a life of celibacy. What I was studying in Ancient Secrets of Sex was utterly unconnected to perhaps the single most amazing creative act on the planet, the generation of life. Me, the potential engineer, I had no appreciation of what a construction that was!

I didn't look so good in this history. In fact, I wondered why Marcia bothered with me at all.

"Why did you come with me tonight?" I asked her on the tower.

"Oh, well, maybe I wanted to go to one Bare-ass Naked and Nude Swimming Party before I turned to a life of prayer."

"Yeah, but . . . "

"Maybe I wanted one more date with you. After all, Mark, you've been the only one . . . the only one I ever really wanted to go out with."

"But . . . I still want to go out with you." I said this as a question, a complaint.

She smiled, touched my arm. "I like boys. But boys turn into men. And men can't seem to get along with women."

Then Marcia explained that her parents were now officially breaking up. Her father had rented an efficiency apartment near the college, but would soon move to St. Louis and a new job. Marcia's mother was returning to her own hometown in Oklahoma, going back to the house she'd grown up in and her ancient but still capable mother.

There had been some ugly scenes in the house behind ours on the Circle. She shuddered when she reported this, and I was surprised I hadn't heard shouting over the backyards, nasty threats, the breaking of furniture. At least there had been no violence directed at her mother or herself. At least Marcia claimed that.

In the end Marcia hadn't known which parent she wanted to go with. She cleverly went between the horns of that dilemma.

Like most of my generation, I never thought about divorce as a genuine danger to my family or the families of those near me. People married for life in our mythology, like Ozzie and Harriet, George and Gracie, all the Moms and Pops of successful little businesses. Even when, just a few years later, one of my aunts left her husband abruptly while I and her children were in college, the whole event remained incredible, remote and almost fictional.

Of course, there had been all along some divorces, a few remarriages, and quite a number of adulteries in the town of Fairfield. But these were just more of those things we blinded ourselves to in those days. We believed so much in the stable family of the stable Circle neighborhood in the stable community of Fairfield, that, in our imaginations, we sealed up fissures and breaks as soon as they occurred. We saw union and harmony despite the evidence of a strained foundation beneath it all. We sensed the 60s, but turned our eyes and ears and minds backwards toward an Eden washed with nostalgia.

That night near the end of my last summer in Fairfield under the wings of my parents and a superficially unified community, Marcia and I climbed down the narrow bending stairway in the middle of the tower, walked the length of the Banner's top floor, took an elevator to the ground level, passed through the end doors out onto the grounds, and started walking home.

As I passed down the hall, I noticed chipped paint on the doorjambs. I realized that many layers of thick green enamel still couldn't cover completely the graffiti etched into the metal above the payphone--"For a good time, call Suzie." The hotel's carpet was worn, the curtains frayed, the concrete steps onto the lawn cracked with age.

In between the hotel and the Dairy Queen, I turned and looked back at this symbol of an age, the Route 66 establishment whose "facilities are far ahead of anything else by the roadside and exceed the average accommodations of first-class establishments in large cities."

"You know, it was a grand place."

From this direction, the magnificence of the building was revived for me. I forgot what Marcia had said about dwindling guests, the cost of needed repairs, the challenge of advertising in an age of interstate travel. The Banner's wings reached across the high ridge as if it might ascend into the night sky, soar above Fairfield, swing west, and follow the great highway, Route 66, toward a wide open American West.

"The hotel?" said Marcia. "Oh, yes. It has been grand, and I'm sorry to leave it. But I know the direction my life should go now." She was going east, not west, to a Catholic retreat near Irontown. I would leave in less than two weeks for Springfield, 100 miles in the opposite direction.

Still, I saw myself and my friends within the framework embraced by Meriwether Clark, builder of the Banner Hotel. We would always be the kids of Route 66 and its attendant structures, optimistic young people following the sun in pursuit of America's dream. Free country, land of opportunity, wide open spaces. Maybe one day I would create a similar monument, something to shape the future.

I had thought I could hold my fellow residents of the Circle and this sense of our identity together as I started the next phase of life. I would go away to college, but keep friends--especially a girlfriend--back home.

As it turned out, I would see Marcia again only after the years had made both of us into different people. During my college days she was as lost to me as if she'd gone all the way to Rome and back to the Middle Ages.

As I walked down Limestone Drive, having come around the top of the Circle from her house toward mine, I had to ask myself again who I was if she was a child of God.

Well, for one thing I was the son of Richard and Susan Landon, who greeted me at breakfast the next morning with unusually close attention. Beth was already up and playing at a friend's house across the street.

"What are you both looking at?" I asked, a bit nervously. Despite Billy's and my assurances to the girls last night, I wondered if my parents could have been awake when I came in. I worried that Dad had seen the hole in the wall again and been reinspired to anger. Had someone informed them that I was an occasional wee-hour customer at The DC? Did they think I had been eaves-dropping on their lovemaking?

(Actually, it was not me who had been spotted at The DC, but Billy and Sheila. I would learn this later, on my first weekend home from college. According to a friend who told a friend what Billy had told him, they were having that post-coitus cigarette so famous in our culture, so sought after by all adolescent boys.)

"Going to work?" my father asked.

"Not until noon, my usual Thursday schedule."

"Hm. Want a ride?" my Mom asked. In general, I walked to Gunn's, less than a mile, accepting Mom's rights to the Studebaker. But if one of them was going my way, I often took the lift.

"Oh, I don't know. Maybe." They seemed to have something on their mind. And I didn't like it.

She giggled nervously. Dad looked rather severely at her and then said, "I would take you, but, you know, work . . ."

"Sure, OK. I guess I'll have some breakfast. I could finish installing those handles later. That about finishes the Buick."

"Oh, that reminds me. We have a problem there. Come out and take a look with me."

"How about later, Dad? I just got up, you know."

Mom tugged on my shirt sleeve. "No, come on. I think you need to see this."

Now I was getting worried. There was clearly something going on here. I checked to make sure this wasn't one of my dreams in which I discovered I was naked, the odd one in a crowd of people who had for unknown reasons failed to put on clothes that morning.

We went through the backdoor in the kitchen, on into the garage, out the front into the driveway. On top of the Buick Roadmaster Estate Wagon, parked to one side of the drive, sat a giant bow, not of ribbon but a broad swath of blue cloth. The car shone in the morning sun.

"Congratulations!" said my father.

I was dumbfounded. What did he mean?

"It's yours, Mark," said my Mom, her smile now completely out of control.

"Mine?"

"The car, son. It's for you to take to Springfield, to college."

"But I thought . . . "

"Oh, it was your father's little joke. Making you think you were fixing it up for him, for his rock finding trips. But, all along, it was for you, of course. You need a car, you know, to come back home for visits." Her eyes were a bit misty.

"You'll need all the places for your stuff. Look here," he pulled open a back door. "Books can go in the side cabinets. You can keep snacks, paper, pencils, odds and ends in these little net pockets you suspended from the roof. And an engineer will need space to put drawing boards, surveying rods, all the equipment."

Opening the back door, my Mom called, "These bins can hold laundry, divided into darks and lights, of course." As she worked a triangular pulldown compartment I had constructed, I remembered her own experience in design, when she had worked first in the New York garment industry and then for the war effort. "You can bring things back for me to wash. You'll want to come home, of course, some."

"The engine's completely overhauled, Mark," said my father. "This baby's going to run for your four years easily. And look at the wood!" That was his favorite part of

276

the car, the woodie's gleaming side panels. I had hated them when I was doing the refinishing--sanding, staining, varnishing--but all of a sudden they looked beautiful.

And maybe I didn't look too bad myself, getting hugs from both parents. Well, as I'd known all along, they were my biological parents.

I had toyed with the idea that there was another me somewhere, another traveler through life temporarily trapped on Limestone Drive in Fairfield, Missouri. Unlike those confused truckers, who sometimes got turned around trying to follow Business Route 66 through town, however, I'd known north and south, left and right, up and down for a long time now. In fact the bearings I'd developed here would steer me right through college and beyond, even in Vietnam, though that's a story for another day.

Right now I accepted, pretty much completely, the conviction that this sense of direction would send me off to college, off to a new phase in life. It was still down Route 66, fortunately, still westward toward a larger future. And I knew I was ready.

The End

Epilogue: Romantic Destiny

Here is the way I now see my love life, the adolescent phase of which came to an unexpected end on top of the Banner Hotel one warm August night in my nineteenth year. Marcia Terrell, my childhood sweetheart, retreated to a nunnery deep in the Ozark foothills, and I piled all my worldly belongings into a 1953 Buick Estate Wagon (last of the great "woodies") and drove off into the sunset--well, west toward where the sun sets but also to Springfield, Missouri, to begin college.

The fates do not, however, deliver a beautiful young coed to me there, the future love of my life and mother of my children. Oh, there are candidates for those roles at Southwest Missouri State College, but some reject my invitations in that direction, and with others I stop short of making any offers. (I do, however, lose my virginity in that first year of college, not unlike, I believe, many in my generation.)

Believe it or not, the true love affair in this history had begun more than a dozen years earlier in a small village in Virginia. The father of a family of four there had been struggling with respiratory problems, his lung capacity severely restricted by numerous bouts of childhood pneumonia. His doctor says he must give up the construction business he founded and with which he stands to become a rich man, if he can remain healthy. But the physical strain is simply too much for him.

There is another solution: "Go west, Bradford," says Doctor Thomas Baldwin, an old friend.

"What do you mean? Leave Tidewater?" Bradford Wilfer asks. He's sitting on the examining table in T-shirt and shorts.

"That's right. This climate's no good for you. Mold in the winter, mildew in the summer, pollen in between. You need to be where the air is clear, away from East Coast pollution and Southern dampness. I'd say Arizona, California, somewhere basically hot and dry."

"California? That's the last place I'd like to be! Los Angeles is home for Hollywood, all that tinsel and glitter."

"Yes, but you'll live to get used to it. There's your family to think of, Brad. You've got two daughters who need to be provided for. And not through cashing in some insurance policy!" And it's those two, Arabella and Mary Anne, who inspire the move.

On a blistering hot mid-summer day in the early 1950s, the Wilfer family pulled away from Greenland, Virginia, passed by Richmond on their way through the Appalachian Mountains, across the Mississippi River, over the Great Plains states, past the Rockies, and into Santa Barbara.

Marie Wilfer was hired to teach seventh grade social studies that fall, and Brad found an office job with a small company kept afloat through contract work with the state government. The girls prepared to start school in a low adobe building facing the Pacific Ocean. But a week later they were all in the car again.

The Wilfer family's car travel was much different than the Landons', by the way, where everyone had a place and stayed in it. In that Missouri family father drove, mother navigated, and the children sat in back in a fixed order--me behind Dad, Beth in the middle, Charles behind Mom.

But the Virginia Wilfers--they were everywhere, or so I've been told. While it's true that Brad drove more often, Marie took her turn at the wheel as well. Pappa played the alphabet game with his daughters or trounced them regularly in Hearts.

The girls generally began each day in the backseat, but Mother was quite willing to trade places with either. And sometimes all three females piled into the back for story-telling, twenty questions, lunch on the go.

Oh, and there's a dog. Brad Wilfer always had dogs, eccentric, generally lovable, family dogs. So riding along with the family of four on the way to California is a slobbery, asthmatic, endearing seven-year-old bulldog. Buster's presence requires constant rearrangement of the passengers in the 1948 Chrysler sedan because only the parents can tolerate his doggy breath and constant drool for any length of time.

On sunny days, he rises up on his back legs and hangs his giant head out one of the rear windows, so Marie puts one of the girls in the navigator's position and moves to the back. On rainy days, Buster wants to be in front on top of Mother's feet, where the car's ventilating system sends a stream of cool air down to the floor and where she shares cool water from a jug. And at night the dog insists on lying at full length on his back to sleep. So the three ladies share the backseat.

They are driving both day and night on the way back from California. Yes, after two months a shared homesickness and Brad's special disgust with all features of West Coast lifestyle inspire the Wilfers to pack up everything they own and head east again. It may kill him sooner than later, he tells Marie, but this Virginia native will not die on foreign soil.

His decision goes against the trends, of course, as the Sunbelt is laying the groundwork for its later emergence as a distinctive region of America. The year-round sun on open beaches, the sense of Disneyland as Mecca, an emphasis on youth as a sustainable lifestyle, and new jobs coming from the very process of growth lead to the creation of a culture of recreation. And citizens from all walks of life and states of the union migrate toward the promised land. But the Wilfers turn their back on all this.

And what I say happened is this: on the drive through Missouri, the Wilfer family of course took Route 66. (The major east/west highways crossing the Appalachians in

281

those days directed you toward St. Louis; from there "America's Highway" is the logical route to Southern California.) And at that time there were no bypasses around small towns, so the Wilfers followed the highway into town, where Fairfield called the route "Kingshighway". Kingshighway, remember, ran near the Circle, just the other side of the Cut through which passed east- and westbound freight and passenger trains.

Bella Wilfer and Mark Landon, then, would have been, at a single moment many years ago, at the ages of five and six respectively, separated only by the Missouri-Pacific railroad tracks and the row of houses across from mine on Limestone.

Or were we really separated by a hundred yards? There is a fuzzy memory I retain from early childhood of straying out of the bounds set by my parents when we first moved to the Circle. I don't know how, but Billy Rhodes and I (and perhaps others whose identities I can't quite drag to the surface of my memory) end up standing alongside a busy street, cars and trucks moving past us at a speed significantly greater than we are used to seeing in our own quiet neighborhood.

I'm going to catch hell for this, I know. And that's probably why I remember it now.

Another muddled area of my brain's memory tells me that my parents had gone uptown for a quick interview at the bank, perhaps to negotiate a mortgage (we'd first rented the house on Limestone). Charles and I were left under the supervision of the mother next door, who could have been distracted by any number of other children passing through in Circle play.

Was it historic Route 66 I gazed at that summer day more than forty years ago? Did the Wilfer family pass directly in front of me that sunny day, with Buster leaning out the passengerside rear window and Arabella perched opposite, Mary Anne the nominal navigator checking road signs? Did the earth pause just the tiniest bit in its daily rotation, the stars shift into a fortuitous alignment, the forces of history and biology coordinate in a miracu-lous coincidence?

Of course, they did. Arabella and I saw each other and fell in love on the spot. A vision for each was etched on the deepest map of memory.

True, the Wilfer car sped past. I watched other cars moving east and west. And we didn't see each other again until after college, nearly twenty years later and in neither Missouri nor Virginia. But we were destined, I believe, to be together from that moment on Route 66.

Bella Wilfer Landon, a down-to-earth sort who has her own version of how we met, thinks this is all foolishness. She didn't see me, she says, forty-five years ago alongside a Fairfield city street. She doesn't remember any part of the Show Me state on that continent-crossing journey.

If she had been looking out the window, she claims, it's fanciful to think she would be struck by the sight of my five-year-old self. Pictures in the Landon family album do not reveal an unforgettable face, she observes. Not much distinguishes one snotty-nosed boy from another, any-way. And, finally, it's absurd to think that the memory of any such encounter, even had it happened, would have remained with her for a decade and a half, predisposing her to recognize, let alone respond to, an adult me.

I nod agreement but still say to her, "Even so . . . "

In more playful moods, I ask her innocently, "Honey?" (She hates to be called "Honey.") "Honey, was it on your way out to California or the way back that we met?"

Usually, she resists my either-or assertion and doesn't even answer. At other times she remarks casually, "I re-member a possum flattened on the highway in Oklahoma pretty clearly. And a pig rooting by the roadside outside East St. Louis. Where did you say you grew up?"

At such moments I recall thinking I'm a child raised by gypsies.

But mostly I hold on to this version of my past, our past. We met and fell in love as children, grew up apart, then were reunited by destiny on a baseball diamond in Atlanta, Georgia. Now we live, we hope, happily ever after in St. Louis, the city with the arch through which America traveled to the frontier. We live along the path by which fabled Route 66 snaked its way into history during the middle third of the twentieth century.

If others continue to find this journey of my generation worth following, I'll pick up the story of how I came to settle for good in St. Louis another day soon. Until then, gentle reader, fare thee well.

The Route 66 Novel Series: Route 66 Kids

Route 66 kids are the generation that grew up in America after World War II, experiencing childhood in the innocent 1950s but coming to adulthood in the turbulent 1960s. But Route 66 Kids are also the "children" of novelist Michael Lund, each book a product of memory and imagination.

Growing Up on Route 66

This novel, first in the series, was published by BeachHouse Books in October 2000. Set in a Missouri small town along "America's Main Street," the story takes places in a neighborhood known to the children growing up there as the "Circle." That time and place are remembered by the novel's narrator as ideal, but closer scrutinyrepeatedly--and often humorously--complicates this innocent picture. In growing up we continually confront things that do not make sense to us. Then, in sudden moments of inspiration the pieces come together. For those growing up in the 1950s, of course, the biggest mystery of childhood was sex. And central characters in this story, Mark Landon and Marcia Terrell, are repeatedly surprised as parts of this great puzzle take shape in and around them.

Route 66 Kids

A sequel of sorts to *Growing up on Route 66*, this novel is a Babyboomers' coming-of-age story, reminding us that children always wonder about their origin. When kids asked "Where do I come from?" in the 1950s, they were really asking about sex, the biggest mystery for those growing up in an age of American innocence. Cold War children also wanted to know more about their parents and the community which surrounded them. Central characters in this novel, Mark Landon and Marcia Terrell, find out about the past in the structures of the Missouri small town they live in, which is located along "America's Main Street." Route 66. Throughout their story this great highway endures as a symbol of the promise this nation enjoyed at mid-century.

Work in progress

A Left-hander on Route 66

Not everyone would share in America's post-war prosperity of the 1950s. Fairfield, Missouri native Hugh Noone knew he had been born on the wrong side of the tracks, and society's reaction to his left-handedness convinced him that he would not be in a position to enjoy new freedoms coming with the Sexual Revolution of the 1960s. In fact, he writes his life story from jail, appealing his wrongful conviction and imprisonment twenty years after the event. But revealing the details of his past and effecting a resolution of his case mean a dramatic rearrangement of his world.

Miss Route 66

In this novel, Susan Bell tells the story of her candidacy in Fairfield, Missouri's annual beauty contest. Now married and with teenage children in St. Louis, she recounts her youthful adventure in this small town along "America's Highway." At the same time, she plans a return to Fairfield in order to right injustices she feels were done to some young contestants in the Miss Route 66 Pageant. Throughout this journey she wonders what, if anything, was feminine in the "Mother Road" of the 1950s.

Route 66 to Vietnam

This novel takes characters from earlier works in the Route 66 Novel Series farther west than Los Angeles, official destination of the famous highway, Route 66. Mark Landon and Billy Rhodes find the values they grew up on challenged by America's role in Southeast Asia. But elements of their upbringing represented by the Mother Road also sustain them in ways they could never have anticipated.

Michael Lund, the author, grew up in Rolla, Missouri, and now teaches college composition and literature in Virginia. He is at work on more books in his Route 66 series about growing up in 1950s middle America.

Books from Science & Humanities Press:

HOW TO TRAVEL—A Guidebook for Persons with a Disability – Fred Rosen (1997) ISBN 1-888725-05-2, 5½ X 8¼, 120 pp, $9.95 **18-point large print edition** (1998) ISBN 1-888725-17-6 8¼X10½, 120 pp, $19.95

HOW TO TRAVEL in Canada—A Guidebook for A Visitor with a Disability – Fred Rosen (2000) ISBN 1-888725-26-5, 5½X8¼, 180 pp, $14.95 **MacroPrint-Books**™ edition (2001) ISBN 1-888725-30-3 7X8, 16 pt, 200 pp, $19.95

AVOIDING Attendants from HELL: A Practical Guide to Finding, Hiring & Keeping Personal Care Attendants 2nd Edn—June Price, (2002), accessible plastic spiral bind, ISBN 1-888725-72-9   8¼X10½, 125 pp, $16.95, School/library edition (2002)   ISBN 1-888725-60-5, 8¼X6½, 200 pp, $18.95

If Blindness Comes – K. Jernigan, Ed. (1996) Strategies for living with visual impairment. 18-point Large type Edition with accessible plastic spiral bind, 8¼X10½, 110 pp, $7 (not eligible for quantity discounts— distributed at cost with permission of the National Federation of the Blind)

The Bridge Never Crossed—A Survivor's Search for Meaning. Captain George A. Burk (1999) The inspiring story of George Burk, lone survivor of a military plane crash, who overcame extensive burn injuries to earn a presidential award and become a highly successful motivational speaker.   ISBN 1-888725-16-8, 5½X8¼, 170 pp, illustrated. $16.95   MacroPrintBooks™ Edition (1999) ISBN 1-888725-28-1 $24.95

Crash, Burn and Learn—A Survivor's Strategy for Managing Change—Captain George A. Burk (2002) Principles of Leadership and Total Quality Management by Captain George Burk, inspiring survivor of a military plane crash, who overcame extensive burn injuries to earn a presidential award. ISBN 1-888725-59-1, 5½X8¼, 120 pp, $16.95

Paul the Peddler or The Fortunes of a Young Street Merchant—Horatio Alger, jr A Classic reprinted in accessible large type, (1998 MacroPrintBooks™ reprint in 24-point type) ISBN 1-888725-02-8, 8¼X10½, 276 pp, $16.95

The Wisdom of Father Brown—G.K. Chesterton (2000) A Classic collection of detective stories reprinted in accessible 22-point type ISBN 1-888725-27-3 8¼X10½, 276 pp, $18.95

24-point Gospel—The Big News for Today – The Gospel according to Matthew, Mark, Luke & John (KJV) in 24-point typeType is about 1/3 inch high. Now, people with visual disabilities like macular degeneration can still use this important reference. "Giant print" books are usually 18 pt. or less ISBN 1-888725-11-7, 8¼X10½, 512 pp, $24.95

Buttered Side Down - Short Stories by Edna Ferber (BeachHouse Booksreprint 2000) A classic collection of stories by the beloved author of *Showboat, Giant, and Cimarron.* ISBN 1-888725-43-5, 5½X8¼, 190 pp, $12.95 MacroPrintBooks™ **Edition** (2000) ISBN 1-888725-40-0 7X8¼,16 pt, 240 pp $18.95

The Four Million: The Gift of the Magi & other favorites. Life in New York City around 1900—O. Henry. MacroPrintBooks™ reprint (2001) ISBN 1-888725-41-9 7X8¼, 16 pt, 270 pp $18.95; ISBN 1-888725-03-6, 8¼X10½, 22 pt, 300pp, $22.95

Bar-20: Hopalong Cassidy's Rustler Roundup—Clarence Mulford (reprint 2000). Classical Western Tale. Not the TV version. ISBN 1-888725-34-6 5½X8¼, 223 pp, $12.95 MacroPrintBooks™ edition ISBN 1-888725-42-7, 8¼X6½, 16 pt, 385pp, $18.95

Nursing Home – Ira Eaton, PhD, (1997) You will be moved and disturbed by this novel. ISBN 1-888725-01-X, 5½X8¼, 300 pp, $12.95 **MacroPrintBooks™ edition** (1999) ISBN 1-888725-23-0,8¼X10½, 16 pt, 330 pp, $18.95

Perfect Love-A Novel by Mary Harvatich (2000) Love born in an orphanage endures ISBN 1-888725-29-X 5½X8¼, 200 pp, $12.95 **MacroPrintBooks™** edition (2000) ISBN 1-888725-15-X, 8¼X10½, 16 pt, 200 pp, $18.95

Eudora Light™ v 3.0 Manual (Qualcomm 1996) ISBN 1-888725-20-6½, extensively illustrated. 135 pp, 5½ X 8¼, $9.95

The Essential **Simply Speaking Gold** – Susan Fulton, (1998) How to use IBM's popular speech recognition package for dictation rather than keyboarding. Dozens of screen shots and illustrations. ISBN 1-888725-08-7 8¼ X8, 124 pp, $18.95

Begin Dictation *Using ViaVoice Gold* -**2nd Edition**– Susan Fulton, (1999), Covers ViaVoice 98 and other versions of IBM's popular continuous speech recognition package for dictation rather than keyboarding. Over a hundred screen shots and illustrations. ISBN 1-888725-22-2, 8¼X8, 260 pp, $28.95

Tales from the Woods of Wisdom - (book I) - Richard Tichenor (2000) In a spirit someplace between *The Wizard of Oz* and *The Celestine Prophecy*, this is more than a childrens' fable of life in the deep woods. ISBN 1-888725-37-0, 5½X8¼, 185 pp, $16.95 **MacroPrintBooks™** edition (2001) ISBN 1-888725-50-8 6X8¼, 16 pt, 270 pp $24.95

Me and My Shadows—Shadow Puppet Fun for Kids of All Ages - Elizabeth Adams, Revised Edition by Dr. Bud Banis (2000) An illustrated guide to the art of shadow puppet entertainment using tools always at hand wherever you go. A perfect gift for children and adults. ISBN 1-888725-44-3, 7X8¼, 67 pp, 12.95 **MacroPrintBooks™** edition (2002) ISBN 1-888725-78-8 8½X11 lay-flat spiral, 18 pt, 67 pp, $16.95

Growing Up on Route 66 —Michael Lund (2000) ISBN 1-888725-31-1 Novel evoking fond memories of what it was like to grow up alongside "America's Highway" in 20th Century Missouri. (Trade paperback) 5½ X8¼, 260 pp, $14.95 **MacroPrintBooks**™ edition (2001) ISBN 1-888725-45-1 8¼X6½, 16 pt, 330 pp, $24.95

Route 66 Kids —Michael Lund (2002) ISBN 1-888725-70-2 Sequel to *Growing Up on Route 66*, continuing memories of what it was like to grow up alongside "America's Highway" in 20th Century Missouri. (Trade paperback) 5½ X8¼, 270 pp, $14.95 **MacroPrintBooks**™ edition (2002) ISBN 1-888725-71-0 8¼X6½, 16 pt, 350 pp, $24.95

MamaSquad! (2001) Hilarious novel by Clarence Wall about what happens when a group of women from a retirement home get tangled up in Army Special Forces. ISBN 1-888725-13-3 5½ X8¼, 200 pp, $14.95 **Macro-PrintBooks**™ edition (2001) ISBN 1-888725-14-1 8¼X6½ 16 pt, 300 pp, $24.95

Sexually Transmitted Diseases—Symptoms, Diagnosis, Treatment, Prevention-2nd Edition – NIAID Staff, Assembled and Edited by R.J.Banis, PhD, (2002) Teacher friendly --free to copy for education. Illustrated with more than 50 photographs of lesions, ISBN 1-888725-58-3, 8¼X6½, 200 pp, $18.95

Once in a Green Room: A Novel—Keri Baker (2001). After being raped and having an abortion while in college, a young woman struggles to deal with her feelings and is ultimately helped by the insights she gains from her special education students. Contact information for help groups throughout the United States.Part of proceeds contributed to RAINN. ISBN 1-888725-38-9, 5½X8¼, 160 pp, $14.95 **MacroPrintBooks**™ edn (2001) ISBN 1-888725-61-3, 8¼X6½, 16pt, 200 pp, $24.95

Ropes and Saddles—Andy Polson (2001) Cowboy (and other) poems by Andy Polson. Reminiscences of the Wyoming poet. ISBN 1-888725-39-7, 5½ X 8¼, 100 pp, $9.95

The Stress Myth -Serge Doublet, PhD (2000) A thorough examination of the concept that 'stress' is the source of unexplained afflictions. Debunking mysticism, psychologist Serge Doublet reviews the history of other concepts such as 'demons', 'humors', 'hysteria' and 'neurasthenia' that had been placed in this role in the past, and provides an alternative approach for more success in coping with life's challenges. ISBN 1-888725-36-2, 5½X8¼, 280 pp, $24.95

Virginia Mayo—The Best Years of My Life (2002) Autobiography of film star Virginia Mayo as told to LC Van Savage. From her early days in Vaudeville and the Muny in St Louis to the dozens of hit motion pictures, with dozens of photographs. ISBN 1-888725-53-2, 6½ X 8¼, 300 pp, $16.95

To Norma Jeane With Love, Jimmie -Jim Dougherty as told to LC Van Savage (2001) ISBN 1-888725-51-6 The sensitive and touching story of Jim Dougherty's teenage bride who later became Marilyn Monroe. Dozens of photographs. "The Marilyn Monroe book of the year!" As seen on TV. 5½X8¼, 200 pp, $16.95 **MacroPrintBooks**™ edition ISBN 1-888725-52-4, 8¼X6½, 16 pt, 290pp, $24.95

Rhythm of the Sea --Shari Cohen (2001). Delightful collection of heartwarming stories of life relationships set in the context of oceans and lakes. Shari Cohen is a popular author of Womens' magazine articles and contributor to the *Chicken Soup for the Soul* series. ISBN 1-888725-55-9, 8X6.5 150 pp, $14.95 **MacroPrintBooks**™ edition (2001) ISBN 1-888725-63-X, 8¼X6½, 16 pt, 250 pp, $24.95

The Job—Eric Whitfield (2001) A story of self-discovery in the context of the death of a grandfather.. A book to read and share in times of change and Grieving. ISBN 1-888725-68-0, 5½ X 8¼, 100 pp, $12.95 **MacroPrintBooks**™ edition (2001) ISBN 1-888725-69-9, 8¼X6½, 18 pt, 150 pp, $18.95

Copyright Issues for Librarians, Teachers & Authors–R.J. Banis, PhD, (Ed). 2nd Edn (2001) Protecting your rights, respecting others'. Information condensed from the Library of Congress, copyright registration forms. ISBN 1-888725-62-1, 5¼X8¼, 60 pp, booklet. $4.95 postpaid

Inaugural Addresses: Presidents of the United States from George Washington to 2008 -2nd Edition– Robert J. Banis, PhD, CMA, Ed. (2001) Extensively illustrated, includes election statistics, Vice- presidents, principal opponents, Index. coupons for update supplements for the next two elections. ISBN 1-888725-56-7, 6¼X8¼, 350pp, $18.95

Plague Legends: from the Miasmas of Hippocrates to the Microbes of Pasteur-Socrates Litsios D.Sc. (2001) Medical progress from early history through the 19th Century in understanding origins and spread of contagious disease. A thorough but readable and enlightening history of medicine. Illustrated, Bibliography, Index ISBN 1-888725-33-8, 6¼X8¼, 250pp, $24.95

Behind the Desk Workout – Joan Guccione, OTR/C, CHT (1997) ISBN 1-888725-00-1, Reduce risk of injury by exercising regularly at your desk. Over 200 photos and illustrations. (lay-flat spiral) 8¼X10½, 120 pp, $34.95 Paperback edition, (2000) ISBN 1-888725-25-7 $24.95

Science & Humanities Press

Publishes fine books under the imprints:

- ◆ Science & Humanities Press
- ◆ BeachHouse Books
- ◆ MacroPrint Books
- ◆ Heuristic Books
- ◆ Early Editions Books

Books by Michael Lund:

Growing Up on Route 66 —Michael Lund (2000) ISBN 1-888725-31-1 Novel evoking fond memories of what it was like to grow up alongside "America's Highway" in 20th Century Missouri. (Trade paperback) 5½ X8¼, 260 pp, $14.95 **MacroPrintBooks**™ edition (2001) ISBN 1-888725-45-1 8¼X6½, 16 pt, 330 pp, $24.95

Route 66 Kids —Michael Lund (2002) ISBN 1-888725-70-2 Sequel to *Growing Up on Route 66*, continuing memories of what it was like to grow up alongside "America's Highway" in 20th Century Missouri. (Trade paperback) 5½ X8¼, 270 pp, $14.95 **MacroPrintBooks**™ edition (2002) ISBN 1-888725-71-0 8¼X6½, 16 pt, 350 pp, $24.95

BeachHouse Books

An imprint of

Science & Humanities Press
PO Box 7151
Chesterfield, MO 63006-7151
(636) 394-4950
www.beachhousebooks.com
E-mail: editor@beachhousebooks.com

Item		Each	Quantity	Amount
Missouri (only) sales tax 6.075%				
Shipping per order)				$4.00
		Total		
Ship to Name:				
Address:				
City State Zip:				